TAKEN BY THE BEAST

CONNER KRESSLEY
REBECCA HAMILTON

EVERSCORCH

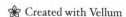 Created with Vellum

CHAPTER 1

I ran through the hallway, throwing open closets like a lunatic. Just shy of two hours—that's what it had taken me to completely screw up what my best friend Lulu did daily with ease. In that time—one hundred and eleven minutes to be exact—I had burned three grilled cheeses, knocked over a vase that I hoped wasn't too expensive, and (most importantly) 'misplaced' her three year old son.

It was safe to say I wasn't the domesticated type.

"Jack, this isn't funny!" I yelled, pulling open the final closet door and coming up empty.

My breathing came more labored now, and not just because I had been running nonstop for the last several minutes. This hall was my last chance. I had now officially covered every inch of this house, attic and all. The little guy was nowhere to be found, and my panic was quickly twisting into dread.

The doorbell dinged, at once breaking me from my train of thought and sending my heart into my throat. What if that was Lulu? What if she forgot her keys? I would have to explain to her how I lost her kid, and that would no doubt send her eight month pregnant butt right into labor.

It might not be Lulu, though. Maybe it was the cops. New

Haven was about as big as a shoebox, and before I'd moved away from here all those years ago, it was certainly the kind of place where your wayward child could show up on your doorstep with police escort. Lord knows I had.

I kicked off my heels, because if my seventeen-year-old self had taught me anything, it was that cops who have come to chastise you didn't really care for the hooker heel look. I doubted that would change just because I'd aged a decade since then.

As I got to the door, I bit my lip, bracing myself for one sort of confrontation or another. The doorbell rang again. *God, help me.* I twisted the handle and pulled the door open in a 'rip the Band-Aid off' sort of way.

Before me stood a polished woman, best guess mid-twenties, wearing a sundress and sporting the sort of unwavering blonde hair that could double as a hard hat if need be. Pearls adorned her neck, she clutched a purse between her hands, and she smirked as she looked me over head to toe.

"How very forceful of you," she said, running her hand up and down the doorframe. "I would be more careful with it. It's palmetto. Imported all the way from the Carolinas."

I grimaced. Before I left for New York, New Haven was a farming town. We had two general stores, a diner, and a movie theater that was always three months behind the rest of the country. You could set your watch by it. I hated the town back then, but not nearly as much as I hated it now. Ten years away had seen this place morph into a sort of retreat for the newly wealthy. The general stores gave way to day spas, the diner was replaced by a Starbucks, and last I heard, the movie theater was vying to house an independent film festival in the fall.

And all of that would be okay. I had never been the type of woman to bat away progress, after all. But it came complete with people like this woman, and that rubbed me the wrong way.

"I'll try to keep that in mind—you know, when handling it," I said, trying hard to keep the smarm out of my voice. "Can I help you?"

"Other than refraining from treating my best friend's door like a jilted lover, you could invite me in," the woman said, and she brushed past me, completely nullifying the need for an invitation.

"Y-your best friend?" I stammered.

As far as I knew, *I* was Lulu's best friend. Sure, she had been cordial with some of these *nouveau riche* housewives, but that was more out of necessity than anything else. It wasn't who she really was.

"That's right," she said. "Though, to be honest, I'm a little peeved at her. Lulu promised to let me know before she hired a housekeeper. I had more than a few qualified candidates in mind." She removed a pastel glove and ran her finger along the counter. She lifted her hand and looked at the pad of her pointer finger with disgust. "Not that you aren't doing an adequate job."

"I'm not a housekeeper," I said, folding my arms over my chest.

"Oh, thank God," she said. "I'd hate to think Lulu was actually paying you for this."

"Who *are* you?" I asked, marching after the woman.

"Ester Jacobs." She gave me a little nod.

"I see. Well, I'm Charisse Bellamy."

"Oh," she said, setting her purse on the chair, careful to miss the apparently dust-ridden counter. "Lulu's new friend. I've heard of you."

"Ha!" I scoffed more loudly than I intended. "Well, given that I've known Lulu since we were crawling around in the dirt, I'd say that makes *you* the new friend."

"What a charming visual. Forgive me for not recognizing you at first. When Lulu told me her model friend from New York was coming for a visit, I naturally pictured someone a little..."

"Thinner?" I finished, noticing the way Ester's eyes traced my curves. I posted my hands on my hips and dared her to look away. "In the real world, there are a lot of different standards of beauty."

"Evidently." Ester pursed her lips. "In any event, I'm here for Jack. Not that this interaction hasn't been delightful."

Uh-oh. That's right. I still haven't found Jack.

"I... He's asleep!" I said before thinking.

"Asleep?" Ester said with narrowed eyes. "Why, it's nearly four in the afternoon. Something tells me Lulu wouldn't be fond of the idea of you throwing off her son's sleep schedule like this." She made a clicking noise with her tongue. "Of course, I suppose that's something only a mother would think of."

I bristled, not so much because she had hit a nerve or anything. Sure, kids were something I wanted...in the far off future. It was sort of the way a person wanted to go to Europe or plan for retirement. I was going to think about it, just not today.

No, the thing that really pissed me off was the slithering notion that she might be right. Lulu *was* a mom, and I wasn't. There were things that she went through that I wouldn't understand—things that this stuffy witch apparently would.

"Look, I don't know what to tell you. He's asleep. Come back later," I said, motioning toward the still open door.

"You sure about that?" She smiled.

I clenched my teeth, wondering what she knew that she wasn't telling me. But I didn't have time to consider that. A shriek—loud and decidedly panicked—sounded from outside.

I darted to the door to find Lulu standing in the driveway, a spilled bag of groceries littered at her feet and her hands clawing at her temples, the way they did only when she was really freaking out.

"Jack!" she yelled, her eyes planted on the backyard. "Jack get back from there!"

Leaving the groceries behind, she bolted toward the house faster than any pregnant woman this close to popping ever should.

"Lulu, slow down," I said, flinching at the fire coloring her eyes. "The doctor said you're supposed to take it easy."

"And *you* were supposed to be watching him!" she said much louder than I had anticipated. She pushed past me, almost knocking me down with her momma bear bruteness as she made her way out the back door to the huge expanse that was her backyard.

I went after her, trying hard not to react to the smug satisfaction that Ester didn't even attempt to hide.

"That's the strangest nap I've ever seen," Ester remarked as she followed me outside.

At first, I didn't see him. The yard was completely empty, save for the customary swing set and sliding board that seemed to be everywhere now. God, people sure loved to procreate around these parts. But as I followed Lulu's running (and bouncing) frame, that quickly changed.

Jack was beyond the white wooden fence that separated the backyard from Bookman's Woods, which traced the outskirts of much of the town but seemed bigger now than it had when I was a kid.

Jack splashed around, running his hands through a shallow running stream and laughing like some sort of carefree hyena.

I bolted toward them, easily catching up with Lulu as she made it to the fence.

"Damn it! Damn it! Damn it!" she yelled, moving down the fence, looking for the break that Jack had undoubtedly squeezed through. "Jack, you get back from there!"

She was breathless, holding her belly and wheezing.

"Lulu, calm down!" I said, scanning the fence. "He's right over there. We can see him. There's no reason to—"

"What the hell do you know?" she barked at me. "You were supposed to be watching him, and you let him go here of all places! Do you have any idea how dangerous—" She bent forward, clutching her stomach and panting even harder.

"It's just a stream, Lulu," I said. I reached for her, but Ester was already there, making soothing sounds into her ear and pulling her away from me.

God, how's that for symbolism?

Jack stood, as if sensing his mother was in pain. His eyes cut to the left, and following them, Lulu pointed.

"Th-there," she muttered breathlessly.

A piece of the fence had broken, leaving the smallest of openings in the otherwise unyielding white wood.

"I'll get him," I said

Lulu was way too pregnant to crawl on her belly, and I had seen enough women like Ester to know that they didn't get their hands —much less their dresses—dirty for anything.

The look Lulu shot me told me she would rather be going to get her son herself. But she was too winded, and I was too ready. I slid through the tear in the fence as as quickly as a woman with curves could. The tear was small and the edges of the fence were jagged. It didn't surprise me when one of them scored my back.

I winced, but kept moving. After wriggling my ample hips and bottom through the fence, my legs came through easily. Looking back, I saw a stain of blood—my blood—across the wood. Whatever. I would bandage up later.

Jack waded out of the stream and hobbled over to me, and I scooped him up into my arms, giving him a half-guilty, half-grateful hug. "What were you thinking, Little Man?"

He mumbled something in baby speak, something that sounded like "He talks" or "He walks."

Kids are so weird.

Letting him go, I ushered Jack through the tear. He made it through much easier than I had, artfully dodging my bloodstain with plenty of room to spare. I, on the other hand, wriggled around like a fish caught on a hook, no doubt ruining my favorite pair of jeans in the process.

Jack scrambled away from me and jumped into his mother arms.

"You shouldn't be holding him," I said, getting to my feet and checking out all the dirt that was now caked into my outfit.

Yep. Ruined.

"I've got him," she said, keeping her eyes away from me.

"But the doctor—"

"Goddamn it, I said I've got him!"

I reared back, knowing better than to push my best friend any further.

"Ester," Lulu said, turning to the prim woman, "I need you to—"

"Get a contractor to fix that fence?" She shot me a look before continuing. "I already sent a text. He'll be here within the hour."

"Thank you." Lulu sighed in the way you would expect to hear from someone who had just heard their husband had come out of surgery fine. But this was a fence. It was a stupid fence that blocked woods that Jack was *barely* in. Yes, I had screwed up, but was it really that big of a deal? Lulu never cared about things like that before.

"Lulu, I'm sorry. I was making lunch. I didn't—"

"Look, I need to lay down for a bit," she said dismissively. "Just...just make sure that fence gets fixed."

"All right," I muttered at her back as she walked away.

"I'll show myself out," Ester said, shooting me another withering glance. "After all, I know when *I've* overstayed my welcome."

She smirked as she walked past Lulu, giving her a gentle squeeze on the shoulder. It was a simple gesture, but it hurt. Maybe Ester was right. Maybe I had been here too long. Maybe after everything that happened, this wasn't the place for me.

I turned back to the woods, staring out into the trees as though I could see my future among them.

I felt so alone. Even here, even with Lulu and in the town where I had spent the first seventeen years of my life, I felt like an outsider. If only Mom were here. If only I could retreat into her the way I always used to when things went wrong. I never felt alone so long as I knew she existed in the world. And maybe that was the thing. Maybe now that she was no longer in the world, alone was all I would ever feel.

I ran my fingers through my hair and tried not to cry. Instead, I just kept staring out at those woods. And the funny thing was, for a second, it felt as though something might be staring back.

CHAPTER 2

By the time dinner rolled around, things had calmed between Lulu and me. I would like to think that was because Lulu realized she had overreacted about the whole 'scary-woods, must-have-fence' thing. But in all honesty, my chicken piccata probably had more to do with it. Lulu had loved that recipe ever since my Grandma No Neck taught it to me during that summer I spent in the mountains.

That, paired with a bottle of wine, and Lulu could loosen up after just about anything. She was pregnant, though, so I would have to hope the piccata was especially potent tonight.

She scooped what was probably her third helping onto her plate and dug in.

Looks like it's doing the trick.

My eyes gravitated from her to Jack, who was half covered in macaroni and cheese and completely over whatever perceived trauma Lulu inexplicably imagined he would face once he got three feet past the tree line.

"It's different this time," she said through a heaping mouthful. "What is that?"

I smiled. "I started adding tabasco."

"Really? Since when?" She stabbed at a cube of chicken with her fork.

"About seven years ago," I said, wincing at all that statement revealed.

"Good God!" Apparently the effect hadn't been lost on Lulu, either. "It has *not* been that long since we've spent real time together."

"High school," I said. "Not that I didn't beg you to come with me."

"Not this again," she said, grinning and wagging her finger at me. "What was I going to do in New York, Char? I'm not pretty like you."

"That is insanely untrue. For one, everyone thought we were twins growing up. You're a freaking supermodel."

"No," she answered, grabbing Jack's leaking juice cup and tightening the lid. "*You're* a supermodel. I got magazines in the attic to prove it."

I leaned back in my chair. "You kept those stupid things?"

"Are you joking? You were pretty much famous."

"Tell that to my agency," I mumbled, pushing food around on my plate with one of Lulu's heirloom forks. I guess Ester hadn't influenced her too much. Yet. "I wasn't 'pretty much famous' enough to keep them from pretty much dropping my ass."

"Morons." She scoffed. "The world is full of them. It doesn't take anything away from you."

"Except an income," I answered. "Speaking of which..." I wriggled uncomfortably in my chair. "I owe you a lot of money. I haven't forgotten about that, and I will absolutely pay you back once—"

"Enough," she said, raising her hand in stop-right-there fashion. "You've had a rough go of things, Char. Money should be the least of your concerns."

"Tell that to Medi-Collections. They've called me twice this week. Turns out chemo isn't cheap."

Images of my mother, of the way she looked at the end—

strapped to machines and struggling for air—assaulted me the way the cancer had assaulted her. As always, tears stung my eyes.

Keep it together, Char. Streaky-mascara-face is not your best look.

I blinked hard and stared at my plate. "I just want you to know I don't expect a free ride."

"And you aren't getting one," Lulu answered, reaching across the table to place her hand on mine. "You're not here for nothing, Char." She gave my fingers a little jiggle. "With Eddie gone so much for work, it's not really feasible for me to be by myself right now, especially with Jack."

"'Cause I do such an amazing job watching him," I muttered. "I really am sorry about earlier. What about the guy who's supposed to fix the fence?"

Lulu sighed and pulled her hand beside her plate. "Ester texted me before we sat down. Some project at the Coleman Mill is running long. They're going to be three days. At the earliest."

The anxiety in her tone didn't make sense. It was only a fence. Not even the whole thing—just a single board...half of a board, actually. What was the big deal? But the way Lulu's hands twisted around her napkin told me it was a big deal to her.

"It's okay," she mumbled. "Eddie left the gun."

"The gun?" I almost choked on the air, my eyes flying wide. "Lulu, I get that your friends probably expect things to be perfect around here—Lord knows Ester seems like the type—but it's *a piece of wood*. What the hell do you need a gun for?"

Her eyes moved over to Jack. Her hands gripped the napkin even tighter. "It's nothing," she said, almost panting. "You wouldn't understand."

"Because I'm not a mom?" I asked, already sick of that notion.

"Because you're not *from* here," she answered. "At least not anymore. New Haven isn't the same place we grew up in, Char. Things have changed, and we've had to change with them. The woods are part of that."

"What are you talking about?" I tilted my head. "How could the woods change?"

"Look." Lulu swigged another sip of water. "It's not important, and neither is this whole money thing. Eddie makes a good living, certainly good enough that you don't have to worry about stupid stuff like paying me back for snacks or whatever ridiculousness is cooking in that whacked out brain of yours."

"I just want to *do* something. I don't want to overstay my welcome," I lamented, remembering what Ester had said.

"Then do something," Lulu answered. "Get a job if you want. I, for one, would love the idea of you sticking around for more than a few weeks. Who knows, you might even find this is somewhere you can call home again. Until then, my guest room is definitely open."

She stood, cradling her pregnant stomach and letting out the sort of belch girls only let out when guys weren't present.

"Dinner was amazing. Thank you." She smiled, the first non-strained gesture she'd made since the fence incident. "But I think Jack here is getting drowsy, and I need to sleep for a week after that." She pulled Jack gently from his booster seat and took his hand. "Just remember to lock up before you go to bed, okay?"

I nodded.

Lock up. Right. Then she won't need the gun.

Ugh.

"And Char," she called over her shoulder from the kitchen doorway. "Do try not to be so hard on yourself. These morons out here, they don't know the girl that I do."

* * *

I should have known better than to ever think Lulu would let one little transgression taint a friendship that had survived almost a decade of not being in the same zip code.

Still, I was a guest in this house, one who had no way to show my host how unbelievably grateful I was to have her—not to mention her guest room—in my life. Pulling out my laptop, I decided that if I couldn't pay for rent, food, or practically anything else (thanks a lot, medical bills), then I could at least try to chip in where I could.

For whatever reason, this fence was bothering Lulu enough to consider brandishing a firearm. Setting that bit of lunacy aside, I figured if I could take matters into my own hands and fix the stupid thing, then that might be a good way to show her how appreciative I was for all she had done and was doing for me.

Never mind that the closest I had ever come to real manual labor was that time I had to provocatively press a sledge hammer against my chest for the cover of Maxim.

Fixing a fence couldn't be that hard. A bit of wood, a couple nails, and some of that elbow grease I always heard the camera people talking about, and the job would be done. Lulu wouldn't have to wait three days for those carpenter idiots to finish whatever crap they were doing at Dumbass Mills. It would be finished. *I* would have finished it, and aside from loosening Lulu's death grip on that pistol, maybe getting something accomplished would actually make *me* feel better.

I opened the browser and searched for the nearest hardware store.

One hour away.

"Seriously?" I muttered to myself.

For all the expanding this stupid town had done, one would think a hardware store would be among the first improvements. Of course, my luck didn't work that way.

A drive out of town for a piece of wood was impractical; I couldn't afford the wood and nails if I spent all of my money on a tank of gas. I would have to go to the town's open market. And I *hated* the town's open market.

I glanced at the clock and cursed under my breath. It was after eight, which meant most of the vendors would have closed shop by now. As much as I wanted to let Lulu wake up to a newly mended fence, it would have to wait until tomorrow. Better than three days, sure, but not the perfect surprise I had hoped for.

An image of a very pregnant Lulu snoring and clutching her pistol flashed through my mind. It would have been funny if it wasn't so...okay, it was still pretty funny. But it was strange, too.

What was it about those woods, and what had Lulu meant when she told me I wouldn't understand?

On a whim, I typed Bookman's Woods into the search engine. Bookman's Woods was a mammoth, a national reserve really. It stretched through pieces of four towns and two counties and held more than three endangered species. But according to the search results, it turned out that wasn't all it held.

A news article from the Freemont Times—the second town to our left—led the search results.

THIRD BODY IN TWO WEEKS FOUND IN BOOKMAN'S WOODS.

When I clicked, a picture of a smiling girl loaded. Beneath it, a caption read "Same strange markings cover the remains." Same strange markings? As what? The other bodies?

When I examined the picture more closely, I shuddered. She was brunette, like me. And she had blue-green eyes...also like me. In fact, she shared more than a passing resemblance with me, which made her death even more unsettling.

I didn't want to read the article. I shouldn't have read the article. But I couldn't stop myself. I scrolled through quickly, learning that the girl who looked like me was named Nancy Redcliff, was a second year pre-med student at Freemont U, and had recently gotten engaged to her boyfriend of a year.

My scrolling finger froze as I neared the picture of her body. A lump grew in my throat the way it always did when I looked at something like this. But it wasn't the gore that gave me pause.

The markings—large scratches that crisscrossed the poor girl's back—looked just like those I saw on Dad that night...the night he disappeared.

The memories flooded my mind as fresh as if it'd just happened, when in reality, it'd been decades ago. Heck, I'd only been eight when he'd walked through the front door, silent and gruff. It wasn't unusual for him, though. Dad was often that way. He laid concrete, and he hated it. Mom and I stayed out of his way on nights like those. But that night, for whatever reason, I decided to bring him cookies, something to make him feel better.

When I walked in, he was changing his shirt. The unexpected markings on his back took my breath away.

"Daddy! Oh, goodness! What—"

He screamed at me get out, said I would be better off as far away from him as possible.

I opened my mouth to tell him he was wrong, but he brushed past me. I hadn't even noticed the bag in his hand until I stood at the window, perched on my tippy toes as I watched him march into the woods. The same woods that Lulu was so afraid of now.

It was the last time I ever saw him.

I slammed the laptop shut. This was ridiculous. So a couple of kids got themselves killed out in the woods. It was probably an animal and had absolutely nothing to do with what happened with my father.

For so long, I had convinced myself that Dad disappeared, that something must have happened to him. Forget the telltale bag slugged over his shoulder. He would never leave us. He would never leave me.

But now that I was grown, I knew better.

My father ran away from us. Anything else was just a story I told myself to try and feel better. I was done with stories, and I was done with towns that told them. Getting yourself all worked up because there was a wolf or a mountain lion thirty miles away didn't make any sense. God, a night in a real city would put all of these bumpkins in the looney bin.

I shook my head. I didn't want to stay here, in some place where they spun tales tall enough to make your best friend sleep with a gun under her pillow.

I didn't want to be that person, not for anything. And something told me that if I stayed here long enough, I wouldn't be able to help it.

No, I would go to sleep, wake up, collect the supplies I needed from town, and fix the stupid fence. Then I would get a job, save up like crazy, and make a break for it. Maybe I could call my (former) agent and beg him to take me back.

Hell, the Sears Catalog always needs models.

I punched my pillow, trying not to think about this ridiculous place, about all it had seen me lose.

"Idiots," I muttered, climbing into bed. "They turn their town into a pressure cooker and then they make monsters out of thin—"

A sudden howling cut off my words.

Tensing, I threw off my covers and lurched for the window. The sound was nothing. A dog, or something. I would prove that to myself.

I glared out into those goddamn woods. See, nothing. Absolutely—

A shadow moved between the trees, hulking and burly, but also tall—too tall to be an animal.

I blinked hard, once, and then again. When I looked back, there was nothing there.

Stop it, Char.

This place would drive me crazy if I let it. It was nothing. An animal.

I got back in bed, trying to feel more New York and less New Haven.

But somewhere in the back of my mind, I couldn't let go of the howl...or the markings...or the dead girl who looked just like me.

CHAPTER 3

I set my alarm for 6:45 the next morning, thinking that if I got a handle on the whole fence issue, I might be able to wrestle the pistol out of Lulu's hand without incident. Of course, after my internet escapades last night and that howl in the distance (which was absolutely positively a coyote...right?) I didn't really need help waking up. I'd completely missed my "window" and was on my second wind when the clock radio sprang to life, blaring 'My Humps' and telling me that the night was mercifully over.

I opened my closet with all the aplomb you would expect in the morning from someone who had spent her formative years sleeping until noon.

Crap. Laundry day.

Scanning the rack, I found the only clean thing I had was a dress the good people at Seventeen Magazine allowed me to keep after a particularly breezy photo-shoot. I wanted to be low key at the stupid open market. How could I do that in a sundress that featured a dangerously low cut top and a sparkling gold sequins?

Oh, screw it. Might as well give these stuffy losers something to talk about.

I grabbed the matching sky high heels, because when you jump down the rabbit hole, you do it with both feet. Quietly, I snuck out of the house, closing the door behind me, my heels clapping against the sidewalk like a runway model on her first trip to Milan.

A slight breeze cut through the springtime warmth, and birds sang in the trees as if they were serenading some cartoon princess. The open market was just through town, a half-mile walk at the most if I went straight. But straight meant I would have to pass by the cemetery, and I wasn't ready to do that. Not yet. I made a quick left and hummed along with the birds, trying to keep my mind in a light place.

The streets were obviously emptier than what I was used to back in New York. Even at this time of morning, the city would be a mass of people all buzzing about. But aside from some joggers (a few of whom did double takes when they caught a glimpse of my outfit), I was pretty much by myself.

To stave off the boredom, I popped in my earbuds and shuffled through my downloads. If people judged me by the way I looked, they would probably assume there was some bubblegum club song jamming through my head, but the truth was, I had always been more of a book girl. After all, there was no law that said models couldn't enjoy Steinbeck.

Ten minutes and half of an audiobook chapter later, I was pulled from my third visit with Holden Caulfield by a hand on my shoulder. I spun around, removing the buds from my ears.

A burly man with a five o'clock shadow and a baseball cap that read 'John Deere' stood grinning at me. A wad of chewing tobacco protruded from his lip, and his tongue flicked disgustingly in and out of his mouth.

"Well, how you doing, sweet thing?" he drawled. His smell—whiskey and sweat—nearly knocked me down.

"Fine 'til a minute ago." I jerked away from him. "You need to sober up, dude."

"Me?" He scoffed, but his half-open, bloodshot eyes agreed. "I ain't the one taking the walk of shame."

"What? I didn't—"

"Save it, sweet thing. That's a club dress if I ever saw one. You leave your car over at Fangs? I could give you a ride. You know, it ain't safe for a girl to be walking around these parts by herself." He looked me up and down, drinking me in with a look that made me glad I'd skipped breakfast. "Especially one like you."

"I think I got it," I said, stumbling backward and feeling one of my heels wobble beneath me. "Besides, it doesn't look like you're in any condition to be driving anyone anywhere."

"Come on," he slurred. "You obviously ain't the type to keep your legs closed for long. What's one more time?"

Okay, so I'd never been the type of girl to get stunned easily, but that sure as hell did it.

I opened my mouth to speak, or barf, or something. Instead, a loud, raucous laugh burst out. To my surprise, I found myself nearly keeling over, grabbing my gut and chuckling.

"Seriously?" I said, cupping my mouth with my hands. "Oh, my God! Are you serious?"

Understandably, he was not amused.

"You think this is a joke, bitch?" He spit tobacco-colored crud at my feet. His meaty hands balled into fists at his sides. "You think this is funny?"

Before I could reply, another voice came from behind me: "It's certainly pathetic enough to be funny."

I turned to find a sleek man with blond hair, angular features, and blue eyes so bright I was sure they could cut diamonds. His arms crossed his chest—his very...nice...chest.

Wow.

"This ain't nothing to do with you, kid," the drunken brute stammered, marching closer. "Step aside. You can't handle this."

The blond man smiled wide. "As the foremost expert on all things me, I'll have to disagree with that."

"He's big," I muttered to the blond man as he settled beside me.

"They always are," he answered. "Just means he thinks he doesn't have to work as hard. You wanna hold my phone while I take care of this?"

He shoved his white iPhone into my hands before I could answer.

"You don't have to do this," I said. "I can take care of myself."

"I don't doubt that," he answered. "Doesn't mean you should have to."

With that, the blond man darted forward, bridging the gap between himself and the drunkard.

The drunk man swung at him, but the blond ducked, causing the bigger man to stagger as he missed.

"Are you sure you want to do this?" the blond man asked, circling the drunk.

"Pfft! You can't hurt me, kid! You ain't nothing but a twerp."

"Whatever you say." The blond man shot me a smile. "This'll only take a second."

The infuriated drunkard lunged at the blond man. As nimble as a dancer, the blond man spun around, pulling a pair of cuffs from his back pocket and slapping one onto the drunk man's wrist. He gave him a swift kick to the knee, which sent him wobbling. The blond man closed the other handcuff onto a nearby stop sign.

"See, just a second." He turned to me, a grin still on his handsome face. He pulled a walkie talkie I hadn't seen before from his hip and spoke into it. "10-94 on Crescent Avenue. Transport requested. Suspect is apprehended. Be aware, he's as big as an ox and drunk enough to be flammable."

"10-4," someone on the other side of the line answered. "Be there in three."

Before long, a New Haven police car screeched up to us. The blond man talked to an officer who helped the drunkard into the back and then promised to "get the girl's statement." Up until that point, I'd just been standing there stunned. After all, here I thought this handsome blond was trying to be my hero, but really he was just doing his job.

"You okay?" the blond man asked as the car pulled away, taking the drunk to jail.

"Yeah," I answered, more sternly than I probably should have.

"I told you I didn't need your help. I could have dealt with that guy fine on my own."

"Of course you could have." He shrugged, stuffing his hands into the pockets of his tight-fitted jeans. "You were always like that, though. I remember that time you and Lu tied me to that tree by the lake. God, you guys used to scare the hell out of me."

"Wait," I said, narrowing my eyes at him. "What are you talking about?"

A blush flared in his cheeks. "You don't remember me, do you?" He chuckled, shaking his head. "God, Char, you're killing me here."

Okay, so he knew my name. And he knew Lulu's name. But who did we tie up to a tree other than...

"No, you're not!" I said, looking him up and down. "Dalton?"

He spread his arms wide. "The one and only!"

Lulu's kid brother was a snot-nosed, piss-ant of a kid when I left town. He had big ears, scrawny arms, and a disposition that would wilt flowers if they were in direct communication with him for too long.

This guy was...hot. He was hot *and* charming. They couldn't be the same person.

"But you're a child," I said, struggling to match my memory with the current reality.

"I'm twenty-four, Char," he said, arching his eyebrows at me. "Tabloids have shown you with younger. Not that I've been keeping up with you..."

The heat in my face spread to my ears, and I looked away. "Yeah, you definitely grew up," I muttered. "And filled out."

"I'm not the only one." When I looked back, he winked at me.

"And you're a cop?"

"A detective, actually," he said. "Hence the street clothes. I live in Milledgeville now. I'm on a case at the moment, so I really need to get going." He moved closer to me with a hint of something devilish in his gaze. "I'm supposed to get a statement from you about that drunken jackass, but seeing how I'm kinda busy right now, maybe I could take it down over coffee tomorrow."

Was he...asking me out? Was Lulu's little brother asking me to go on a date with him?

I wasn't quite sure how I felt about that. On one hand, he was definitely cute enough to warrant a second (and probably third, fourth, and fifth) glance. But he *was* Lulu's brother. Wouldn't that make things weird?

Ugh! I shook my head. What did it matter? I wasn't here for that. I wasn't even here to stay.

"We can meet for coffee, *but only while you take my statement,*" I answered firmly.

He smiled. "What else did you have in mind?"

"Look, I—"

"Oh, stop." He waved me off. "Does it look like I'm hiding a diamond ring in my pocket?" He kicked a pebble in front of him. "Just coffee is more than okay with me. I'll text you the address." He shot me another smile and started to walk away. "You know," he said, turning around and walking backwards, "they were right about you. You went off to the big city and got all full of yourself."

My face grew even hotter now, and my hands balled at my sides. "I did not!"

"Yeah, you did," he said, looking me up and down. "But I never said you didn't have reason to be."

❧

I HAD BARELY MANAGED TO BEAT DALTON OUT OF THE forefront of my mind when I made my way into what passed for the heart of town. *Good*, I thought. That meant I had successfully dodged the cemetery. Coming face to face with that place right now, with my mother's headstone in the western corner, would only serve to send my mind down a path it didn't need to go right now. I was here to reset, and I couldn't reset if I kept rewinding.

The extra-crowded marketplace came into view. People

smothered the streets and, the drunken would-be rapist aside, my dress and shoe combination had its expected effect. I could barely contain my glee at seeing the distasteful looks that graced the faces of the old farts as they caught sight of me.

A woman whispered, "She's either charging for it or giving it away," to her friend, and as I was about to spin around and give her a challenging glare, something more alarming caught my attention. A missing person poster. I wouldn't have stopped normally, but aside from missing posters being something of an oddity in a town like New Haven, the girl's picture was oddly familiar. She looked like...

Well, she looked just like me.

As I read over the poster, checking out the girl's brown curls, her full cheeks and bust, and the curve of her hips that could have been a reflection of my own, I shuddered. Sure, her nose was a little bigger, and her eyes were a darker shade of blue. But, for the second time in two days, I was face to face with a picture of a woman who looked a great deal like me. And, for the second time, it was clear something horrible had happened to her.

Annabeth Girts was last seen heading to her car on the night of April 16th. At the time of her disappearance, she was wearing an orange sweater and jeans. Any persons with information on her whereabouts are to contact—

I would have kept reading, except right then, my heel broke.

As I went winding down a nearby stairwell, I thought about a lot of things—none more than the fact that the piece of garbage Italian shoes were *eleven thousand goddamn dollars*!

I braced for impact, envisioning a bloodied face and broken teeth that would no doubt come as a result of tumbling down concrete stairs, and mused at how I could have sold these shoes on Ebay. I wouldn't have gotten more than twenty dollars for them, despite their value—that was the only reason I had kept—but now, they were likely about to kill me. All because New Haven liked half of their stores to have cellars.

I wonder who I could sue at this point.

. . .

BUT THERE WAS NO PAIN, NO METALLIC BLOOD TASTE, NO BROKEN teeth or bruised tailbones. Instead, I found myself in the arms of a man—the second inexplicably attractive man I had crossed paths with in a single day.

Either I was losing it, or Lulu was right. This town had changed. Especially with the selection of...er, well...men.

My rescuer this time had dark eyes and even darker hair that slicked back on his head. His cheekbones were dusted with stubble —I would bet he was the type that always had a five o'clock shadow. He stared down at me for a long moment before his lips, pink and inviting, finally parted to speak.

"You-you have a freckle in your eye," he said.

"I got it from my father," I mumbled, staring at him hesitantly, as though his face were the sun and I didn't want to blind myself.

He shook his head. "What are you doing down here?"

"I...I fell," I said, bristling at the steel in his voice.

"I can see that." His scowl set firmer. "I mean, what were you doing skulking around at my doorstep? And what did you do with my barrier?"

He glared at the street above, at the decidedly barren stairwell that apparently was supposed to be blocked off.

"I didn't see any barrier," I said, trying—and failing—to squirm my way out of his arms.

"Damn children," he growled. His chest, firm and impressive, rose and fell in deep, sharp intakes of breath. "Look, no one is supposed to be down here. It's not safe."

"Obviously," I said. "Now can you put me down?"

He sighed heavily and sat me on the pavement. I winced as pain shot up my ankle and my leg folded under me.

"Damn it, you're hurt," he said, scooping me back up, but sounding more perturbed than concerned. "I suppose you'll have to come in now."

"Well, don't put yourself out or anything. Wouldn't want you to overdo it with the compassion and pull a muscle."

He glared down at me and huffed, marching me through a door he unlocked by pressing a series of numbers against a keypad.

I bit at the inside of my cheek, debating if I might be better off hobbling home with my injuries or letting this jerk help me. Considering he was a very handsome jerk, I went along with the latter.

We entered a huge, barren space that, upon first inspection, was probably almost definitely a murder dungeon.

On the off chance I was wrong, I muttered, "What is this place?"

"A club," he answered flatly. "Or it will be in two weeks."

"A club?" I asked, looking around at the dark, dank void, thinking about how big of a turnaround two weeks would have to bring for this to be anything even close to such a thing.

"Yes," he said, setting me on a lone, dusty stool. "For dancing, mingling...you know, general merriment."

"*General merriment?*" I asked, giggling. "Why would you even want a club in a town like this? There's no market for it."

"There are young people here," he answered. "This will give them someplace to go. Someplace safe," he finished under his breath. "Let me get you ice and get you on your way."

"You're a ray of sunshine, aren't you?" I said as he disappeared off into a backroom.

Looking around the space, I saw it was even more pathetic right side up. There was no way this guy was going to turn this place into a club in two weeks. It would take someone of immense taste and talent to pull that sort of thing off. It would take someone who had been around the block a time or two, someone who knew what she was doing and had the foresight to get it done. Someone like...

My gaze fell on a 'Manager Wanted' sign.

While it was true I didn't want to stick around, this was the sort of thing that could really help me out. I could help Mr.

Deadpan get this place up and running, make a little scratch, and then take off once I got my legs back under me. Plus it would give me something to do so I wouldn't feel like such an anchor around Lulu's neck.

"You're looking for a manager," I yelled into the distance.

"No," he yelled back.

"You're not?"

"I am, but it's not you," he answered, still in the other room. "There's a form and protocol. But that aside, you wouldn't be a good fit."

"I wouldn't?" I asked, narrowing my eyes. "I spent my formative years in New York hobnobbing with Hollywood starlets and athletes. And you think I wouldn't be a good fit? I can't see why, given that it would take me all of fifteen minutes to give this place a fighting chance."

"Look, I understand you're—"

A loud rumbling noise came from the back, like thunder or a large machine malfunctioning.

There was silence for a long time after that—so long that I leaned forward and shouted, "Hey, bud, you okay?"

The noise amplified and a muffled "Goddamn it!" came from the back room. Then there was a loud clanking and crash, as if a set of dishes had shattered against the floor. This guy was going to get himself killed.

I slid off the stool, careful not to put much pressure on my ankle. I moved forward. Sure, it ached a little, but if you could walk a runway with half a placemat and light bulbs on your head (thank you, Fall line 2011), hobbling around on a banged up ankle was cake.

Really it was more annoying than painful—walking around with one fill heel and one broken one—but not impossible. I inched toward the backroom, following through the hallway the man had disappeared into. It stretched out a hundred feet and then split off left and right. Making my way to the 'fork', I passed a room on the right with a huge padlock on it. The door was wooden and looked even older and more neglected than the rest of this place. But that wasn't the strangest part. There was a symbol, like a crescent moon, painted red with a few dots on the inside.

"Damn!" came another shout from the left.

I turned to find him on his knees, soaked to the bone, jabbing at what looked like an ice machine. A plastic bag, no doubt where my ice was intended to reside, lay empty on the floor.

He growled. "This blasted contraption!"

"Blasted contraption?" I asked, arching my eyebrows.

"You shouldn't be standing," he said, giving me the briefest of glances. "I don't have the time or resources for a lawsuit, so if you could kindly limit the amount of damage you inflict upon your body, I would appreciate it."

"I bet you're popular," I said, leaning against the wall and taking the pressure off my foot.

He stood, his dripping shirt clinging to his hulking chest. Well, damn. He probably actually *was* popular, regardless of how he treated people.

He pressed his hands against his knees and shook his head. "I can't get this ridiculous machine to work."

"I gathered that."

"There are so many buttons, and so many different kinds of ice. Who would want their ice to be crushed, anyway?"

"Me."

"Figures," he muttered.

"So how are you going to run an entire nightclub if you can't even fill a bag of ice?"

He threw his hand toward the machine. "No one could work that stupid thing."

"Press the crushed ice icon," I said. "It will light up. Then push a cup against this lever." I hopped over to the machine and filled the bag the way I had a million times back when I was still working at that restaurant before my agent landed me my first real gig. "It's pretty standard. It works the way you think it would." I gave him a quick look over and amended, "Well, maybe not the way *you* think it would."

His mouth fell open, but he snapped it shut it before mumbling, "I have a soda machine on the way."

"I can work that."

"And an espresso maker." This time his raised his eyes to me. He looked defeated and hopeful all at once.

"I can work that, too."

"What if I put a stipulation in your contract saying you can't sue me for throwing yourself down the stars?"

"I didn't throw myself anywhere, but sure, I'll sign it." I grinned. "Boss."

He picked himself up off the floor and stepped out of the room and into the hall with me.

"Abram Canavar," he said gruffly—or perhaps he was just bitter over conceding I knew my way around a club. "When can you start?"

CHAPTER 4

"I can't believe you," Dalton said, taking a sip of his coffee and staring at me over the brim of his mug. His blond hair hung lazily in his eyes, and though I couldn't see his lips, there was no doubt in my mind he was smiling.

I tried a swallow of my cappuccino, but it was way too hot. "I'm not sure what you mean."

"Yeah, you do." He wiped his mouth. "Not to toot my own horn or anything, but it isn't every woman who'd make me wait two weeks for a date."

He swept his hand to indicate his body, and I couldn't argue there. He was dressed down in a gray t-shirt and corduroys; his pistol dangling visibly from his hip sure as hell didn't hurt. He was, indeed, not the type of guy you expect to wait for you. But I wasn't going to tell him that.

I lifted my eyebrows and grinned. "Did you really just use the phrase 'toot my own horn'?"

"I know. It's sexier than you thought, right?"

Coming from him, yeah, just about anything would be sexier than I expected. But the whole situation was still strange. I mean, this was Lulu's little brother. I basically watched him grow up.

He'd at least traded in his taste for earth worms for expensive coffee. And seeing how we were flirting shamelessly, apparently my tastes had changed, too.

"Who said this was a date?" I asked, half toying with him and half genuinely not sure if I wanted to commit to that idea.

"Nobody," he admitted, plunging a stirrer into his coffee and twirling it. "But nobody came out and said the sun was up, either. Doesn't mean we don't need shades. We're both grown now, Char. Let's not pretend we don't know what's going on here."

He bit his lip, which was admittedly much sexier than I would have liked it to be.

"I've been busy," I said, trying—and failing—not to stare at him. "That's why it's taken me so long. It's not because—" I cleared my throat. "I don't know if Lulu told you, but I got off my ass and actually found a job."

Well, the truth was that I *fell on* my ass and got the job, but he didn't need to know that.

"She said something about it," he answered, his tone firmer than I expected.

I leaned in ever-so-slightly. "Something wrong?"

"That night club, right?" he asked, running a hand through his hair.

"That's the goal," I answered. "The truth is, it was barely a pit in the ground when I got there. The guy who owns the place wouldn't know contemporary from alt contemporary if the theming slapped him in the face."

Dalton's eyes glazed over, and he blinked. "I have no idea what you're talking about."

"Which is why *you* shouldn't open a night club, either," I said with a reprimanding point of my finger. "But I've made good headway since I got there. I actually need to get back before long. Tonight is the grand opening, and there's—"

"I don't think you should work there anymore," he said, then he swigged his coffee again.

I narrowed my eyes. "Excuse me?"

"I mean, I'm sure you're good at what you do—great, probably. But I've been around since the last time we've seen each other, Char. I know things now—things I sometimes wish I didn't. Places like that and girls like you...they don't mix."

Suddenly, I felt acutely aware of what I was wearing, of every inch of exposed skin and every fleck of makeup. I was right back there with that drunkard, being judged on my clothes and appearance.

"*Girls like me?* What the hell is that supposed to mean?"

"I'm sorry. That came out wrong." He shook his head and pushed his coffee aside. "This case I'm on...it's getting to me more than it should."

"The girl on the missing poster?" I asked.

"I'm not really allowed to talk about that."

"Do you have any idea who did it?" I asked, my heart racing. He knew about this more than I did, and we were both avoiding the elephant in the room—that the missing girl looked a helluva-lot like me.

"There are a lot of awful people in the world, Char." His hand fell and hovered over his pistol. Did he even realize he was doing that? "And they tend to congregate in those sorts of places... clubs...the nightlife scene."

"I meant it when I said I could take care of myself," I said, splaying my hands across the table. "It's cute that you're worried about me. Really, it is. But if you're curious about what kind of girl I am," I said, harkening back to his earlier phrase, "I'm going to tell you that I'm not the sort who gets scared off easily. All this talk of missing girls and howling things in the woods—it just doesn't do much for me."

"Doesn't much matter what it does for you. Still poses a threat to the women in our town."

"Uh-huh," I said, ticking my head to the side. "Well, buddy, let me tell you. I've lived in scarier places than New Haven." I had to hold back a giggle at the thought. *Big Bad New Haven. Yeah.* This single murder and one missing girl was the most action they'd had in decades. "I've lived in the city, Dalton. I've worked the graveyard shift for a year and a half. Had pervs glaring at me with every step down the runway—"

"This is making me feel better, Char," he said, his mouth setting into a grim line.

"My point is, this 'small town gird your loins' nonsense isn't going to change the way I sleep at night." I huffed. "Now this might not be the best job in the world, and Lord knows Abram is far from the best boss," I said, thinking of his cold attitude and barking nature, "but the pay is good, and it gives me something to do besides take up space at your sister's house."

"Okay, okay," he said, spreading his hands. "I get it, and I totally respect your decision. Now get back to that part where you were calling me cute."

I chuckled out loud, surprising myself. "I didn't call *you* cute. I said what you were doing was sort of cute. Sort of."

"Potatoes, tomatoes, Char. Don't run from your feelings." He smiled and rested his chin flat against his hands, which were folded on the table. Suddenly he looked like a puppy—cute, harmless, and ready to show submission.

"Don't give me that look," I told him, noticing the way his bright eyes got wider, rounder, and even more adorable.

"You didn't mind it when we were kids," he teased.

"It didn't have the same effect back then." I nearly choked on my words. I was determined not to let him affect me. At least not until I knew where these feelings were leading us. "Look, I don't like to talk about this, but it's been a rough year for me. Losing my mother, losing my job—it took a toll on me. And while your sister has been better to me than I have any right to expect, coming back here hasn't been the best thing in the world for me, either. Everyone's moved on around here. Their lives are different...fuller. I have to find something to do with myself. This might not be the place I want to be forever, but it looks like the place I'm going to have to be for a while. And I can't just keep mooching off your sister."

"You could always move in with me," he said, wiggling his eyebrows. "I'm sure I could find *something* to keep you busy."

"Slow your roll, Puppy Dog." I leaned back, resting my arm on the back of my chair. "Usually, a guy takes me to dinner before inviting me to move in."

"Deal!" Dalton said, snapping his head upward. "I'll pick you up Friday night at seven."

"Hey, wait a minute!" I said, sitting forward again. "That wasn't—"

"Too late. I already accepted." He finished off the last of his coffee. "And I don't like to be disappointed."

"Fine," I mumbled, following him to the door, "but—"

Before I could finish my thought, he turned toward me, putting us inches apart. The tension rendered whatever I was about to say pointless. My breath caught in my chest. I couldn't deny my attraction, even if whatever was happening between us felt...wrong. Would I ever be able to see him as something other than my best friend's little brother?

"There's something about you, Char, hiding right under the surface," he said quietly into the silence between us. "I'm not sure how I missed it before."

I could say the same for you, I thought, blushing uncontrollably.

His arm reached past me, bringing his face a hair's breadth from mine. Oh, no. This wasn't good. He was going to kiss me, and I so wasn't ready for that.

My hands shot up to stop him. "Dalton, wait!"

He pulled his arm back, coat now in hand where it wasn't before. "Just had to grab my jacket, Char." He winked. "See you soon."

Then he left, and I stood at the door for a good ten minutes waiting for my heart to stop beating so wildly in my chest.

* * *

In the two weeks I had been working at Abram's club, I had

made several changes. I switched out the lighting (who wanted fluorescent tube lights in a club, anyway?), I canceled his furniture shipment and changed it out for something a little hipper (which wasn't hard considering he had ordered wicker), and I even convinced him not to put mirrors on the ceiling (since, you know, it wasn't the seventies). But the most important change I had implemented since coming here was definitely when I convinced Abram to change the name.

It wasn't easy. Things never were with Abram. Even when he was there, which wasn't nearly as frequently as you would expect from an owner, he was stubborn as an ox and completely closed off to the idea of change. Luckily for him, I could be just as stubborn, *and* I didn't have the taste of somebody's grandfather.

"*I named it the Cellar because it's in a damn cellar! How much more explanation does it need?*" he'd said when I'd confronted him about his choice of name for his establishment.

I'd combated that quite easily: "*A cellar is dark and dank, you idiot! Who wants to go there? You might as well name it The Cesspool!*"

We settled on 'The Castle' since it was old and majestic-sounding enough to suit Abram and because, well, it was better than The Cesspool. I mean, The Cellar. Either way.

As I passed the club sign, I gave it a little wink, seeing it as proof not only of my effectiveness here, but also of how misplaced Dalton's fears had been.

'*That kind of girl', my big, gorgeous ass.*

Descending the staircase (much more gracefully this time than the first time), I was surprised to see Abram locking the door.

"What the hell are you doing?" I asked. "We only have three hours until opening. We need to be inside."

"You're late," he growled, which I absolutely expected at this point.

"Pfft, twenty minutes. I had a date. Besides, I figured you'd be—"

"It's almost dark!" He spun toward me. The stubble on his face was fuller now, almost too full given that, just yesterday, he was nearly clean shaven.

"Newsflash," I said, "nightclubs are open at night."

Actually, come to think of it, I wasn't sure if I had ever seen Abram around here in the evenings, much less at night. Certainly he couldn't keep that up, though. We were about to open. He *had* to be here for that.

"Where are you going anyway?" I asked.

"I have to attend to some business," he answered, gaze firmly directed toward the pavement.

It was then that I noticed how labored his breathing was. He practically huffed at me. And the look seeping out through his eyes spoke of either pain or anger. Maybe both.

"This is *your* business, Abram," I said, planting my fists on my hips. "We open the doors in just a few hours. You *have* to be here."

"I have other things to consider." He clutched at his gut, folding into himself just a little.

"Are you okay?" I asked, inching forward instinctively. "Should I call an ambulance?"

"You have a job, Ms. Bellamy." He grunted again, obviously hurting. "I expect you to be on time, and I expect you to do what's required of you." He moaned, bowling over.

"Jesus, Abram, let me call somebody."

He threw a hand in front of him, stopping me in my tracks. "If you want to help, you can get the hell away from me and do your damn job!"

His teeth ground together, and his muscles clenched, flexing under his tight-fitting black jacket.

I stepped back, eyeing him up and down. Sweat poured off every exposed inch of his body as he sat hunched-over on the pavement.

"Are you stupid?" He growled. "Get inside! Now!"

Normally, if a man spoke to me like that, I would introduce his crotch to my Louboutins. But something was going on here, and I didn't have a full picture of what it was.

So instead of flipping out all over this hardheaded douchebag, I just glared at him and said, "I know what my job is. You don't have to be such a beast about it."

He got up slowly, tensing his muscles as if he was afraid his insides were going to come pouring out. Turning from me, he began up the stairwell. "Ms. Bellamy, you have no idea."

CHAPTER 5

The next few hours flew by quicker than I had hoped. In my mind, I would have plenty of time to get everything in order before The Castle's grand opening. In reality, though, I probably looked more like a Milan noob on a greased runway.

There was just so much to do, and until the trail bartenders and wait staff got here, I was the only one to do it. And whose fault was that?

So, while I bustled about, arranging and rearranging the chairs, tables, and centerpieces, I couldn't help but curse Abram under my breath. He should have been here. Hell, he should be the one doing most of the heavy lifting. This was, after all, *his* nightclub. Shouldn't he be at least a little concerned about how the place looked once the floodgates opened?

Still, he *had* been sick. He was practically bowling over in pain when he left, all gritted teeth and clenched muscles. I should have called the ambulance. For all I knew, the brute could be lying in a ditch somewhere. But the idiot had a head like Monday morning. You just couldn't get through it.

So, sensitive and caring woman that I was, I found my irritation with him tinged with a little concern.

That really pissed me off.

Once I was absolutely sure (for the third time) that the contemporary decor was all centered and the 'feel' of the room was perfect, I moved my attention to more utilitarian matters. There was a huge cooler behind the bar, and it needed to be filled before thirsty customers arrived. I always found getting people drunk was more about timing and less about actual desire. Nobody liked to wait for their 'whatever on the rocks,' and I sure as hell wasn't going to be the hostess/manager/woman who did everything because the damn boss couldn't be bothered to.

Sure, I could have waited for the new bouncer to get here and help. God knew he was probably going to be bored to tears tonight. New Haven wasn't the type of place to support a line past the velvet rope. But I was too type A for that. So I kicked off my giant heels and made haste toward that troublesome ice machine.

I was three trips into what was certainly going to be double digit treks when a noise from inside the room across the hall stopped me in my tracks. It was loud but nondescript, like white static or distant rainfall. I hadn't been outside for a few hours now, and the downstairs of the club didn't have many windows. The sky had been clear last I'd checked, but if it was raining now, it sounded as though Abram had left a window open.

I set the ice bucket down and stepped into the hall, and as I neared the other room, the strange red symbol painted on the door began to take shape. Still, I couldn't tell what it was. I grabbed the handle and turned, but the door was locked.

Maybe I should call Abram.

Whatever was in that room would no doubt be ruined if it was raining as hard as it sounded. Then again, he *had* been a super dick to me earlier...

You know what? Let it pour.

Maybe that would teach him to be a little more responsible with his club.

By my seventh trip, the noise quieted, so at least the rain was dying down. But there was another layer to the sound now. A melodic whisper...a song...as if someone was singing on the other side of the door.

Well, that didn't make any sense. As far as I knew, I was the only person in the club. Abram must have left a CD playing. I pressed my ear against the door to get a better listen as the song continued.

It was...hmmm...I had to be hearing that wrong. It sounded like it was whispering my name.

I bristled and pulled my head away.

"Hello?" I rested just my palms against the door now. "Hello? Is someone—"

The door flared with heat, and I jerked backward as the metal burned my hands.

What the hell!

The song got louder, whispering my name over and over again.

"Real funny, Abram!" I said, hoping it was a joke. I knew better, though. Abram wasn't the joking type. And besides which, he wasn't even here.

A knock on the door startled me so much that I shuddered.

"Charisse," a voice sounded from the alleyway outside, and I jumped again, then caught my breath.

Get a hold of yourself, girl! It's just the bartender.

I flipped open my phone and checked the time. Almost seven. The club would open in just over an hour. I needed to get back to work.

I gave the weird door one last look before sprinting down the hall to let the bartender in. She stood waiting for me with a big smile on her face, dry to the bone and not a puddle in sight.

* * *

An hour later, you could have knocked me over with a feather. I didn't see New Haven as the sort of place to have much of a market for a night club. A bar, sure. A backwoods pool hall, definitely. But the sort of quasi-refined establishment I had in mind, not so much.

As such, I didn't allow myself to entertain the possibility of

The Castle filling up. Half-full would be a good night, I told myself. So you can imagine my surprise when not only did the place fill to capacity, but a line formed outside the door.

I guess the bouncer won't be so bored after all.

Things moved quickly after that, and despite myself, a sense of pride started to build inside of me. *I* had done this. This place was popular, in part, because of all the hard work I had put into it in the last few weeks.

It sure as hell wasn't Abram's doing.

I thought about calling him. After all, it was his pockets that the thirsty crowd was lining tonight. And despite how infuriated I was with him, I wanted to make sure he was okay. And what was more, I kind of just wanted to talk to him.

No, that can't be right.

My specific role changed a bit as the night progressed. I hadn't really expected the influx of people, and Abram's wallet hadn't exactly been open during all of our planning, so I had hired accordingly. In other words, we were wildly understaffed. So as the hours passed, I went from proud manager, to equally proud hostess, all the way to down to haggard (but still proud) waitress.

I had just spilled three vodka tonics all over my white blouse when I heard the first words in hours that weren't commands or drink orders.

"Lulu, I thought you said she ran the place," came a familiar voice. "From here she just looks like a barmaid who's showing too much cleavage."

I quickly found the source. Ester sat at a nearby table beside Lulu, eyeing me up and down like a cat staring at a goldfish she deemed too small to worry about.

God, why couldn't it have been a drink order?

"Char, your shirt..." Lulu mumbled, her gaze landing on me. There was a soda water in her hand, and the look on her face was a mix of shock and discomfort.

"I know," I said. "It's ruined." I bent down and picked up the spilled glasses. "And it was Prada," I said, cutting my eyes over to Ester. "Very expensive."

"Well, now it's very see-through," Ester announced, grinning and taking a sip of her drink. Looking back at Lulu, she muttered, "I told you she wasn't wearing a bra."

Of course I wasn't wearing a bra. Bras weren't exactly designed for open-backed tops. But how would *she* know?

I followed her gaze down to my breasts only to find that the vodka tonics had bled through the fabric, exposing—well, everything I had that was exposable.

My face ran hot as I realized everyone was staring at me.

"Damn it!" I muttered, crossing my arms over my chest.

"I didn't expect you to be so modest." Ester pursed her lips. "I guess models are only comfortable showing skin when they have Photoshop to correct those little imperfections."

"Ester!" Lulu said, her gaze shooting daggers at her new friend.

"What?" she asked, motioning to my unintended display. "So they're not perfect? I'm not judging her or anything."

"You'll have to excuse me," I said through clenched teeth. Without waiting for an answer, I bolted off, arms still crossed to salvage what dignity I had left.

This was *so* not how I wanted the night to go. Not only had I exposed myself in front of basically the entire town, but I had made a fool of myself in a place I was supposed to run. This officially could not get any worse.

"Char?" Dalton's voice boomed like a firing squad cocking their guns. He had just walked in, and (if there was a God in heaven) maybe he hadn't seen everything I had to offer.

"I can't right now," I said, trying my best to move away from him.

The place was crowded, though, and the guys here didn't seem as though they wanted to help a buxom—and basically topless— woman run away.

"I just wanted to say hey," he said, weaving through the crowd with irksome ease.

"Hey," I said, over my shoulder, still moving, still intent on getting out of this with at least a little of my self-respect intact.

"Well, I mean, and to say congrats." He was close now—so close I could feel his breath on my neck.

He swung in front of me, stopping me where I stood. My shirt dripped onto the floor, I stunk of alcohol, and worst of all, every inch of breast that wasn't covered by my hands, might as well have had a blinking arrow pointing to it.

I sighed, accepting defeat. "Thanks."

"Oh, wow," he said. His gaze lingered where everyone else's had, but to his credit, he forced his attention upward to my face. "That's a lot of—"

"Yes, it is," I answered. "And there are a lot of people here, so if you don't mind—"

"Right!" Dalton said. "On it." He shrugged off his jacket and tossed it over my chest. "There we go," he said, looking at me again. "I wanted to tell you congratulations on the opening." He grinned. "Though, if I'm being honest, I sorta want to congratulate you on other things now."

"I'm mortified," I said with a groan as he scooped me up into a hug. "I just flashed the entire town."

"Lucky bastards," he muttered.

Though I tried to fight it, I couldn't help but smile. Sure, I had embarrassed myself. And I had probably given Ester at least a month's worth of ammunition. But things felt better in Dalton's arms. He was warm. He was dry. And what was more, he was inviting—the sort of inviting I hadn't felt in a long time.

"It's going to be all right," he said, in a slightly more serious tone.

And the thing was, at least for a moment, I believed him.

That was, until a huge boom rocked from above. I jerked, looking up. Another boom shook the roof, followed by the creaking and breaking of wood beams.

. . .

THE ENTIRE CLUB GROUND TO A HALT, MUSIC AND ALL. Everyone stared up at the source of the strange noise. Then another crack erupted, and something crashed through the ceiling.

A woman screamed. Her scream became many screams. People ran, some filing for the door, some too drunk to know where the door was. I weaved through the crowd, easier to part than it had been minutes ago.

And as I neared where some of the crowd had gathered, I saw exactly what had shaken them up so much.

Lying lifeless and bloody on the floor, covered in scratches and bite marks, was a woman.

A woman with dark hair and bright eyes.

A woman—another one—that looked a lot like me.

CHAPTER 6

I hadn't been inside The Castle in days. No one had, what with the crime scene tape stretched across it, blocking the entrance with its creepy yellow and black barrier. That didn't stop people from talking about it, though.

Not five minutes went by without me overhearing someone recall that gruesome moment. Either they were recounting what they saw firsthand—with a few embellishments thrown in for good measure—or they were repeating what they heard from a friend who *had* been there. No one seemed to have seen exactly the same thing. The only thing everyone agreed on was that they were absolutely, never ever, under any circumstance, without question, going back to that club.

They had even taken to calling it "The Casket" instead of "The Castle."

Turned out the only thing worse for a business than a small town murder was an *unsolved* small town murder. And worse for me, the girl—like every other who seemed to get herself in trouble within a twenty mile radius—looked disturbingly like me.

But she wasn't me. *I* was me.

In the two days since that girl came crashing through the roof, I had been through three rounds of police questioning, and within the confines of those sessions, I learned that Abram had only moved to town a few months prior. I also learned that he came from old money. I did not, however, find out Abram's address. And since he had deliberately been sending me to voicemail for days now, I was starting to worry.

It wasn't that I cared, per se. He was, after all, an arrogant prick. But his business had fallen through, the last time I saw him, he was sick, and if I knew the people in this town the way I thought I did, there were probably more than a few who thought he was the murderer.

Which was absolutely ridiculous. Abram was a lot of awful things, but he wasn't a killer. He just wasn't.

Right?

And while the town and the police had already asked him their fair share of questions, I wasn't about to let him off the hook from mine. I had waited long enough, and damned if I was going to wait any longer.

I checked back at the club every day until finally he returned, furious that he had avoided me this long. It wasn't just his livelihood on the line. In fact, if he was as rich as I'd been informed, he had nothing to worry about.

But *I* did.

So when I saw him standing at the bottom of the stairwell leading to The Castle's entrance—his back to me, arms folded, staring at The Castle's door—I nearly charged.

"Be careful," he said without looking up at me. His black slacks matched a t-shirt that hugged his arms, chest, and shoulders in a way that made him look impossibly large and defined. "I'm not in the mood to catch you today."

Gritting my teeth, I padded the rest of the way down the steps. "Don't worry," I answered, infusing a light tone in my voice that I didn't really feel. "I think I've got this much under control."

"Really?" He swerved to face me, cutting those dark eyes right in my direction. The stubble on his cheeks had been shortened since last I saw him, but there was still a hint of darkness in his expression that matched his stormy eyes.

"What's that supposed to mean?" I asked, settling next to him.

"It means it would be the first thing you had under control." He sounded more tired than angry, but that didn't stop the rage from bubbling up in my chest.

"You can't be serious." I pitted my hands on my hips. "You're not seriously going to blame this on me!"

"No," he said, raising a mitt-like hand to shush me. "You didn't kill that girl."

"Carla," I said, moving closer. "The paper said her name was Carla Rogers."

"I know her name, Ms. Bellamy. Trust me, in the last few days, I've learned more about that girl than I ever cared to know." One of his hands balled into a fist at his chest. "She was a graduate student, she came here from Anchorage, and according to her friends, she had just went through a bad breakup with her boyfriend and wanted to go out that night to 'relax a little'." He shook his head morosely. "She was a baby."

His words broke at the end, and my heart ached to tell him everything would be okay.

"Abram, I—"

"Stop," he said, his voice sharp enough to silence me. "You didn't kill her, but that doesn't mean you didn't facilitate the tragedy. Make no mistake, that girl is dead because of your actions."

If I could have seen my own face, it would have no doubt been a trip. What the hell was he talking about?

"*My* actions?" I balked. "I didn't do anything."

"Precisely." He growled, turning to me, his arms crossing across his massive chest. God, why was I always looking at his chest? I forced my attention up to his face as he continued. "The upstairs was supposed to be closed off, Ms. Bellamy. No one—*no one*—was supposed to be up there. I made that explicitly clear to you many times!"

He was closer to me now, his mammoth chest heaving in huge, infuriated breathes. His teeth ground together, his lips curled back, and there was a fire in his eyes that would have scared me if it didn't intrigue me so much.

"So how did it happen, Ms. Bellamy? How did that poor girl end up in a place inside *my* club that *you* ensured me no one would enter?"

Maybe I should have been afraid. Maybe I should have been repentant. He had, after all, made it crystal clear to me that upstairs was off limits to everyone but me, employees included.

But it hadn't even been the balcony she had fallen from, and what's more, who knew how long her body had been on the roof before it fell? The police said it wasn't the fall that killed her. She'd already been dead.

So, no, I wasn't repentant. And I sure as hell wasn't afraid. I was angry, outraged, and what was more, *I was right.*

"She fell through the *roof*, Abram," I said. "Not over the balcony."

A vein pulsed along his temple. "You can't *get* to the roof without access through the second floor," he said through gritted teeth. "So I ask you again—How. Did. This. Happen?

"You know what?" I jabbed his chest with my index finger. His pecs were firm and unyielding, which I probably would have paid more attention to if I wasn't enraged. "None of this would have happened if *you*"—I poked him again for good measure—"would have done *your* job!"

His dark eyes widened, but I didn't let him respond. I had too much to say.

"That's right, you *arrogant asshole.*" Jab, jab, jab. The last poke of his chest hurt one of the knuckles in my pointer finger, so I finally dropped my hand away. "If you would have actually taken the time to be where you were supposed to be instead of laying it all on my lap, then maybe things would have turned out differently."

"Don't you dare," he said. He stepped so close to me that our chests pressed together. He had to crane down his head to look at me, and I think I trembled a little then, but not out of fear. "I'm not the one who allowed a murderer through the front door."

Abram was a big guy, even compared to a tall, curvy girl like myself. But I swallowed the lump in my throat and steeled my gaze up at him. "And what the hell was I supposed to do about that?"

"What I hired you to do!" he said. "You told me you could do this. You sold yourself as some street savvy siren who knew everything there was to know about running a nightclub. Where's that woman, Ms. Bellamy? Because, from where I'm standing, all I see is some blubbering little girl making excuses!"

Before I could stop myself, my arm reared back. My hand flew toward him, ready to smack him in his smug, gorgeous face.

Instead of taking the hit, however, he grabbed my arm with his hand and held it steady in the air, staring at me with fierce eyes and flared nostrils. He was so close to me, his chest heaving against mine, that his breath mingled with my own. I sensed he was angry enough to want to do *something*, but I didn't know what. He was a brute, but he wasn't the type to hurt a woman.

He *was* the type to not completely control his temper, though.

"Maybe I should find a new place to work," I said breathlessly, his hand still cupping my arm.

"Maybe you should," he answered, his tone firmer than my own.

I tried to muster up some of that confidence I felt the first day I strolled—or rather fell—into this place. "Your club will never recover from this without me, though."

His grip on my arm faltered a little, but he didn't let go. "I guess we'll see."

For a few more moments, I stared at him, my breaths matching his. What the hell did he want from me?

I pulled my arm away and glared. Turning around, I huffed as I made my way back up the steps.

"The police tape comes down on Wednesday," he said from behind me. "We're open for business again the next day. Will I see you here?"

"I guess we'll see," I muttered, rolling my eyes and walking away.

* * *

As I drove back to Lulu's, I tried shaking off thoughts of Abram, but it wasn't all that easy. He was such an ass—such an absolutely infuriating prick—but I couldn't stop thinking about him.

Did he hate me as much as he seemed to? And if he did, why did I care?

It was a stupid job. Sure, it paid well, but even if I lost it, I could get another one. It would probably be better, too, because I wouldn't have to deal with a boss like him.

I jacked up the volume on the radio, but Florence and the Machine didn't help. All the chords either made me think of how mad I was at Abram or how mad I was at myself for still thinking about how mad I was at Abram. For thinking about him at all.

By the time I got home, I knew what I had to do. The only way to stop thinking about a bad guy was to start thinking about a good one.

I scrolled to Dalton's name in my phone and placed the call from the driveway—only because it was sort of awkward to talk to someone you are hot for in front of their sister.

Lulu's little brother. God, what was I thinking?

But when he picked up on the other end, I actually grinned a little.

"Took you long enough," he said. "I was beginning to think I lost my charismatic charm."

"Remember that time you saw my boobs?" I asked playfully.

I practically heard him blush on the other end of the phone. "I do."

"Well, usually a guy has to buy me dinner before he gets a look at the goods. It's time for you to pay up, Big Boy."

* * *

The next night at Luigi's, Dalton was an entire forty-three minutes late. Still, when he came rushing through the door, a frazzled blur of apologies, he *was* carrying a bouquet of fresh white roses.

"An interrogation ran long. I would have called, but I was this close to a confession," he said, coming tableside with his thumb and forefinger inches apart in front of him.

"Really?" I asked, taking the roses and setting them on the table. "How did it go?"

"Better than this date so far," he said, spying the placement of the flowers. "Are you mad?"

"Not mad, just hungry," I answered.

He ran a hand through his hair and sighed. "Can we start over?"

"No," I said. "You're doing fine."

"Am I?" He smiled and waved away the waitress before she could make it to the table. "Because you seem a little preoccupied."

"Don't be ridiculous."

Of course, I *was* preoccupied. I had spent the entire day fuming about Abram, counting down the hours to this date, and hoping that Dalton's easy-going demeanor would help clear my mind. But here we were, him standing as though he was patrolling our dinner table, and me still unable to stop thinking about my boss.

But Dalton's presence *was* melting away my stress. He was sweet. He was funny and charming. He bought me roses and apologized when he did something wrong. He didn't scream at me and blame me for things that were beyond my control.

He wasn't Abram.

More importantly, we clicked. He knew me. We grew up together. He wasn't some snide mystery man who pushed me away every time I got close to him.

Why was I still thinking about Abram?

Ugh! That man was so infuriating that he made me mad even when he wasn't around!

As Dalton sat down and started perusing the menu, I pretended to do the same, even though I had already read it six times. The fact was, Dalton was a good guy—the perfect guy, actually. It could be good between us. No, scratch that. It could be *great*. We could be 'Nicholas Sparks, clutching each other in the rain and dying in bed together' great.

I couldn't let my anger toward my jackass boss ruin something that wonderful, could I? Nope, not today. I knew what I had to do.

I reached over, took Dalton's hand in mine, and squeezed it. "Thank you for the roses, thank you for the jacket the other night, and thank you for the lobster roll I ordered before you got here. If I'm preoccupied, it's because I've had a lot on my mind. But that doesn't matter anymore, because you were right. I have to quit my job, and I'm going to do it tonight."

CHAPTER 7

Dalton managed to stop me from getting up in the middle of dinner to rush over to The Castle and quit, which turned out to be a good thing, since the date turned out to be pretty enjoyable. Especially because Dalton couldn't be happier with my decision. Even before dead sorority girls started falling from the rafters, Dalton didn't think I belonged there. And, while I still wasn't sure what he meant when he said I 'wasn't the right type of girl for a place like that,' after everything that had happened, I wasn't sure I disagreed with him, either.

I wasn't a good fit for that place, and I sure as hell wasn't a good fit for Abram. Our last interaction would've told anyone as much. All I wanted to do was stop thinking about him—about his brooding eyes, about his hard, sculpted chest, about his stupidly handsome (and always scowling) face. Most of all, I didn't want to think about the electricity that sparked between us more and more every time we were near one another.

I promised Dalton I would give it the weekend and let myself cool off before I officially quit. He didn't want me running in there and saying something I would regret. So I sat around all weekend, twiddling my thumbs, chewing the scenery, and all around chilling out. Turned out Dalton was right. After I got a hold of myself, the fire in my gut—the thing that was pushing me to run away from Abram and The Castle so quickly—died down. Even the desire to leave faded.

I was left only with this: the knowledge I would be better off away from there, away from him. Away from my unexplainable feelings that threatened to ruin a good thing between Dalton and me.

And that was as clear as it was pertinent. It was for that reason I knew I still had to quit.

I moved down the stairwell to the club as carefully as I had every time, save the first. Expecting to see Abramr standing outside an unbroken sphere of police barricades, I was stunned to find the alleyway empty and the pavement littered with shredded crime scene tape.

"Damn him," I muttered.

I hurried the rest of the way toward the door, ready to type my security code into the pad and get this over with, but the door was already open. In fact, it was swung out so far it had practically fallen off the hinges.

"Abram," I called through the door. "Abram, you're not supposed to be in there. They could throw your dumb ass in prison for this!"

When he didn't answer, I stepped inside. I was going to kill this man even if I ended up in an orange jumpsuit. I flicked on the lights to get a better look, but what I saw took my breath away.

The entire place was in ruins.

The furniture was tipped over, destroyed with its pieces splayed across the floor. Glasses lay shattered in shards on what was left of the bar, and scorch marks spotted the drapes and carpeted areas. All my work in tatters around me.

"Somebody set this place on fire," I whispered to myself.

"Among other things."

I jumped back a step. Even though I had expected Abram's presence, his voice still startled me. But nothing was more alarming than his condition.

Abram sat ass against the floor, his knees to his chest, his eyes transfixed on the destruction surrounding him. Though he remained his hulking self, dressed in a gray pair of pants and a tight matching blazer, he looked smaller somehow.

It didn't take me long to recognize the look on his face. It was the same one I felt on my own when my agent told me I had aged out of modeling, when I had to move to a smaller apartmdent, when Mom was diagnosed. It was utter defeat, the sort one only earns by watching everything they've built melt away in an instant.

Maybe I had been wrong about Abram not caring about The Castle. Whatever things in this world were important to him, this club was among them.

I walked a few steps toward him but decided it prudent to keep at least some distance between us.

I splayed my hands. "What happened?"

"Looters, I suppose. That's what the fire department told me." He shrugged lightly. "They took the beer, all the alcohol. Smashed up the place pretty good. I'm told I'm 'lucky' they were able to contain the fire. Some *luck*, huh?"

My hand flexed into a fist at my side. "My God, why didn't you call me?"

"I didn't think you would care," he mumbled.

"That's not fair," I said, shaking my head. "I know we didn't leave off in a good place, but if you needed me, I would have come." I cleared my throat, turning to hide the blush creeping up my cheeks. "I mean, it's my job."

"Is it?" he asked, arching his eyebrows. "After the other day, I wasn't sure. What are you doing here anyway? You obviously didn't know any of this was going on, and you're not on the schedule."

"I came here to quit." I sighed. "But it's not—"

"Quit then," he said. "I wouldn't blame you." His gaze panned the room. "I know I gave you a hard time before, but you shouldn't have to go through this. It isn't your mess to clean up."

Turned out that was all it took. Looking at Abram, so humbled, so downtrodden, and hearing him tell me that none of this was my problem...well, it made me want to *make* it my problem.

He was a dick, sure. But he was also right. I shouldn't have to go through this. No one should.

Not even him.

"I can't believe how selfish people are," I said, and I crossed the rest of the way to kneel beside him on the floor—even though it would likely ruin my designer skirt. "To hit you when you're down like this, all for a couple bottles of beer and whiskey."

"Please." He scoffed. "Tell me you aren't as blind or ignorant as the firemen and police officers in this town."

"What?" I narrowed my eyes. "You don't think this was a burglary?"

"The fire started upstairs," he said, his gaze lifting up. "Where that girl was killed."

I wasn't sure whether it was what he said or the way his dark eyes bore into me after he said it, but suddenly it was hard to form words.

"I—you..." My hands twisted together in my lap. I wanted to reach out to comfort him, but for some reason, it felt wrong. "You think someone was trying to destroy the evidence?"

"No," he said, scowling. "I think someone *succeeded* in destroying the evidence. The entire attic is gone. Most of the bottom floor was ravaged."

I didn't know what to say. Nothing would make him feel better.

"There's nothing left here, Ms. Bellamy, at least nothing you can help me fix."

"So that's it?" I asked. "You have one bad week, and you just give up?"

He smirked, challenging me with his gaze. "Says the girl who came to quit."

I lowered my head and stared at my hands folded in my lap. "It's not like that."

He sat up straighter, some of his old self shining through again, and I didn't know whether to be grateful or annoyed for that. "Then tell me what it is like."

Yes, I *had* just come in to quit, in no small part because I saw this place, and my boss, as a lost cause. That didn't mean I wanted Abram to feel the same way, though, and I wasn't sure how to tell him that without letting on to thinking the place was doomed no matter what.

"I—uh—"

He tilted his head to one side. "You what? Are you at a loss for words, Ms. Bellamy?"

I slammed my fist against the ground between us. "You are extremely aggravating!"

Abram leaned back against the wall, hands folded behind his head, and closed his eyes. "There's the door," he said. "No one's making you stay."

That was probably *why* I was so upset right now. Because if I was being honest with myself, a small part of the reason I had done this—a very, very small part—had been because I wanted him to fight for me to stay. Now here I was, trying to convince him he still needed me.

Something wasn't right here.

And still I tried.

"I get that it'll be a lot of work—"

"Too much work, Ms. Bellamy." He brushed himself off and stood up. Even now, after having known him for this long, I was still shocked by the sheer size of him. "And for what?"

"For this!" I answered, waving at the wreckage and hoping he could see it for what it could still be. "You worked really hard on this."

Well, whenever you weren't disappearing for the night.

"*We* worked really hard on this!" I added, following him as he marched toward the hallway. "We worked our asses off for this stupid club, and now you're just going to walk away because things got rough?"

"Is that what you think this is about?" He turned to me so

abruptly that I took a step back. His eyes bore into me again, and I could barely catch my breath. "What's happening here is dangerous. These disappearances, this murder, that howling thing in the woods—this is not pretend, Ms. Bellamy. This is not some dark fairytale you can dismiss or ignore. Real people are *dying*. Do you think I care about this ridiculous club, about these walls and floors? This was supposed to be a place they could go! A place where they would be safe while—" He bit his lip hard and looked at the floor. Looking back up at me, he added, "It was never about this *place*."

"Then what?" I asked in a small voice. "What is it about?"

"Don't you get it?" His brow furrowed, as though he was surprised that I didn't already know the answer to my question.

"It's about...the people?"

"You, Ms. Bellamy," he said, softening his tone. "It's about you, of course. Ever since you fell into my arms, ever since the moment I saw you, with that freckle in your eye and your take-the-world-by-storm nature, it's been about you."

My heart jackhammered in my chest, beating so hard I was sure it would shatter my ribcage. Was this actually happening? Was Abram telling me he had feelings for me? But that couldn't be right.

"What are you saying?" I asked, too stunned to move.

"I'm saying there are things happening here that you don't know about, that you shouldn't have to worry about." He set his jaw. "You need to leave this club, leave this town, and don't ever look back." He gave me a long stare—one that I might describe as longing if I was forward enough to believe it—then he added, "Your final paycheck will be in the mail by the end of business today. Have a good life, Ms. Bellamy."

He turned and lumbered toward the back room.

Oh, hell no. He was not just going to say that and walk away! I rushed after him just in time to watch him head through the 'symbol door.' I grabbed the handle, but it scorched my fingers, and I yanked my hand back.

What the hell? It was way too hot to touch, let alone turn.

I chewed my lip, eyeing the door, thinking about shouting at him through the hunk of wood to come back out here. But even the thought of doing that made me feel pathetic. I had come here to quit—to get away from him. And now I was running after him, on the verge of begging him to talk to me?

No, I couldn't be that girl. But I certainly wasn't going to be the girl who took commands from some man who didn't even know how to work a damned ice machine.

Yes, there were things going on here. Things I didn't know about, and things that I *did*. There were reasons for me to stay in this town. Dalton, for one, and for two, well...Abram.

Ugh.

I closed my eyes and leaned against the wall beside the symbol door, tilting my head back. I was here for Lulu. That's why I came in the first place, even if most days it felt more like she was helping me. I promised I would be here when she had her baby, and if for no other reason, that was why I would stay. I certainly wasn't going to run away just because some asshole told me I should.

I moved back to the club's main area, deflating as I surveyed the mess. Dalton aside, this club had been the only bright spot in my last few weeks. Fixing this dive up—making it a place people wanted to be—filled me with a sense of purpose that I hadn't felt since Mom died.

That's when I knew what I would do.

Instead of *telling* Abram what I was thinking, I would *show* him. I would fix this entire place up and let him see for himself that I was stronger than whatever dangers he feared for on my behalf. He might have been ready to throw in the towel, but I wasn't. We would worry about the rest later—add security, do a night of free admission to show this place wasn't a murder barn...whatever necessary, we would do it. But Milan-be-damned, this club wouldn't be left for dead.

Mom didn't raise a quitter and, soon enough, Abram would know that, too.

CHAPTER 8

It took three phone calls and all of forty-five minutes to get help putting The Castle back together. I would have liked to give myself a huge pat on the back for proving myself to be a competent and effective manager (if that was even what I was anymore), but the truth was, for all the upper crust snootiness New Haven had garnered in the last decade, work was still few and far between—which meant the lowly middle class couldn't turn away employment opportunities.

Even if those opportunities happened to be at a murder scene.

I couldn't, of course, actually do any of the refurbishments until the police tape officially came down. And since that wasn't happening for a day or two, I had plenty of time to load up on supplies. Unfortunately, the only décor store I could find that didn't have the word 'Barn' in the title was a good fifty miles away, but I wasn't about to let that stop me.

It was that want for supplies—or, more precisely, the hunt for the perfect replacement tables—which had me on the road that night.

I should have gone earlier, but Lulu had woken up short of breath and, as the designated freeloading best friend, rushing her to the emergency room fell under my jurisdiction. It was just gas (thank God), but when you're that preggers, they apparently have to run three dozen tests no matter what brings you to the hospital.

By the time I got her back home, fed, and safely in bed with Jack snoring in the next room, the sun had already set.

I thought about putting the trip off until tomorrow. I even thought about asking Dalton to come with me. It could be a date, of sorts. But I was behind schedule, and if I was going to be serious about this, then I needed to get a move on, and Dalton would have been...distracting.

I cut onto the main road, my mind firing off one stressing thought after the next. Things were supposed to be simpler here. This was supposed to be the place I could chill out and start over after my mother's death.

But here I was, dating one man, thinking about another, and strutting down a runway surrounded by an ever-growing audience of dead bodies that looked unnervingly like me.

Why was I doing this? I never wanted to run a nightclub, and I sure as hell didn't see myself settling down in New Haven.

I pressed harder on the gas pedal, accelerating as though I was already making a run for it from that miserable town. But there was a hesitation there I hadn't felt before. Something that made me feel tethered to New Haven.

Maybe the reason I wanted club manager job was for the control. Maybe, with so much spinning in orbit around my head—so much that I couldn't grab or change or fix—I felt compelled to find any situation I *could* control. And The Castle was just that.

Thinking of the club brought an image of Abram to mind, and I sighed. Was it The Castle I was drawn to...or was it *him?* I tried to think back to other jobs I'd had before, and never had thinking about work made me think about my employer's eyes, or arms, or chest, or lips.

I gripped the steering wheel tighter and gave myself a little shake. *Snap out of it, Char.* The truth was, I was only thinking of Abram right now because I felt bad for him. He had seemed so defeated. Of course I couldn't get that image out of my mind—

who could? All I wanted to do was save him from that misery. Lord knows I couldn't save myself from mine.

I mean, it was either that, or I just wanted the job because he didn't want me to have it.

So I either want to help him or piss him off. Real healthy, Char.

Those thoughts, along with a little concern about whether the tables would look like they did on the website, swirled in my mind.

On a long, dark stretch of highway with woods on either side, Lulu's car made a loud pop. I had never been much of a driver. It wasn't really a necessity in New York. As such, I didn't really know what was going on when something about the steering changed and the car startled swerving across the emergency lane.

I jumped, gasping. Tightening my grip on the wheel, I jerked back hard the other way. The car fishtailed and spun across the empty highway until it skidded sideways into a tree.

Despite being thrown back, my seatbelt kept me in place. Still, it hurt like a bitch. .

Once I pulled myself together, I stumbled out of the car. I kicked off my heels and cursed my incessant need to dress up even when only the employees at a furniture supply store would see me. A quick assessment of the car revealed the culprit for my distress: a flat tire.

That's pretty special.

Only I could have such a disastrous reaction to something so basic. The flat tire may as well have been ancient hieroglyphics for all I knew about it.

As I stared at the shredded rubber, chewing my lip, my agent's voice scrolled through my mind. "Pretty girls shouldn't do that sort of work," she'd said one day in reference to women learning to change the oil in their car. "It ruins the hands."

I looked down at my hands now. They were useless, but damn if they weren't stunning. I rifled through the front seat until I found my cell phone. No signal.

Ugh! I hate this place.

So much for Triple A. Maybe if I walked back toward town, I

could get a signal. It was only a couple of miles, and for all I knew, only a few steps until the signal kicked back on.

I grabbed my purse and took a look around. The road was dark, sandwiched by thick tree lines and without a single street lamp. Not exactly my idea of an inviting nightly stroll.

A sense of uneasiness crept over me. Here I was, all alone, in the dark, and without any way to call for help.

Would walking down that road even be safe?

Would staying here with the car be safe, either?

I thought about the girl in the club—her dead, open eyes. I thought about the missing girl, about what might have happened to her. I thought about the girl in the next town over, the one who had been found in these woods...not too far from here. She'd had markings all over her and a face that could easily be confused for my own.

But if I worried about that now, I was just as bad as the backwoods townsfolk who spun tall tales about forest monsters being the culprit.

A howl, sharp and terrifyingly close, spiked a shiver down my spine. My muscles tensed as something primal and instinctive turned on in my brain. I grabbed at my phone, fumbling for my flashlight app and squinting as its thin white light forced a narrow cone into the darkness.

I spun slowly, looking around for the source of that howl and hoping to God I didn't find it.

The woods were even closer than I thought, almost swallowing up the road on either side. Had they grown in the ten years since I had been gone? I didn't remember them being so...encroaching.

I shone my light back toward town. Maybe if I waited here, locking myself in the car, someone would come by.

I inched backward, grasping for the door handle while scanning the area with my light.

Then I heard it—low, even breaths accompanied with a simmering growl. It was worse than the howl, mostly because of how close it was. I couldn't dismiss it this time. It rumbled so near that every hair on my arms and neck prickled.

A whoosh of something darted in front of me, knocking into my hand. My phone flew from my gasp and landed screen first onto the road, the light shooting straight up into the nighty sky.

I jerked back as I saw what it now illuminated. A thing—some sort of animal—reared in front of me, huffing wildly.

Dark auburn fur covered its body. Its head stretched into a long snout, and fangs jutted from its open mouth. It had all the characteristics of a wolf—a massive torso, pointed ears, and powerful hind legs.

Except it wasn't a wolf. Wolves weren't this big.

It threw its head up and howled again, loudly into the moonlight. Never one to run toward a fight, I spun away and took off, my bare feet smacking the pavement. But I knew it was no use. This open road would make it a foot race, and an animal that size would have a gait I couldn't outrun. My only chance, if I had any at all, would be to somehow lose this beast inside the woods.

The animal took off behind me, first two feet, and then four, clapping against the pavement.

I darted into the woods, stumbling as the ground shot up a little at the tree line. My heart raced ten times faster than usual. Fear sent beads sweat crawling down my spine.

My eyes adjusted to the near-absolute darkness just in time to alert me I was about to crash headfirst into a tree. I stopped, bracing myself against the bark. I dodged out of the way, but the animal chasing me wasn't so lucky. It slammed into the tree trunk and let out a surprisingly human-sounding yelp.

I zigged to my left then zagged to my right, remembering something from a television special about some kind of animal that couldn't keep up with that sort of thing.

No such luck, though. The beast gained ground on me.

Oh that's right. It was an alligator.

The beast's breath, hot and terrifying, brushed against the back of my neck. I was even hotter now, pouring sweat as I spun around a nearby tree, changing directions.

I had no idea where I was headed or even what direction I was going in. But the quick thinking earned me a much needed split second. Using it, I slid to the ground, wincing and throwing my hands in front of me as the beast jumped over me. It skidded to a stop and turned.

Getting back on its hind legs, it paused with bright yellow eyes trailing down my body before baring its teeth again. Then, slowly, it started toward me again.

My eyes stayed locked on the creature, but my hand went for my bag. Back in New York, I kept mace in my purse. You know, because of the crazies.

As the monster neared me, my fingers fumbled for the small rounded bottle. It growled again, and I sensed a bit of hunger, but then, I suppose it wasn't chasing me down just to say hello.

Grabbing the bottle, I cursed my luck. *Empty*. But there was something beside it—something small, hard, and bumpy.

That's right. A stupid exfoliating soap my agent used to make me use—the one Mom said could take paint off the walls.

I wrapped my fingers around it, unsure what I was going to do. It was a rock, at best. And what good could a rock do against a monster? Even David had a slingshot.

The monster settled in front of me, leaves crackling under foot, paw, or hoof—whatever this thing had. Its breaths were not labored like mine. It hadn't even exerted itself.

Its hands folded in a claw-like manner, probably preparing to shred me to pieces, to mark me up the way it had the woman on the internet. And, like her, tomorrow I would nothing but a statistic—an unanswered question posted alongside a picture in the newspaper.

It opened its mouth wide, howling as it had before, and I reared my arm back and flung the soap. God must have been feeling cheeky, because it landed right in the monster's open yap.

The creature grabbed its throat and starting heaving, choking on the soap.

I scrambled to my feet, not sure where I was going, but ready to get anywhere where this beast wasn't.

As quick as my bare, pedicured feet would take me, I ran deeper into the woods. The monster probably wouldn't choke to death on soap, but I might be able to find a hiding place to duck into to wait the horrible thing out.

I ran so far and so fast that my lungs burned. I kept imagining the monster behind me again, paws galloping after me. I had to keep running. Maybe there was a ditch, or a cave, or a...

Or a two story house with front porch furniture?

I slid to a stop, bracing myself against the pain in my bloody and bruised feet. There, sitting in the middle of the woods, like the greatest mirage anyone could ever imagine, stood a house. A light shone from a second floor window. Not only was there a house out here, where a house had no business being, but there was someone in it.

I might actually survive this.

A howl shot through the woods; the monster was undoubtedly back on track, so I pooled what little energy I had left and made a beeline for the front door. My hands slammed against it in panicked knocks.

"Help me!" I screamed. "Help!"

No one answered. With little time to waste, I turned the knob, and to my great relief, the door actually opened.

I clamored in, slammed the door closed behind me, and bolted the lock.

The first floor was dark, but I switched on a nearby light.

"Hello?" I yelled again. "I know I shouldn't be here, but there's something out there!" Tears stung my eyes. "I need help!"

No answer.

I ran toward the stairs, to the burning second floor light. At the very least, if the monster found me here, I needed as many closed doors between us as possible.

Two rooms sat at the top of the stairs. I grabbed the handle straight ahead, but it was hot and singed my fingertips. For an instant, my mind traveled to the door inside The Castle. But then a sickeningly close howl shook me back to the present.

I darted inside the other room. But no sooner had I crossed the threshold than the window shattered in front of me. Glass flew everywhere, and when it settled, the monster stood before me.

It was on its hind legs again, like a man. Bits of the soap were clutched in its 'hand,' and the look in its yellow eyes said it would enjoy whatever hell it was about to put me through.

I turned toward the open door, hoping I could at least run for it, but to my utter shock, I was met by a second beast. This one was even larger than the first. Its body was even more hulking, covered in coarse black fur. It, too, stood on its hind legs, but this one looked past me, toward the other monster.

Just when I was about to burst into defeated tears, it leapt over me. I had never seen anything so big move so quickly, so fluidly.

In an instant, it was on the other monster, tearing into it with claws and teeth.

Before they could finish fighting over which of them would get to eat me, I turned toward the stairs to make my escape. Maybe they would kill each other, or maybe they would get over their differences and split me down the middle. Either way, I wasn't planning to hang around and find out.

I grabbed hold of the railing to start down the stairs, but the old wood snapped beneath my touch. I fell in a series of painful tumbles. My head hit hard against the floor, but only enough to rattle me—not enough to stop me from trying not to die.

But when I attempted to stand or even move, it was no use. My vision darkened. I struggled, pulling myself across the floor.

I didn't even make it half-way to door before things went black.

I was about to become the world's best-dressed doggie treat, and there was nothing I could do about it.

CHAPTER 9

Stretching against the cool, soft sheets, memories filtered in the way they often did in the morning. But when the image of the beasts came along, my mind snapped to attention, and my eyes flew open.

I wasn't on the floor anymore. I was in a lumpy bed, satin sheets covering me and pillows propping up my head. How did I get here? What happened to the monsters that seemed so intent on making a meal out of me?

The vision of their yellow eyes and bared fangs clouded my thoughts. Surely they hadn't left such an easy meal passed out at the bottom of the staircase, and even if they had, that didn't explain how I'd ended up in this bed.

I leaned forward, my body aching all over as I scanned the room for danger. Not that I would be able to defend myself should anything pop up. My head was spinning, my vision blurred, and worse than that, my phone was nowhere in sight. Embarrassingly, my stomach rumbled, as though food should be the most of my concerns.

Flinging the sheets back revealed a cut red rose lying beside me on the bed. It had been pruned, too, free of thorns.

Okay, things just went from weird to weirder.

I still had no idea whose house I was in, but it was pretty clear someone had been here. Maybe the owner of this place, the one responsible for the burning light on the second floor window, had saved me. Maybe he had beat back those animals, and when he was done with that, scooped me up Rhett Butler style, put me to bed, and sat a rose beside me for good measure.

Thinking it over, I couldn't decide whether that was cute or pervy.

"H-hello?" The word scraped my throat.

No answer came.

I threw my legs over the side of the bed and stood, taking the rose in my hand. I cleared my throat. "Is anybody there?"

For the first time, I had a chance to really look at the house I had broken into. It was plain, the walls free of pictures or paintings and the furniture sparse and nondescript.

A pair of slippers waited at the bedside beside my high heels, which were now cleaner than they had been before I took my unplanned trip through the forest.

At the thought, I froze.

I hadn't worn those shoes in the woods. I had thrown them off the instant I saw the first creature. That meant whoever put me by this bed went all the way to my car, got my shoes, and brought them back here.

All that, but they clearly hadn't called the police...

Suddenly, a new dread—a more human one—seeped into my soul. I grabbed my heels and made a beeline out the door.

I was on the first floor. Evidence of the fight lay strewn all around me; chairs and tables had been smashed in a way that reminded me of The Castle after the looting.

I had never met this person, and he had just saved my life, but I wasn't about to take a chance on dodging a wolf-shaped monster bullet just to end up like Clemp's backwoods bride.

I shoved my feet into my heels, wincing against the pain, and darted toward the front door, chancing only the slightest glare in either direction. When I got to my exit, though, I found a note hanging from the handle.

Leave this place. Don't tell anyone about it or anything you saw here, and don't ever come back.

Of course, I took the advice.

* * *

It took me an hour to find my way back to the main road, stumbling over hills and valleys on my heels so hard that I soon wished I had reached for the slippers instead. Lord knew the damage from running barefoot last night was enough on its own to slow me down.

I must have come out of the woods at a very different spot than I left it, because my car was nowhere to be seen.

Sighing, I brushed the hair out of my eyes and started the long trek back to New Haven.

I had been gone all night, and I didn't even have any furniture to show for it. How would I explain all this? Something told me the truth wouldn't go over so well.

So, a monster chased me into a weird house where another monster attacked it. I hit my head, and then I woke up with turn-down service.

Yeah, not so much.

A mile of hot asphalt later, I had my heels in my hands and two throbbing, bloody feet. But nothing was worse than the head full of questions I would never get the answers to.

New Haven appeared before me, as quaint as ever. Still, even a hick town like that was a beautiful sight for eyes that had witnessed what mine just had.

I looked down, instinctively primping myself. Just because I had been through hell didn't mean I had to look like it. But there was no way I was putting those heels back on.

"Hey!" a voice called out from behind me.

I jerked, my entire body trembling. The whole experience must have shaken me up worse than I thought.

"Hey, you!" A kid, maybe seventeen years old, came darting out of the woods toward me. "Get over here!"

Panicking, I flung my shoe at him. My Gucci knocked him in head.

"Goddamn it!" he shrieked, grabbing his skull. "What's your problem, lady? I'm trying to help you."

"W-what?" I asked, suddenly feeling pretty ridiculous. "What the hell are you talking about?"

"You're the model, right?" He looked me up and down. "Dude! The whole town's looking for you!"

"Did you just call me dude?" I asked before registering the rest of what he had said.

"Are you hurt or something?" he asked, scratching his head. "I mean, you don't really look hurt..." he started, but then his gaze continued down to my feet. "Shit, do I need to call an ambulance?"

I wasn't sure how to answer his question. I *had* been through a traumatic experience, sure, and maybe I was in shock...but I doubted there was much a hospital could do for cut up feet. And I certainly didn't feel like having some doctor poke and prod at me all day. I just needed some Advil, a warm bath, a lot of bandages, and my own bed to crawl so I could try to forget everything.

Of course, if the entire town was looking for me, then it definitely wouldn't be that easy.

The boy waved his hand in front of my face then grabbed his phone. "I'm calling somebody to help you, 'kay?"

"No," I said, shaking my head.

But it was too late. The kid already had emergency services on the phone, and within ninety seconds, the sirens blared toward us.

I wasn't surprised to see a patrol car cresting the hill, blinking lights shining from the cab. And when it screeched to a stop in front of me, leaving skid marks on the pavement, I wasn't surprised to see Dalton jump out of it, either.

But the look on his face—the pain mixed with unimaginable relief and hesitant hopefulness—pinged at me. It was the sort of look you only get when someone you *really* cared about was in trouble.

"It's her," he said, slamming the door shut and sprinting toward me.

He scooped me up into his arms and squeezed me just enough to let me know I was really here...really alive. And, for whatever reason, I instantly hoped he would never let me go. That he would tuck me away somewhere safe, where it would just be him and me.

The way it should have been last night, if only I had done what I told him I was going to do.

"Thank God," he muttered, his face pressed against the crook of my neck. "We thought you were..."

"I'm okay." I breathed against his chest, nearly crumbling in into his embrace. "Just a little shaken up. And tired. But I'm definitely not...well, you know."

He set me down and started to turn away, but not before wiping a tear from his cheek. Meanwhile, Lulu lugged herself out of the backseat of the cop car. My guilt over not being where I should have been doubled at the sight of her, then tripled at the sight of her overripe belly.

She was *so* pregnant. So. Damn. Pregnant. And here I was, blowing out the tire on her car and disappearing into the woods.

"It's all right," I said, tears burning behind my eyes. "I'm fine, really I am."

I stepped toward her and hugged her the same way she had hugged me after Mom's diagnosis.

Her whole body was trembling. "They found the car—"

"I'm sorry about the car," I said.

"Shut up about the stupid car," she said, wiping her eyes, smiling through her tears. "What happened? Where were you?"

My mind flickered back to last night, to running through the woods away from monsters and finding myself mysteriously moved inside a seemingly abandoned house. Then I thought about all the girls who had disappeared, all of the girls who looked just like me. And the note on the door of the house, warning me to keep my mouth shut.

My lips parted, though I was still unsure what to say. It wasn't so much the note that gave me pause. After all, I was free of whoever wrote it. But, even if I told the truth, who would believe me?

Monsters running through the woods at night? Wolves that stood on their hind legs like men? It was one thing for people to make up stories about missing girls and wild animals, but it was another to say you knew those outlandish stories actually had merit.

None of it made any sense, and it would have likely either branded me a lunatic or an unreliable witness. Or, ya know, maybe they would eat the story right out of my hand—this was New Haven after all. But did I want to take the risk? Once I said it, there would be no taking it back.

So I did what any woman would do when faced with a similar situation: told as much of the truth as possible without making myself look bad.

"The tire blew out, and then I heard some weird noises..." I started, trying not to pause too much as I filtered out details of my story on the spot. "My phone didn't have service, and I saw a...an animal or something on the road. It started chasing me, and I headed out into the woods." I swallowed hard. "It took me this long to find my way back out."

"Oh, my Lord. You poor thing," Lulu said, taking my hand.

"You didn't hear us?" Dalton asked, cocking his head to the side. "After we found the car, a few of us went out into the woods with hounds, looking for you. We weren't quiet about it."

"I...I must have been a long way out," I answered. "Not that I would have been in the mood to come running toward the sound of dogs."

"Understandable," he muttered.

"There's a house, Dalton," I said, my stomach twisting in knots. "Out in the woods, there's an old house. It looks like someone might live there."

Someone who wanted to protect the secret of what was really

going on in those woods, I thought. But I couldn't say that—not without explaining more than I cared to.

For a long moment, Dalton glared past me and into the woods. I wasn't sure whether he could tell I was withholding something, but it was clear that a bit of his ease melted away.

His teeth ground together, and his jaw set. "I'll look into that."

* * *

Although Dalton and Lulu insisted on me going to the hospital, the choice was ultimately mine. They settled for me heading back to Lulu's house with both of them to keep an eye on me.

On the ride home, I learned I wasn't the only person who went missing last night; there was one other woman—a real estate agent and mother of three—who disappeared while walking her dog a few hours before they found my car. Her name was Rachel, and judging by Dalton's description of her, she looked a lot like me.

Of course.

We pulled up in front of Lulu's house, the events of the previous night chasing so close behind me that I shivered at the sight of the woods stretching across Lulu's backyard, just past the fence Dalton had parked in front of. He came around to my side of the car and opened the door, while Lulu let herself out and headed up the path to unlock the front door.

"Things are kind of falling apart around here," he said, taking my hand and guiding me out of car much more than I actually needed. "This is the third woman, not counting you, who's vanished in the last month." He shook his head. "Throw in the woman found in your nightclub and the lady from the next county over who was mauled to death, and people are understandably on edge."

"Well, that's why you're here, right?" I asked as he led me up the front steps and held the door open for me.

"I'm afraid it's bigger than me now, Char," he said. "People want to feel like they're in control, especially when they're not."

He guided me through the door, as careful as if I was made of glass. Lulu was in the living room with Ester, the two whispering as not to wake Jack, who was sound asleep on the couch. Some cartoon movie about a genie and a magic lamp emanated a soft glow from the screen.

Great. My disappearance had completely uprooted Lulu's quaint family life. I was supposed to be a help, not a burden. Ester glared at me as she carried Jack past us and up to his room.

"So now what?" I asked, turning back to Dalton. "You have to do something."

He nodded emphatically. "We are, Char. I promise you. They town council held an emergency meeting this morning. Some of the townsfolk had concerns, and we're going to institute a curfew for the woman in town."

"What?" I asked, pulling my arm back from his gentle grasp. "A female-only curfew? Are these idiots living in the stone age?"

The idea of it, of basically segregating people because women weren't strong or capable enough to fend for themselves, rubbed me every way but the right one.

"Perhaps." Dalton winced, then added, "The notion passed nearly unanimously."

I scoffed. "What kind of idiot would even suggest something like that?"

"The same kind that would hire you, I suppose." His gaze slowly shifted from looking out the front window to my face. "It was your boss."

Abram did this? Had he lost his mind?

"No. He didn't. He *wouldn't!*"

What sort of chauvinistic asshole was I working for anyway?

"Char, please try to relax," Dalton said, reaching for me once more. "You've been through enough."

I huffed and stepped back. "Would you stop treating me like the five million dollar bra for a second?"

"I have no idea what you're talking about, but if that means—"

Ester strode right between us, a smug look on her face, and exited through the front door. Dalton glared after her, then shook his head and returned his attention to me.

"If that means I value you, then the answer is no," he said. "No, I will not stop treating you like 'the five million dollar bra'." He smirked and stepped to close the distance between us. "You've been through hell. You're dehydrated, you might be hurt, and you're definitely in shock."

As much as I wanted to be angry, right about now, I didn't exactly mind the idea of a knight in shining armor swooping in to rescue me. And damn if that wasn't what Dalton was trying to do.

He put his hand on my arm. "Now, I know you can take care of yourself. You wouldn't have made it through half the crap you have if you couldn't, right? But I'm a guy," he said, moving even closer, "and my pride is at stake."

I wanted to tell him he need not measure his manliness by his ability to protect me, but I was too distracted by the heat radiating off his body at this close proximity. I couldn't form words as the warmth soaked into my own skin next. With everything that had happened in the last twenty-four hours, I was in sensory overload, and every time Dalton moved, every nerve in my body tingled in response.

He brushed my cheek with his fingers. "My girl was in trouble, and I couldn't save her." He leaned in closer, and my breath caught in my throat. "So, for the sake of me and my fragile, manly pride, let me take care of you now. Okay?"

"Okay," I whispered, just barely managing words.

He leaned in closer and pressed his lips against my ear. "Good. Not let's get you some rest. You can battle the townsfolk over that curfew after a good night's sleep."

CHAPTER 10

The next day, once I had thoroughly convinced Dalton I was perfectly capable of going on about my business as usual, I made it my personal mission to show the idiots serving the town council just how stupid and antiquated the idea of a 'women only' curfew was. Unfortunately, the town council only met on Thursdays and, according to his secretary, Mayor Altman was busy "herdin' up a mess of cattle" and couldn't be reached.

God, I hate this town.

Luckily for me, there was someone else I could vent all my pent up indignation on—someone who might be guiltier than all of the town council-folk put together.

Abram.

As I marched toward The Castle, I couldn't believe I had ever thought of Abram as anything other than a ham-handed jerk. To think I had felt sorry for him enough to try to save his dump of a club, let alone long enough to stop me from quitting.

Well, that was a mistake I would gladly remedy today. I would serve him my walking papers along with a piece of my mind.

I was almost on fire as I descended the stairwell, muttering aloud everything I was going to say to him. I had just gotten to the part where I would tell him to "kiss my fat, gorgeous ass" when I saw him.

He was outside, shirtless and sweaty as he stroked a paint brush across the front door. The hot sun glistened off his body, illuminating the tight muscle that corded his arms and shoulders as well as the pelt of coarse dark hair sprinkled across his chest and abdomen.

Ridiculously, I found myself biting my lip.

"Hey," I said, my voice breaking a little at the end.

His head snapped up, moisture plastering his hair to his forehead, and he mumbled to himself. Standing, eyes narrowed at me, he took a bottle of water and poured it over his head, letting the moisture run down his body. Droplets settled at his navel and on the trail of dark hair that disappeared behind his low hanging jeans.

I swallowed around the lump growing in my throat, dismissing the warm flush in my chest and face as a reaction to the unusually hot day. I mean, clearly it wasn't just me overheating out here. Abram was...drenched.

"Ms. Bellamy," he said, grabbing a towel that hung from a nearby chair and drying himself off. "Forgive me. I didn't expect to see you today." He slung on a flannel shirt, leaving it unbuttoned and hanging loosely around his chest. "I take it you're feeling better."

His tone was almost indifferent—a world away from the intense concern that colored every interaction I'd had with Dalton since my return.

He kneeled over the paint tin to dip his brush and tipped his head toward a paint pan to his side. "Grab a brush."

A brush? Was he joking? First of all, I was wearing Dolce. Secondly, I wasn't here to work. I never intended on working for him ever again.

I clenched my hands at my side and growled. "You've got a lot of nerve!"

He sighed and dropped the brush in the bucket. The paint

splashed up, dots of white speckling the parts of his chest that were still exposed. Then he stood tall—taller than I remembered. Had he always been this intimidating? My breath caught in my throat.

"As always, Ms. Bellamy, being around you has been the most frustratingly mysterious part of any adventure." He grabbed the handle, careful to miss the still-wet paint, and opened the door. "Why don't you come inside? You can tell what fresh irritant has you disheveled today." As if verbally rolling his eyes, he added, "I'm sure it'll be interesting."

I followed him into the club, already more furious than I had been when I'd arrived. This son of a bitch was belittling me. Maybe I shouldn't be so surprised, considering the recent turn of events.

"So this is what you think of women?" I asked, shaking my head in disgust. "Really?"

Though the workers I'd hired wouldn't come for a few more days, The Castle was starting to come together. The rubble had been cleared and a fresh coat of paint had been slapped across the walls. It was gray, which wouldn't have been my first choice. Still, the fact that Abram had done it all by himself was more than a little impressive.

But not impressive enough.

Abram arched one of his dark eyebrows. "As you seem intent on me knowing the other end of this conversation, I have to ask —" He leaned closer. "—what are you talking about?"

"What do you think I'm talking about?" I scowled. "The curfew."

He nodded. "You're welcome, of course. But I was referring to what it is that's *bothering* you."

I blanched, sure the heat in my face would come pouring out as smoke from my ears. This man—this ridiculous man—was *trying* to push my buttons. And worse, it was working.

"You smug bastard," I said, jabbing the part of his hard, bare chest that peeked out from beneath his shirt. "I don't know who you think you are or what right you think you have to—"

"To what?" he asked, smiling. He didn't move my finger; instead, he leaned in further so that my entire hand was now splayed against him. "To do what was necessary to keep you safe?"

His skin was burning, and his pulse beat rapidly against my palm. I steeled myself against the confusion swarming through my mind. I knew how I felt. Angry.

Only angry and nothing else.

Right?

My eyebrows pulled together in that way my agent warned me not to let them. Not unless I wanted wrinkles. Right now, I didn't care.

"Don't you dare make this about me," I said through gritted teeth. "This is about what you think of women!"

"I assure you I am a fan of women, Ms. Bellamy." Abram stared down into my eyes, more of a calm in his gaze than I'd ever seen before. "That is why I prefer to keep them alive."

"By making them second class citizens?" I didn't realize at first, but my nails were beginning to dig into Abram's chest. "You're aware that this curfew does nothing but assume the women here can't take care of themselves."

He grabbed my hand and pulled it away from him. I flinched when I saw the scratches on his chest, but he didn't show any signs of pain.

"I'm sorry. I didn't—"

"Judging by what's happened in the last few weeks, Ms. Bellamy, I would say protecting yourselves isn't among your strongest attributes. Collectively speaking, of course."

I tried to pull my hand from his grasp, but he held firm. "Women are every bit as capable as men."

"Perhaps," he answered. "But men aren't the ones who are being targeted. And, given that you were almost killed the other night because you couldn't change a flat tire, I wouldn't use this as your opportunity to boast of capabilities." His tongue appeared, licking his lips. "Say what you want, but we both know you need someone to take care of you. No," he amended, glaring at me as my heart hammered in my chest. "You *want* someone to take care of you. Don't you, Ms. Bellamy?"

I reared back to slap him with my other hand, but he grabbed my wrist. Now both my hands were captive, and in that instant, we were nearly nose-to-nose, breathing in the same air—a musky air that had been permeated by his scent.

"Let go," I said, hating the way both my breathing and voice had shifted.

His gaze bore into mine, as though he could see something deep inside of me, something I couldn't even see myself. Or, rather, something I didn't want to admit. Something that went against everything I believed and all of who I thought I was.

"Is that what you want, Ms. Bellamy?" His lips parted. "For me to let go?"

He inched a fraction closer, closing that last bit of space between us so that his chest pressed against mine. Suddenly, and against my volition, my nipples hardened. My heart jackhammered against my ribcage, and a flush crept up my body, warming every part of me.

Abram tipped his forehead down so that it rested against my own. "Is that what you want?"

The temperature of the room shifted. The sensation of his hands pinning mine sent sparks through my body. He pushed against me, and the evidence of his arousal stiffened against my thigh.

I opened my mouth, ready to push him away, to tell him that yes, I wanted him to let me go. But the words did not come. Instead, only a whimper escaped my lips.

"Not good enough," he said.

He dipped his head, his lips brushing warm and rough against my neck, and my knees wobbled so abruptly that I wasn't sure I could keep myself upright if not for his grip on me. Another damned whimper trickled from my mouth.

"Not near good enough." His breath was hot against the side of my neck. "Ms. Bellamy, I'm not sure you want me to let go. I think you want me to take care of you. But if you want that—if you want me to *really* take care of you—then you have to say it."

His mouth traveled to my earlobe, the same earlobe Dalton had kissed not twenty four hours before, and Abram gave it a sharp nip.

I moaned, arching my back and pressing hard against him. The entirety of me trembled as pleasure vibrated up my legs and into the rest of me. I moistened, as if to prepare for him, as if to answer his question without saying a word.

"You have to say it," he commanded. "If you want it, you have to say it."

I hadn't felt like this in...well, I couldn't remember a time I'd ever felt *this* way. The attraction—the *need*—was all-consuming. I didn't care about anything else anymore. Just this moment. So I told him what he wanted to hear—what deep down was really true.

"I...I do," I murmured, heart in my throat. "I want it."

He let go of my hands and grabbed either side of me, thrusting me up and wrapping me in his massive, muscled arms.

The world spun as he pressed his face against mine, ravaging my shoulder, neck, and jaw with his mouth.

Finally, mercifully, he took my lips with his own. The rush was almost too much to handle. When his tongue pushed past my lips and into my mouth, I thought I might faint. The warmth of him caressed me, exciting me and comforting me all at the same time.

I wrapped my legs around his waist, and we slammed into a wall still slick with fresh paint. I smelled it all, the paint that now covered us both, the sweat that slid between our bodies, the scent of him that urged me to go further.

My fingers tangled in his hair as he kissed me deeply. He throbbed against me now, and I ached for him to quench the fire he had lit.

His hand, covered in paint, ran under my blouse, inching up from my navel. He bit my lip as he tugged off my bra, freeing my breasts and sending a needy shiver through my body. I moaned again, clutching against him and thrusting my hips into his.

His mouth still pressed against my own, I felt the smile creep across his lips as he scoured my breasts hungrily, electricity in his fingers and desire coursing through my every nerve. He pinched my nipples between his thumb and forefinger until my moans turned to begging, then he pulled at my blouse, ripping it open.

"Your dress," he muttered.

"Fuck the dress," I whispered. "Just keep going."

He trailed kisses down my neck, my chest, my breasts. My body shuddered as he took them in his mouth, one and then the other. His tongue flickered across my nipples, sending shockwaves through me and beating past the very last of my defenses.

But it wasn't enough. I wanted him everywhere. As my body rocked against his, his hand traveled lower, past my navel, in between my thighs. His face came back up near mine, his nose brushing across my cheek and his lips tracing my jawline. When I tried to push my body back against his, I was met with the resistance of him holding me still and his soft chuckle in my ear.

"What are you waiting for?" There was a pleading in my voice, a pleading for him not to stop, for him never to stop.

"You're not ready," he mumbled. His hand slid over the silk of my underwear, and his thumb rubbed my clitoris through the thin material. "I've never known you to be so quiet. Are you all right?"

My nails were digging into him again—his back, this time. "I'm going to kill you, Abram."

"Not yet, you're not," he whispered. His fingers dipped in the welcoming darkness of my underwear, and I gasped as he slid one into me, but his free hand flew up and pressed over my lips.

I stood, trembling against the paint-soaked wall. With Abram's hand against my lips and his other hand inside of me, pushing deeper than I ever imagined anyone would go, it seemed as though I might explode.

After a moment, he removed his hands from me and stepped

back, but when I whimpered, he just grinned. "Shh, Mrs. Bellamy. These walls are thin. You wouldn't want the whole town to hear."

I felt vulnerable, needy, and weak—but I didn't care. My whole face burned as he assessed me with his gaze while sliding off his shirt to reveal the rest of his upper body. The paint had smeared across both of us, and he was covered in streaks of gray and desire. My heart leapt in my chest as his fingers trailed down to unbutton his pants, but there was one more thing we needed to do first.

"Wait," I breathed.

He blanched. "Is this too fast for you?"

I replied with a devilish grin. "Not fast enough," I said, both my voice and body still trembling with desire. "But now *you* have to say it. If you want me, you have to—"

"I do," he said. "Since the first moment I saw you, I have."

Well, that was a lot easier for him than it had been for me, but more importantly, I knew he was telling the truth.

His pants fell, revealing the fullness of his body. He was a sculpture, a masterpiece of skin, hair, and heart. Our bodies collided, and I wrapped my legs around him. He tore away my underwear, the shreds falling to the floor at his feet.

"You're the most beautiful thing I've ever seen," he said, just as breathless as I had been.

And that's when it hit me.

The most beautiful thing I had ever seen just called me the most beautiful thing *he* had ever seen.

All of the sudden, this town didn't seem so bad.

He moved again, slower this time, to lay me across the bar. I was naked—trembling and exposed—but the look on his face told me I was safe, that he would never let anything happen to me. And, for the first time, I knew what he meant about me wanting someone to take care of me.

He was right.

He settled over me, all caresses and kisses, his hands finding my wrists and gliding them against the marble-top, pushing my arms over my head and pinning my hands against the counter. I felt completely out of control, and it felt...good.

As though not satisfied with all that had already transpired, his hands explored my body again—pinching, twisting, teasing. Biting, nibbling, scraping. I was near tears with need when finally he finally rolled on a condom and guided himself inside of me, white stars shooting across my vision as he thrust himself deeper.

I bit my lip, trying to keep my whimpers and moans from turning louder, but when he thrust again, my mouth flung open and, like an audience welcoming the hottest model of the season, a scream of ecstasy escaped my lips.

So much for quitting, and so much for taking care of myself.

But as good as Abram was in bed—or rather, on the bar countertop—I had to wonder...

Could he really keep me alive?

CHAPTER 11

I woke with a sweet ache pulling at my bones. I was on the upstairs floor for The Castle—that was much was clear from the way my body was contorted. But it didn't matter. I was a world away from uncomfortable. I had just experienced the most magnificent thing in the world, something so amazing I was sure it could never be duplicated.

I opened my eyes slowly, blinking away the sleep and stretching out the satisfaction. The sun seeped low through the windows, indicating the fall of evening.

I reached across for Abram, yearning to feel him against my fingertips again. When I came up empty, my eyes flung open. He was gone. Go figure. He'd probably snuck off as though I was some convenient booty call.

Is that what I was?

Well, that would make things awkward. Regret for my actions trickled into my mind. Looking over to where Abram should have been, I found a crumpled note.

I had to go.

I was going to wake you, but then you made this little moaning sound and pursed your lips.

I didn't have the heart to disturb something so beautiful.

I have a lot I want to say to you, a lot I think you need to know.

But a letter doesn't seem like enough, and those texts machines are confounding.

Let me make you breakfast tomorrow instead.

I would love to show you what a real pancake tastes like.

-Abram

A smile broke across my face, and suddenly I didn't feel like a booty call after all. I felt...wanted. Sure, it was a stupid note on a crumpled napkin smeared with barbecue sauce, but for Abram, that was a big thing. I knew that, and because I knew that, it meant something.

I sat up, folding the crumpled napkin and slipping it into my purse, which at some point while I slept had been placed neatly beside me along with my shoes and clothes.

I had never been the type of girl who did the whole 'keepsake' thing. Reminders were just that, and I didn't want to be reminded. But there was something about this note, something about this man, that made me feel differently somehow.

My stomach rumbled, and I was instantly glad Abram wasn't here to hear it. I wasn't about to apologize for being hungry, but something about the idea of being stark naked on the floor of a demolished club with your tummy growling like a grizzly bear didn't seem very attractive.

I stood, ran my fingers through my hair, and slipped on my clothes. Leaving my shoes off and trying ignore the ugly, yellow-green bruises and scrapes on my feet that would surely scar, I sauntered barefoot across the long upstairs hall, looking down over the balcony into the main area.

I felt comfortable here. Really comfortable. And it had little to do with the fact that my bare ass had touched the paint-splattered walls.

Something about fixing up The Castle, about molding it into the sort of place that might have been successful under different circumstances, made me feel better. It was like building this place up built myself up, too. Maybe that was why I was where I was now. Maybe it was this piece of confidence, this accomplishment, which gave me what I needed to let Abram in.

I sighed, breathing in the smell of drying paint. Abram was still here, his scent wafting long after he had left. Every muscle in my body relaxed. For the first time since returning to New Haven, I was at peace.

Moving toward one of the windows, I closed my eyes and let the light of the fading evening sun tingle against my skin. A murmuring tickled at my ears, and at first I thought I just imagined it. But then the sound came again like a soft call, whispering my name.

"Chaaarriiiissse."

Without moving, without flinching, I knew where it came from. I had heard that noise before, singing from behind the painted moon door downstairs.

Before I registered what was happening, I was downstairs, across the main floor, and down the hall leading to the back room. And, though I had no memory of picking it up, I found a crow bar in my hand.

Did I even know where Abram kept his tools?

I stood in front of the door, the voice singing my name to me again.

"Chaaarriiiissse. Chaaarriiiissse."

Last time I'd tried to open the door, I'd ended up with burns on my palms. Now the crow bar was heating to match it. I didn't let go, though. I couldn't. Besides, the heat didn't hurt this time. There was no pain, nothing more than the sensation of warmth. It was almost inviting.

I found the crow bar pulling back in my hands, which were now raised over my head. I could feel the bar being pulled back and then toward the door. It slammed hard against the painted moon, which had begun to glow red.

"Aaaaggaaiiiinnn," the voice sang after the bar shook against the door.

My arms sprang into action again, pulling behind my head. But my phone dinged loudly, indicating I had a text.

Something jarred inside my head, and a crow bar fell from my hands.

Why was I holding a crow bar? Why was I standing in front of this creepy door?

Shaking the fog from my mind, I looked down at my phone.

The text read: Dinner tonight?

It was from Dalton.

Oh no.

I hadn't made him any promises. I hadn't even kissed him, unless you counted a hot peck on the ear. But there was no denying something was going on between us. He had even called me 'his girl'; a definition I hadn't rebuffed.

I hadn't confirmed it, either, though. And certainly I didn't *have* to be his girl just because he wanted me to be. Yet, I knew how some people felt about woman owing men things...

And now here I was, planning morning-after breakfast with my boss while this man was waiting on me for dinner, sending me texts with cute smiley emoticons and being an all-around standup guy. I might not not owe him a hot date, but he certainly at least deserved an explanation.

I wasn't cheating on him, but the whole thing still felt too close to hurting him for comfort. I couldn't let this go on. Dalton deserved better than this. He had been nothing but amazing to me. Not to mention we had grown up together and he was my best friend's baby brother.

This was getting complicated.

But complicated didn't change facts, and the fact was I wasn't attracted to Dalton in the same way I was attracted to Abram. And maybe I had always known that. Maybe running from my growing feelings for Abram was part of the reason I threw in with Dalton so quickly.

That wasn't fair to him, but there was nothing I could do about the past. And now that I knew, not telling him right away would be even worse. I needed to nip this thing in the bud and deal with whatever fallout came from it.

I shot him a text.

Hey. We should talk. I'll meet you at the diner. —Char

I could have broken it off with him via text. God knew it would be easier for *me* that way. But that would be impersonal and, as Abram had said, a letter didn't seem like enough.

Begrudgingly, I slipped my shoes on. I used to love my shoes, but lately, with my feet still sore, wearing them felt like a punishment. Maybe one I deserved at the moment. I sighed as I stuffed my phone back into my pocket. After locking up The Castle behind me, I ascended the stairs, not wanting to do what I knew I had to.

The sun was almost gone from the sky, tinting the clouds red and orange and elongating all the shadows. It would be dark soon, and with that damn sexist curfew in effect, I wasn't legally allowed to be on the streets right now. But since I didn't give a warmed-over damn about that, I kept toward the diner.

I was about halfway there when the unnerving thought struck me: I hadn't been outside and alone in the dark since *that* night. The monsters surged to the forefront of my mind. I still hadn't told anyone about what really happened, and since I didn't fancy being fitted for a strait jacket, it was going to stay that way. Besides, it had probably only been shadows playing tricks. They were dogs...or something...

Dogs with glowing yellow eyes. Dogs that stood straight up like men. Dogs that were way too large to be dogs.

I shook my head, passing by an entrance to those large and encompassing woods.

I didn't want to look at them, not after everything that had happened. But something caught my eye.

A man was wandering into the woods. And not just *any* man. I knew that back. I knew those arms. I knew that ridiculously tight ass.

It was Abram.

CHAPTER 12

What was Abram doing in the woods? And why so close to the area where I had gone missing?

My heart bounced around in my chest like a pinball. I shook my head. Whatever he was doing, I would find out tomorrow. I would just ask him, and he would tell me.

Yeah. Right.

I wasn't kidding anyone—not even myself. This man—a man I had just let into my heart *and* my body—had secrets. He had always had secrets. It was part of his appeal. But now it seemed very likely that his secrets were connected to things that happened to me...things that I still didn't really understand.

Maybe a different type of girl would be okay with asking him tomorrow and taking whatever he said at face value. But the type of girl I was—she just flung her heels off and followed him into the woods, battered feet and all.

At first, I stayed far enough back to be sure Abram couldn't hear all the noise I made storming after him. It was strange. Here I was, after the most intense night of passion with this man, snooping around at his footprints like some sketchy TMZ photographer.

It wasn't as though I was the jealous girlfriend type. In all honesty, I didn't even consider myself to be Abram's girlfriend. I was his—well, I had no idea what I was. But I didn't suspect he was marching into the woods to be with another woman. He struck me as too old school for that sort of thing.

I wasn't sure what I thought was going on. The only thing clear was that weird things had been going on with me since I returned to New Haven, and these woods (and this man) were pieces to a puzzle I needed to solve.

As leaves crunched underfoot, a shiver ran up my spine. The last time I had been here, I was running for my life. It was one of the worst moments of my existence, and the thought that Abram —this man who I had just given myself to—might have something to do with it, sickened me to the core.

No, I was being ridiculous. He was just going for a walk.

A sunset walk through the middle of a tract of woods that had seen the murder of at least one woman. Yeah, that made sense.

Still, there had to be a reason for this, and it couldn't have had anything to do with the myriad of crazy theories running through my mind.

It's just...there was so much about Abram I still didn't know. So much that still didn't make sense. Where did he live? Where did he go at night? Why didn't I ever see him at the club (or anywhere, for that matter) after the sun went down? That wasn't even the whole of it. I'd had so many questions since meeting him, that I couldn't even remember them all—but I knew there was more than just this.

Abram marched quickly through the forest, the sort of speed one only takes when he or she knows exactly where they're going and just how to get there.

My stomach was in knots, and my poor yo-yo of a heart was racing again. Whatever was going on, one thing was for sure: New Haven was no longer the sleepy town I remembered from my childhood.

My phone buzzed, and I hit the ground.

Goddamn it!

Served me right for not having sense enough to turn off the ringer. Just my luck. When I was stranded in the middle of the night, I couldn't have made a call to save my life. But now that I was being (sorta) stealthy, my ringer was blowing up like Lady Gaga at a nightclub. If Abram saw me here, following him, how would I even explain myself?

Hey there. Was just taking a stroll through the place where I almost got killed. Funny seeing you here.

I huddled behind the stump of a nearby tree, hoping that if I was still and quiet enough, he would assume the ringer had just been the wind. If he had heard it at all, that was.

Why should I have to explain myself to him anyway? *He* should be the one explaining himself to *me!*

And yet I kept myself hidden, unable to overcome the guilty feeling I had over not trusting him. It made no sense for me to feel this way, and yet, there it was.

Pulling the phone from my purse, I lowered the ringer down to silent, noticing a text from Dalton had been the source of the disturbance.

Hey. I'm at the diner. Ordering you juice and eggs Benedict. I know how u like breakfast 4 dinner. How long r u gonna be?

Oh, great. I was supposed to meet him to break things off, and here I was standing him up to prance through the woods after the guy I was leaving him for.

It was like I was inadvertently training for the bitch Olympics.

I considered texting him back, telling him to wait there, or ever just telling him it was over like this. But just because I seemed to be in training didn't mean I wanted to take the gold. So, after shooting him a quick, *Sorry. Something came up,* I slid the phone back into my purse.

Slowly, I peeked from behind the stump. Not only was Abram not marching back toward me, but it seemed he hadn't heard anything at all. Because he was nowhere to be seen.

But how could that be? This particular stretch of woods was flat and expansive. It would have taken him at least five minutes to make it out of my line of sight, and it hadn't been near that long.

I stood, brushing leaves and twigs from my dress, cursed my current trend of ruining all my designer things, and took a long look around. Where the hell was this guy? I had never seen him run and, given the sexual encounter I had with him earlier, he didn't seem like the type to do anything in a rush.

I clutched my purse and thought about turning around. But I knew that was no good. If I didn't get to the bottom of this, I would never have a clear head around Abram again. I would ruin this relationship before it even started.

Well, Char, there's only one thing to do.

I didn't know everything that was going on—in fact, the only pieces I *did* have about what was happening didn't make sense when I tried to put them together—but I did know it had something to do with that old house, and I was pretty sure I could find my way back to it.

So long as Abram wasn't there, I could make peace with the idea he didn't have anything to do with this—that whatever he was doing in these woods was as innocent as I hoped it was. And peace, it seemed, was in short supply these days.

* * *

The mile up the road out of New Haven seemed shorter when full of anxiety instead of fear, but the trek through the woods was as unenjoyable as ever. Considering I had never been a nature lover —heels and hills don't mix—I wasn't particularly thrilled with the trip, regardless how much shorter it was this time. But something about that house seemed to draw me to it, as if a piece of myself was waking up and guiding through this place where all the trees and paths looked the same.

I barely had to think as I moved toward my destination, which was good considering my mind had basically melted into paste by this point.

The house came into view. First that awful peak, jutting out from the tree line. Next, I saw the top floor, with the beckoning light still burning in the window.

It had taken me nearly an hour the other night to get away from this place, and I was a bit stunned to realize how close to the road it actually was. Maybe being disoriented from the attack had slowed my escape.

As I drew nearer, the chipped paint and quaint structure exposed beneath the waning sunlight made the old house look less monstrous and more lonely. As lonely as a house could look anyway.

Here was this house, sitting untouched and outpaced by the rest of the world. It was sort of sad. But, more than that, it was almost beautiful. Or at least it would have been if this hadn't been the location where I'd nearly been eaten alive by a pair of quarreling monsters.

I stepped closer to the house, pursing my lips at the already repaired window. For a house that looked as though it hadn't been touched in fifty years, it sure had an efficient handyman.

I pushed all of that out of my mind. At this point, I didn't care about solving this mystery. The only thing that mattered was ruling out Abram as a participant in it.

Inching forward, I bit my lip as the door revealed itself to me. He wasn't going to be here. He was a good man—a bit of a dick, sure, but not the sort to lie, not about something like this. He was old fashioned in a way I couldn't really describe. He was untouched by time, sort of like this house. Sort of like—

Sort of like the kind of man I would find standing in the threshold of the doorway, his arms crossed over his chest. Apparently.

My heart sank at the sight of him. *No, Abram. Please, no.* However small a role he played, this man I had just slept with had a part in all of this.

His dark eyes scanned the periphery of the woods and, for an instant, I thought he was looking for me. Maybe he *had* heard my ringer go off. Maybe he had sprinted away from me quickly enough for me to lose sight of him.

He turned and walked into the house. The door slammed shut behind him, and I was alone, gasping in shock and slumping against a nearby tree.

Shock soured in my stomach, turning to hurt and finally to anger. He had lied to me. It must have been Abram himself who found me in the house that night. Of course, that would have also meant he'd fought back those monsters and saved me. But if that was the case, why didn't he just tell me? Why did he let me limp back to town with cuts, bruises, and a mind so rocked with questions that it barely functioned?

I wanted answers. Abram *owed* me those answers. And, by God, I was going to get them.

But I couldn't just barge in there. He had lied to me at least once. I would have to be sneaky about this and gather some clues, or else he might hide more from me before I ever had the chance to find out. But I also couldn't wait for him to leave. It was getting late and, if I didn't show up soon, Lulu would worry.

Going missing twice inside of a week was the last thing my extremely pregnant and hyper-worrisome best friend needed.

I was going to have to go inside now. I would have to sneak around without Abram knowing I was in there. It was a terrible plan, and yet, it was all I had without the risk of losing this opportunity forever.

Ducking low, I scampered across the field toward the front door. My feet fell lightly onto the porch and, quietly as possible, I turned the knob.

I had no idea what I was going to do if Abram had locked it behind him. Or if he was standing right on the other side of the door. I had never been the sort who thought things through. But the house was in the middle of nowhere, so it wasn't likely he was expecting company.

Luckily for me, the door sprang open. After slipping inside, I crouched down and looked around cautiously, praying Abram wasn't standing there watching me. The quickly setting sun tinted the entire living room orange and red, but thankfully, the room was as empty today as it had been the other night.

I listened for sounds, trying to gauge where Abram might be. Suddenly, heavy footsteps stomped from a back room. Crap. They were headed this way. I sprang to my feet, bolted toward the steps, and pushed up them, hoping to get out of sight before he found me.

I shuddered as my feet fell across the staircase. The last time I had been on them, I had been tumbling down like a discarded sequin on a McCartney original. Shaking my head, I moved into the upstairs hallway just before Abram crossed into the living room.

Pressed against the wall, I found myself guarded in shadow. The sun would be down soon, and getting home from here would prove troublesome. But I needed answers. And right now was the best opportunity to get them.

Sorry, Lulu.

Abram stopped in the living room, and I shivered, thinking he would move up the stairs. I darted farther into the hallway. Remembering the layout from the last time I was here, I knew there were only two rooms at the end of the hall. One of them was the room I had almost died in and the other had been locked the last time I was here.

Now, with little bit of daylight remaining, I could actually *see* the door. And when I did, I nearly choked on air. The door was stamped with a similar crescent moon symbol to the mysterious room inside The Castle.

Realization slammed into me with a sickening thud. How could I have forgotten the way the doorknob had burned me that night? *Of course* Abram had something to do with all this. I was just the idiot girl who needed a damn symbol to spell it out for me. But that still didn't explain what was going on. I needed to hide before Abram came upstairs. I needed to find answers before he found me.

I moved toward the marked door, knowing it would probably be locked but also knowing I would regret it forever if I didn't at least check. Suddenly, a strange noise poured from the other side. It was a song; someone was singing one word.

My name.

A repressed memory from earlier in the night tried to push its way through. The room in the hall at The Castle... I couldn't quite grasp the picture, though. It was like a lost dream. I tried to retrieve more from my mind, but footsteps bounding up the stairs interrupted my efforts.

Abram would be here in mere seconds, and unless I found someplace to hide, he would know I had followed him.

The crescent moon symbol began to glow, and I jerked back just in time for the previously locked door to fly open. A whoosh of cinnamon-scented air burst from the open space, almost knocking me down.

I slid into the room quickly and, without touching it, the door closed behind me.

Okay, so, that's not a good sign.

A loud crashing and then a sound like glass shattering stole my attention before I was able to take the room in. A picture had fallen off a nearby counter. When I looked down at it, my heart skidded to a stop.

The old photograph lay face up under shards of broken frame. Two men stood by a lake, smiling for the camera and showing off their latest catch: a huge catfish.

I recognized both of the men instantly. I had seen one of them in my dreams almost every night since I was a child. When I was little, it seemed I would never stop seeing his face, watching him walk away from me night after night. It was my father.

And, beside him, untouched by time or trend, stood Abram.

"He looks exactly the same," I muttered, mouth agape. "How is that...that's not possible."

"Miss?" a tired voice croaked, breaking me from my

concentration and startling the hell out of me. "Are you here to help me?"

I spun around, the picture and frame slipping from my hand to crash to floor once again. A woman sat on the floor in the fetal position. She was pale and disheveled. Her face was gaunt, and she seemed as though she hadn't slept in weeks. She looked up at me expectantly. When she shuffled, I realized both her hands and feet were fastened with chains connected to the wall.

I recognized her, too. With sickening clarity, I realized where I had seen this face before. It had shone, bright and smiling, from the missing poster I had seen when I first returned to town.

This was the missing girl. She was being kept here, in a house that Abram had something to do with.

This—the missing woman, the mutilated bodies, the strange creatures that chased me to *this* house—was all connected.

And Abram was at the center of it.

CHAPTER 13

"*Are you here to help me?*"

The words couldn't have been more off the mark. Here I was, staring at this woman, mouth agape and wide eyed. I couldn't help myself, let alone someone else—not with my mind spinning like a top.

"H-hurry," the woman begged. "He'll be here soon. He's never gone for too long."

There was such hurt in her eyes, such unadulterated broken fear; it sickened me. Could Abram—the Abram that I knew—be the source of that? It didn't seem possible.

Cuts and bruises spotted her filthy face. Her hands hung limply at her sides, useless appendages bound by chains. As shocked as I was, I managed to shake it off and kneel beside her.

She reeked as though she hadn't bathed in weeks, which I realized with stomach-churning horror was probably the case.

"Is there a key?" I asked, mouth dry.

"There's always a key," she answered, narrowing her eyes. "We just don't always see it at first glance."

Her hand jerked toward my own, striking at me with long, unwashed nails. She sliced into my palm, breaking the skin and sending a trail of blood dripping to the floor.

"Ah!" I jerked away.

Her gaze transfixed on my blood, she ran her forefinger across the splatter. Then she looked back up at me, her eyes wide and sparkling.

"Chaarriissseeee," she said in the sing song voice that had seemed to taunt me from behind closed doors.

I stumbled to my feet, grabbing my palm and glaring at her. There was a hunger in the way she looked at me now, something almost feral in her eyes.

"How do you know my name?"

"Did you know fear has a scent, Charisse?" She tilted her head to one side, her brow furrowing thoughtfully. "It's sweet, like sugarplum. You stink of it at the moment, but it won't be enough to make up for the blood. It won't ever be enough."

I was too stunned to reply. I stepped back, torn between helping her and being terrified she might hurt me.

"Let me out," she hissed. She pulled toward me, jerking against her chains.

"I...I don't have the key." I almost tumbled with the next step back I took.

She held her forefinger up; it was coated with my blood. She grinned. "Just say the word."

"Leave her alone!" Abram growled from behind me.

I spun, shuddering at the sight of him. He was just as big as he had ever been, but suddenly that size seemed more important, more threatening.

"*You* leave her alone!" I yelled, steeling myself. He wasn't about to get away with this, not if I could help it.

"I wasn't talking to you," he said, looking past me. "Wipe it off, or I'll take the hand. I mean it."

The woman's eyes slid from Abram to me. Slowly, she ran her forefinger across the wall, wiping it clean. She sneered. "We're not done."

"We never are." He sighed and turned his attention to me.

As they always had, his dark eyes disarmed me the instant they met my own. But this time, I couldn't afford to let myself get lost in them, not when it was clear what sort of a person he was.

"Let her go," I demanded.

Sure, the chick was acting strange—one charm short of a bracelet—but who was to say that being held captive for so long wouldn't do the same to me? She was probably in shock, starving, dehydrated, and certainly scared to death.

"We need to talk," he answered flatly.

"You can talk to the police. How about that?" I said, balling my fists.

I had been so blind, so stupid. How could I have let myself be seduced by someone like this, much less fall for him?

"I can't let you do that," he said, stepping closer to me.

I flinched, lunging backward and fumbling for my phone.

"It doesn't work out here. Don't you remember?" he asked. "Though I hope you know by now that I would never hurt you."

"Tell that to her." I motioned back to his prisoner.

"She's a different story. A *long* story." His jaw flexed. "I said we needed to talk, and we need to do it alone. Now, you can come with me, or I can throw you over my shoulder and take you."

Though I couldn't see myself, I was sure I paled.

"Listen," he said, his tone a little softer now. "She hasn't been harmed."

"Save the bull. There are cuts all over her. She obviously hasn't eaten or bathed in days."

"She hurts herself, and if she hasn't eaten or cleaned herself, it's because she refuses to do so." He moved closer, something dangerous darting through his gaze. "So what's it going to be?"

"I'm not going anywhere with you."

"See it yourself," he said, and before I could turn to dodge him, he had already slung me over his shoulder.

I could have sworn he grinned as he did so, but before I knew it, I was nearly upside down, my hips high at his shoulder and his strong arm pinning my legs to his chest.

I struggled against his grip, but between gravity and his hold on me, it was useless. He crossed the hall into the room I had been nearly attacked in and mercifully set me down on the edge of a bed. I tried to stand, but his hand came quick to my shoulder to hold me in place.

"Stay," he ordered.

"Or else you'll tie me up like you did her?"

A grin broke across his face, but he bit his lip and looked away.

"Not quite the same way," he muttered suggestively. But before I could even chide myself for blushing, he added, "Hear me out, and then if you want to leave, I will not stand in your way."

My mind and my instincts were at odds. There was a woman in the other room, beaten and captive. But as intimidating as Abram was, nothing about him seemed nefarious, and if he was going to hurt me, wouldn't he have done so by now?

I squirmed beneath the weight of his hand on my shoulder. I was a fool. Now was not the time to test my instincts, which had a history of failing me enough as it was.

A loud crash came from the other room, followed by screeching. When Abram turned to look down the hall, I used the opportunity to escape from under his hand. I made it to the door within moments, but so did he. His arms circled around to grab to me, his breath hot on my neck.

Gritting my teeth and praying for a little luck, I drove my elbow hard into his gut. He didn't crumble as much as I'd hoped, but I darted toward the steps regardless. Stairs were not my friends. I had fallen on both these and the stairs leading down to the Castle. So I hopped onto the bannister instead, sliding down it toward the first floor.

My feet thudded against the carpet, and I bounded toward the door, pushing through it with elbows in front of my face to break the impact.

The air hit me hard and cold, gusting through my hair and prickling my skin. The sun was almost down, and here I was—again—in these goddamn woods.

I barreled into the quickly darkening gray. Visions of that

monster, the one that chased me, sliced into my thoughts. Would it be back tonight? Was it lying in wait right now, itching to pounce on me?

Couldn't think about that. I might not have been able to save that girl myself, but I knew where she was, and the instant my phone went back into service, I would have Dalton on the line. Abram would never hurt anyone again, not so long as that poor girl could hold out until help arrived.

A whoosh of wind shuffled past me, and then he was standing there. Abram. His massive chest heaved up and down in ragged breathes.

"Stop!" He growled, his eyes glowing bright red and his already huge frame somehow even more hulking. "You. Need. To. Listen."

I dodged to the left, but he was there, too, appearing in front of me with impossible speed.

"I said listen!" He grabbed me by the shoulders, wrapping his huge meaty hands around my arms.

"That girl," I coughed out, tears pouring down my cheeks. "How could you do that to an innocent girl?"

"She's not innocent, and she's not a girl," he answered, red eyes burning into me. "No more than I'm a man. Not anymore."

"What the hell are you talking about?" I asked, trying and failing to pull away from him.

"This is going to sound peculiar, Ms. Bellamy, but I'm going to need you to trust me, regardless of how fantastic it might sound."

I continued my futile attempt to free myself, which only resulted in him tightening his grip on my arms. His chest heaved, pressing against mine forcefully.

Swallowing hard, he said, "Ms. Bellamy, there's a beast in me."

For whatever reason, the revelation weakened his grip. I pulled away, spinning and running as quickly as my tired legs would carry me. The setting sun glared in my eyes, making it hard for me to see, but I pressed on. Even if I ran headfirst into a tree, it would be better than whatever Abram had in store for me.

There's a beast in me...

He couldn't possible mean—

He was in front of me again, once again huffing, once again staring at me with glowing, inhuman eyes.

"Fine," he huffed. "Have it your way." He grabbed me again, jerking me toward him in a fluid motion that both terrified and excited me.

"I suggest you brace yourself," he said flatly.

And then he threw me.

CHAPTER 14

As I sailed through the air, surpassing even the tree line, one through pressed in my mind even stronger than my fear of coming back down:

How is this even possible?

Even if I wasn't what my agent generously described as 'full-figured,' no person could toss another one so high into the air. No one could—

Oh God. Look at how high I was. There was no way to survive this. I was going to splat against the ground like a bug, if the branches didn't impale me on the way down.

A scream, shriller than I thought I was capable of, escaped my lips. Suddenly, I felt colder. I would die out here in this woods, just like all the other women who looked like me.

And the worst part was I would never get the answers to the questions swirling about in my mind. No one would. They would all think I was just routinely murdered. Or maybe Abram would cover it up as a hiking accident. Hell, maybe my body would just go missing and no one would ever know what became of me. I would be a fixture on those Walmart missing poster boards, forgotten by time.

I began to fall. The earth sped toward me at lightning speed. I would have screamed again, but what use would it be? Screaming wouldn't stop this. Nothing would. And I didn't want my last moments to be spent howling like some doomed idiot. Even if that's exactly what I was.

Instead, I shut my mouth, closed my eyes, and tried to settle both my stomach and my mind. If this was the end, and it most certainly was, then I was going to face it with as much dignity as I could muster.

Still, if I was gonna die, I wished I could do it in Versace.

Something caught, and I jerked to a stop.

Was that the ground? Was I dead?

I opened my eyes, fully expecting to see either nothing or the golden (and hopefully bedazzled) gates of the afterlife. Instead, I had to begrudgingly admit what I saw was just a beautiful.

Abram had me in his arms, cradling me like I was Scarlett friggin' O'Hara.

I brushed windswept curls out of my eyes. "How did—You just—"

"I told you. There's a beast in me."

"But you didn't kill me."

He growled as though I'd either hurt him or offended him. "Of course I didn't 'kill you,' Ms. Bellamy I only threw you to prove that even the most unbelievable things can be true."

"Mission accomplished," I muttered as I pushed my way out of his arms.

He didn't fight me.

"So explain this unbelievable thing then," I continued. "Tell me what 'there's a beast in me' means."

"Let me ask you," he said, lowering his brow. "What do you know about magic?"

I fumbled through my purse, fingers grasping at the metal cylinder that held my mace. Abram's eyes bore into me, though they lacked the sort of delusional flair you might expect from someone who just seriously asked you whether you believed in magic or what you knew about it or whatever.

Finding the fresh can of pepper spray (replaced after the last incident), I yanked it out of my purse and emptied its contents right into Abram's glowing red eyes. He jerked away from the mist, covering his face with his hands and growling.

It was strange. Not twenty-four hours ago, I would have told you this man was someone special. Okay, so I probably wouldn't have actually admitted that out loud, at least not before our massive sex session. But the truth was, deep down, in a place within myself that I so rarely went that I barely recognized it, there was a piece of me that felt like I might be falling in love with him.

What a difference a couple hours could make.

I turned to run again, but before I could make even a step, he was in front of me. His eyes were watery, puffy, and still red. He grabbed me hard on either arm and somehow looked even larger than he had just a moment ago.

"It is entirely too close to sunset for this sort of dalliance, Ms. Bellamy." He ground his teeth. "Now, I've already thrown you halfway to Jupiter. Should I plant you at the top of the nearest pine? Would that be enough to convince you that what I say is the truth? Or would you prefer this?"

His lips receded, revealing long hooked fangs where his teeth should be. They were huge and crowed out of his mouth. Suddenly, in the light of the setting sun, Abram looked less like a man and more like a monster...as if everything he had said was true.

Maybe there *was* a beast inside of him.

Whatever that meant.

I pulled away hard, stumbling over my feet and falling to the ground. The mace fell from my hand, not that it had done much good anyway.

"You're...You're..." I stammered.

He just stared at me with the saddest, scariest eyes I had ever seen.

It all came together. The missing girls, the glowing red eyes, the monster that chased me through the woods and into the strange house I had just ran away from.

There *was* a beast in him. He was the monster that had chased me.

But no, that wasn't right. Those eyes, I recognized them. Monster or not, I knew them.

"You were...you were the beast that saved me," I said quietly. "Weren't you?"

His fangs receded, and he stepped toward me. "Yes."

I flinched back. "What *are* you?"

He ran his hand through his hair. "There is magic in this world, Ms. Bellamy—things that can't be explained by reason or logic."

"You expect me to believe that?" I asked, although it wasn't lost on me that he *had* just sent me soaring to the heavens.

He stood and looked around wearily. "I don't *expect* you to believe me. I *need* you to. For your own safety."

"And you—you are saying you used magic to throw me?"

"No."

My brow furrowed. "Well, spit it out. You didn't hunt me down just to keep it a secret, did you?"

He shook his head, but his lips moved wordlessly several times before he finally spoke. "Ms. Bellamy... What I mean to say is, there are beings who can channel magic, called Conduits. And in addition to being extremely powerful, they are also exceedingly rare. That woman you saw inside my home...she is one of them."

"What does that have to do with why you have her?" I pressed my lips together, my legs trembling beneath me. "Are you a Conduit too?"

Abram shook his head. "No, but what she is...has everything to do with what I am."

"And that is...?"

"Something unlike anything else. Or at least I used to think so." He looked away from me, deep into the woods. "I was something of a scamp in my younger days, Ms. Bellamy. To put it bluntly, I was crude, lazy, and worst of all, incredibly selfish. I used people, women chiefly. One day, a beautiful traveler named Satina wandered into our village."

"Your village?" I asked, my nose crinkling.

"She was beautiful," he said. "The most beautiful thing I had even seen." He blinked hard. "Or she used to be." He cleared his throat. "I was a handsome man even then, if a bit boyish. And my charms were quite effective when I wanted them to be. Nature took its course with us, and after that, I took mine. She thought we were in love, that we would be married. I, of course, never saw her as anything other than a conquest. That is, until she killed herself."

My skin went cold. "What?"

"She was a Conduit. I didn't know what that meant at the time, but her bloodline was one of the most potent in recorded history. A few nights after I left her, she climbed to the top of the bell tower. She cursed me in front of the entire village, told them of all my shortcomings and that very soon the ugliness inside of me would be seen by everyone. Then she spouted some incantation to invoke the harvest moon." An aching smile etched across his face. "You know, I actually scoffed when she jumped. All I could think, when she hit the ground, was how foolish she must have been and how lucky I was to be rid of her." His eyes flickered back to me. "That's the kind of person I was. As much a beast then as I am now. Maybe even more so."

His hands found their way into his pockets, and his eyes moved away from me again. "A month after Satina died, I was already with another woman when it happened for the first time. It came on me like a sickness. I was on top of her." He bit his lip. "In the middle of it all. I felt myself heaving. It was so painful the first time that I couldn't stop myself from screaming. And her eyes, if I live a thousand years, I'll never forget those eyes. That poor girl was terrified, and with good reason. One look in the mirror showed that I was a monster; a horrific hairy thing that no one could ever love."

Abram folded his arms as I stood motionless, half terrified and half enthralled.

"What happened next?" I asked, too stunned and too curious to move.

"The girl tried to run," Abram said softly, as if the memory had taken him by surprise and he was afraid he might drown in it.

"Tried?" I asked, hoping that didn't mean what I thought it did.

"You have to understand, when the change happens, it doesn't just affect my body. Everything is heightened. Every sensation is a thousand times stronger. Anger, grief, lust—even love; it's all supercharged. I wasn't equipped to handle it then, especially not on that first night." He shook his head hard. "She called me a demon. She said she was going to tell her father what I was, that she was going to have me burned with all the other abominations."

"Burned," I muttered, thinking how long ago that must have been. "How old are you?"

"I didn't want to kill her, but I was so afraid and so angry that I almost did. It took all I had in me to run." He slid down the trunk of a nearby tree so that we were nearly level with each other. "Satina came to me after that, as an apparition of sorts. That's when she told me what she had done. She'd cursed me, made it so that the monster I was on the inside would be what I was on the outside."

"But you're a man now," I answered, waving my hand at him.

"She'd called on the moon to perform her curse, so it's only in effect at night."

"That's why you could never be in The Castle after sunset," I said quietly, realizing how close to sunset we were right now.

"I am this thing," he answered. "I will always be this thing. But I thought I was the only one." His back straightened. "Something is here, though, in New Haven. Someone else like me. He's taking women and hurting them, including the girl currently chained up in my family home."

"But *you* have her," I challenged him, doubt creeping back in. "Not someone else."

"I found her in the woods. She was near death, and though I figured it was a lost cause, I took her home hoping I might be able to save her. At the very least, I thought I would be able to make her final moments more comfortable. But then something strange happened."

When he didn't continue, I waved him on. "*What* happened, Abram?"

"Well, after she died...the body reanimated. It was hijacked...by Satina."

I gasped, reacting more as though what I was hearing was a telenovela than my actual reality.

"It was the first time I had seen her since the first time I changed. I didn't know until then that she's always been with me, always following me. Because she cursed me with her death, her spirit is connected to mine either until I die or until the curse is broken." He scoffed, ticking his head to the side. "She said it was time to break it."

"Break it how?" I asked.

"It doesn't matter!" He growled. "She's a liar. She wants nothing more than to torment me. Besides, this isn't about me," he said, lowering his brow again. "It's about you."

"Me?" I asked, scrambling to my feet. "How could any of this be about me?"

"Because of what *you* are."

"I'm *nothing* like you!" I yelled, blinking away whatever momentary crazy allowed me to listen to that story and actually take any of it seriously. Calling himself a monster was one thing, but pulling me into it, that was something else entirely.

"If you would calm down, Ms. Bell—"

"Oh, for God's sake. You've been inside me. I think you can call me by my goddamn name." I gritted my teeth. "Or better yet, don't call me anything. Don't call me anything at all."

"Get mad if you like, but I'm not the reason this is happening. You are. And until you accept that, it won't stop. If you would just let me explain—"

"Why? Because those girls look like me? That's why I'm in danger, right? That has nothing to do with who I am."

"You've got it half right," he muttered. "You're not in danger because you look like those girls." His gaze traveled from my toes up to my eyes. "Those girls were in danger because *they* looked like *you*."

Now he moved closer to me. "You're a Supplicant, Ms. Bell—Charisse. Your blood has magical properties—the magical properties that a Conduit needs to perform their magic. And there is someone out there like me looking for you, to use you for just that. And it's obvious he'll stop at nothing to get to you."

"How do you know I'm a...whatever it is?" I asked, backing away. "How do you know someone is after *me*?"

"Because I knew your father," he said evenly. "He was a Supplicant, too. You have his eyes."

My mind flickered back to the first time I ever saw Abram and to the first thing he said to me.

You have a freckle in your eye.

Just like my father.

"You're insane!" I said, my mind spinning. Maybe magic was real, and he certainly was a beast, but I had nothing to do with this. And to bring my father into it—I refused to hear another thing he had to say.

"You stay the hell away from me," I said, stumbling back away from him. "Do you understand? Stay away!"

I turned and ran, bolting through the woods. When I glanced back, he was just staring after me. As promised, he was letting me leave now that he had said all he had to say.

I swallowed hard, resisting the tug in my heart and stomach that made me want to erase all I had learned.

"Don't ever talk to me again!" I screamed, more to cement my resolve than to rebuke him. "Not ever again!"

This time when I ran, I didn't look back. And I swore to myself, right then and there, this would be the last time I ever laid eyes on him.

CHAPTER 15

It was strange how easily I found my way out of the woods that night. Maybe I had been up and down this path enough to know my way around. But, given my astonishingly bad sense of direction, it probably had more to do with the way my thoughts were racing.

Monsters and witches, curses and fangs—all these things filled my mind. Conduits—whatever they were—and all that other garbage Abram expected me to believe, mentally batted me around like one of those hacky sacks Lulu and I used to kick back and forth in grade school.

While my subconscious guided me to the main street of New Haven, my actual conscious was trying to make sense of all the senselessness that was now my life.

If he expected me to believe him—that magic was real and he was a douchey product of some Conduit witch's temper tantrum—then he had another thing coming. It was too farfetched. Well, except for the douchey part. Abram definitely fit the bill where that was concerned.

But what about all the crazy things I had seen? I couldn't ignore them. Like it or not, I couldn't explain half of the things that had happened to me since I returned to New Haven. But magic? Could that really be the answer?

My head was still swimming when I made it up Lulu's walkway. It was after dark now, which technically made me a fugitive thanks to the town's ridiculous 'women only' curfew.

Screw that. If I could deal with strange woods monsters, possessed witch prisoners, and a boyfriend who could throw me around in all the wrong (and right) ways, then this one-horse-town's Barney Fife patrol was the least of my worries.

I heard the baby crying before I even settled in front of the doorway. The sound of his wails, haggard and tired as though they had been going on awhile, sent shivers down my spine. Something wasn't right. When Jack cried, his mother dealt with it. She was freaking Super Woman.

Instantly, I thought of the fence, of the way Lulu freaked when she saw it was broken. It made sense now. If there were creepy kooky monsters doing creepy kooky things one hundred feet from where my kid slept at night, I would want to keep the fence up, too.

My entire body went cold as I fumbled through my purse for the key to the house.

"It's okay, Jack. It's gonna be okay," I said, my hand shaking as the key found its way into the doorknob.

Of course, I couldn't back that up. For all I knew, there could be an army of Conduits or weird wolf-monsters or hell, leprechauns, waiting to hijack me as soon as I walked through the door. And what could I do? I was a plus-sized model whose only knowledge of self-defense came from last winter's ill-fated trend of designer combat boots.

Oh, that's right. What was it Abram said? I had magic blood that could do spells or something. And apparently that meant my blood was in high demand. *How refreshing.* Whether it was true or not, it didn't speak well for my safety, let alone my ability to save others.

God, please tell me I'm not considering it's true.

As the door swung open, I saw the reality in Lulu's home was a bit more ordinary in origin, though no less horrifying.

My friend lay on the floor of the foyer, her face pained and tense, a puddle circling her body. Her water had broken. She was in labor.

I ran to her, forgetting all my worries as I knelt beside her on the floor.

"Are you all right?" I asked as she did her breathing exercises. "How long have you been like this?"

"The phone," she said through grunting breaths. "Get the phone."

She was calmer than she had any right to be—definitely calmer than I would have been if my glorious ass was in the same position. Looking over, I saw her cell phone was out of reach. She mustn't have been able to get Jack to bring it to her.

I lunged for it and was already dialing 9-1-1 before I realized I could have used my own phone without the dramatic dive into the living room.

I didn't even let the operator finish her intro before I cut in. "My friend is in labor. I need you to get somebody to—"

This time she interrupted me, reciting the address.

"Yeah, that's it. Hurry. I think she's about to blow!"

Lulu crinkled her eyebrows. "About to blow? I'm not a whale, Charisse."

"Forgive my lack of etiquette. I'm trying to get them to hurry," I answered. Then, realizing I was still on the phone, I said, "Not you, 9-1-1 lady. You're awesome. Just send someone."

Ending the call, I flung the phone back onto the couch and joined Lulu at her side.

"Relax, please, Charisse," she said, wincing. "People give birth at home all the time. It's not—" She moaned, keeling over farther where she lay on the floor. "—life or death."

"You look like you're dying to me," I said half-heartedly. Truth was, her pain terrified me, no matter how normal the Discovery Channel said this life event was.

"Thanks," she muttered. Somehow, she was smiling between

the bouts of pain, but it never lasted long. She seemed to only get a few seconds' break between each of her moaning fits.

I think I was squeezing her hand tighter than she was squeezing mine. Man, those birth shows she was always watching had it all wrong!

"Do I need grab the sheets or boil some water or something?"

"That depends on if you're trying to get stains out of my bedspread." Lulu grunted. Obviously she was in pain, and obviously I wasn't the type of person you wanted to bring with you to a medical emergency.

"I'll be fine," Lulu said, sweat forming on her brow. "Just try to calm Jack down until the paramedics arrive."

Trying to calm Jack down sounded much easier than it actually was. I was bitten, I was scratched, I was punched, and I was called the only word he knew how to say—which wasn't really a word at all, but more like a sound I could not replicate. But the kid was scared, and since I was basically peeing my pants myself, I couldn't blame him.

When the paramedics finally arrived, they were quick, guiding Lulu onto a stretcher and assuring her (and Jack and I) that everything would be just fine. For Lulu, that might be true, but for me it was anything but.

After his mother left, Jack went from simmering to full-blown nuclear. It took every rabbit I could pull from my hat to keep him quiet for even a minute. I did my best baby voice. I tried pirate cartoons. I attempted to feed him cookies (which were thrown back at me). I even tried to pay the stupid kid, but it turned out twenty bucks wasn't as big an incentive to a toddler as I imagined it might be.

It may have been for the best, though. The more Jack screamed (and there was a lot of screaming) the longer my mind stayed occupied. It was when he was actually quiet, in those moments of silence, when my own internal monologue got noisy.

I started to worry about Lulu, and not just for the obvious reasons. Sure, she was in labor, and yes, the hospital in New Haven was about as big as a Quizno's (with all the technical advancement). But what was really pulling at my mind was what Abram had told me.

The dead girls...they all looked like me. And, according to Abram, that was the reason they were all dead. Someone was looking for me, because my blood was magic and they could use it to take over the world or make some supermodel fall in love with them or something.

You know, that old chestnut.

But as crazy as all of that sounded, I was actually beginning to believe it. And that was what was upsetting me so much.

Because as much as all those dead girls resembled me, none of them looked as much like me as Lulu did.

For our entire lives, people confused us for sisters. We had the same dark hair, the same light eyes. Of course, Lulu was missing my father's eye freckle, but that distinction hadn't saved any of the other girls.

A horrible howling echoed from the woods behind us. Jack erupted back into screams, and though my entire body shook, I rushed to grab him. The monster was out there, but which one?

God, I was actually taking all of this seriously.

How could I not, with all I had seen tonight?

Another howl. From the same monster or another one? Maybe it was from an ordinary, run-of-the-mill, non-monstrous wolf. Hey, a girl could hope.

My mind raced to the worst possible scenario. What if Lulu was attacked on her way to the hospital? What if the monster who chased after me—the one Abram saved me from—had ripped into that ambulance in an effort to get a hold of her?

Would she be running through those woods right now, scared and in labor? Or would she not even be able to run, same as she hadn't been able to get to her phone? Did the Discovery Channel say fear can stall labor? Or was that with animals?

No, if something was after Lulu, labor or not, she would be trying to get back to her child. But what chance would she stand against a beast? She would be ripped apart, just like the rest. And it would be all my fault.

I reached for my cell before I realized who I was intending to call.

My mind shouldn't have gone to him. I had just told him how awful he was and how I never wanted to see him again. But if Abram was here, he would fix this. He would run those meaty wonderful hands through my hair and tell me everything would be all right. And I would believe him. Just like, God help me, I believed him now.

I set the phone back down and curled up in a ball on the couch with Jack, squeezing my eyes shut to try to keep the tears from falling.

How had my life gotten to this point?

CHAPTER 16

It was halfway through a symphony of Jack's screams that a knock sounded at the door.

My body tensed, causing all my other thoughts to screech to a halt like Saturday night traffic in Queens.

As if he sensed it, too, Jack's high-pitched hijinks stopped as well, allowing the next knock to echo through an otherwise silent house.

I inched toward the door, looking out of the corner of my eye for something that might be used as a weapon. As the third knock banged along the door, I settled for the first thing in the kitchen I could find—a cheese grater.

Never one to put off the inevitable, I pulled the door open, holding the grater out in front of me like a magic talisman.

"I appreciate it, but if I was going to present someone with a kitchen utensil, I think it would be the blender. Just feels more personal."

Dalton stood in the doorway, a sly smirk plastered across his otherwise adorable face.

Okay, so the smirk was adorable, too.

He was dressed in a police uniform: brown slacks and a matching shirt with a star shaped badge pinned to his chest. If I wasn't so scared and embarrassed, I would have said it was hot. Because, you know, I was a red-blooded female and there was nothing—nothing—sexier than a guy in uniform.

Well, unless you count a sexily aggressive nightclub owner who may or may not moonlight as a giant wolf-monster or psycho kidnapper. Somehow, though, I sensed the latter wasn't the case, and I wasn't sure if that was more alarming or less.

Why was my life so weird?

"Are you—" I started, then shook my head. "Is Lulu—"

"Still in labor," Dalton answered. "It's gonna be an all-nighter. Lucky for you, I'm an all-night kind of guy."

A bolt of guilt ran up my chest. Dalton had been such a great friend to me. And, if I was being honest, he had been a great 'more than a friend', too. And how had I repaid that awesomeness? By bumping uglies with the first sexy guy who looked at me twice.

His eyebrows rose. "Can I come in?"

Well, that was awkward. Here I was just staring at him in silence.

"Sure," I answered, because after all, it was his sister's house, and who was I to say he couldn't come in? "Have you called her husband?"

"His phone's going straight to voicemail. He must still be in the air." Dalton moved past me and gave me a peck on the cheek.

God, he still thought we were together.

I should have flinched away from him. I hadn't been the type of girl who deserved a kiss from a guy like Dalton, someone capable of making me feel so safe and loved. I was the kind of girl who threw all that away for someone who kept secrets from me, someone who spouted nonsense when questioned about those secrets. But, for all that, Abram made me feel alive in a way that Dalton hadn't, in a way I feared Dalton never could.

"How have you been?" he asked, moving through the foyer and scooping up Jack, who instantly perked up a thousand percent. "I missed you today at the diner."

"Right," I answered, remembering the text I had sent him. I

was going to break up with him, but then the world turned upside down. And here he was, being so gracious about me standing him up, too.

Break up with him now, dummy!

I opened my mouth, but no words came. The moment felt all... wrong. My world was still spinning. I wasn't sure where I (or anything else) was going to land.

I should have broken up with him anyway, on the sole basis I didn't deserve him. We weren't officially together, but there was something between us. I was certain he wasn't sleeping with anyone else, and yet I had.

I couldn't even bring myself to defend my actions with the notion that we had never agreed to see each other exclusively. I'd never been one to see a problem with women dating as many men as they liked, but in this situation, the fact remained Dalton wasn't aware of me seeing anyone else, and this would hurt him, and that was what made it wrong. The only *right* thing left to do was tell him.

Yet my mouth still couldn't form the words.

"Sorry about dinner," I said lamely. "Things came up."

"They usually do," he answered, tousling Jack's hair. "No worries. Though I did have to brave the diner crowd shooting me pitiful looks. And on my first day in uniform and all."

"Yeah, what's that about?" I asked. "I thought detectives wore plain clothes."

Not that I was complaining.

"It's for the curfew." He shrugged. "The town thought it would be more effective if the people on patrol looked like officers instead of—"

"Studs?" I finished.

A blush crept up his cheeks. Oh, no. I was doing it again, feeding into the relationship monster.

"Sorry," I muttered instinctively.

Dalton's eyebrows pulled together. "For what?"

Kill me now. "I don't know. I'm not feeling right tonight."

At least that was true. I felt wrong. All wrong. I shouldn't be playing this game, and yet selfishly, I wanted Dalton to be here. Abram was either literally or figuratively a monster, and the reality was, if Abram wasn't in my life, I would be with Dalton, no questions asked. But I didn't deserve him after what I'd done.

Dalton nodded as if it was no big deal. If only he knew...

He looked at Jack, who was giggling now, but whose face was still streaked with tears and red blotches. "He's been crying?"

"Only every second since before I got here," I answered, squinting at the way he seemed so at ease with Jack in his arms and trying to decode the secret.

"Well, he's better now."

"Thanks to you."

He smiled. "I have my talents."

"I have no doubt," I answered. Now a blush crept up my cheeks.

"Have you eaten?" he asked. "How about I put him to bed and throw on some spaghetti? How does that sound?"

"Like you've been reading from my dream journal," I answered, realizing how hungry I was.

As he set Jack down and moved from Jack's room to the kitchen, eyeing the place from top to bottom, I realized why he was actually here.

I crossed my arms. "Lulu sent you to check up on me, didn't she?"

It all made sense. I was here, as useless as a soaking wet parachute, and she sent her brother to make sure I wasn't destroying her home and her kid.

"Don't be ridiculous." His smile faltered as he put the pasta on the stove. "I'm sure you're doing a great job."

"Save it. She thinks I'm going to make a mess of things."

"I believe the word 'sinkhole' was used." He grinned, his hand moving to rake through his hair. "But it's not bad."

I arched my eyebrows.

"Well it's not *that* bad." He chuckled.

"Don't laugh. This isn't funny," I said, surprised at how angry I was becoming. "We're in a crisis, and my best friend doesn't trust me!"

"Well," Dalton said, inching closer. "First of all, it's not a crisis. She's in the hospital. You know, where pregnant women go when they're in labor."

I would have pointed out not all of them, according to Lulu, but I really didn't know enough to argue. I frowned.

"She'll be *fine*," Dalton said. "And if she's a little bit concerned about your abilities in certain areas..." He cleared his throat. "And, for the record, I am *not* saying she is concerned. Mostly because she'd kill me if I told you that. It'd only be because she knows this type of thing isn't really your bag."

Disregarding his retro usage of the word 'bag', I said, "That's just a nice way of saying I don't fit in with her anymore."

And there it was, the truth of what had been simmering between Lulu and I since I returned to New Haven.

"Face it," I continued, "if it had been Ester who found her, you wouldn't be having this conversation."

"You're right." He shook his head. "If that stuck-up snob would have found my sister, I wouldn't be having this conversation. But I wouldn't be here, either." He leaned in, kissing me on the cheek. "Because you are." Dalton brushed a strand of hair out of my eyes and continued. "You're amazing. You have to see that. God knows everybody else does. It's why Ester hates you. It's why Lulu loves you so much. It's why..."

His hand lingered on my cheek as his voice trailed off. Heat ran through his fingers, tingled along my cheek. It was all around me, thick and warm, almost like—

"Your pasta is burning," I said, noticing the billowing smoke.

"Not the impression I wanted to make." He grinned, still looking into my eyes.

Biting my lip, I answered, "You're doing just fine."

* * *

Two phone calls to the hospital to check up on Lulu and an

absolutely breathtaking (if a little overdone) pasta-and-eggplant dish later, Dalton and I were snuggling on the couch.

It would have felt wrong if he hadn't been so right. Sure, he wasn't strong in the way Abram was. After all, Abram was massive. Abram was a thrilling, intimidating, and exhilarating thing. Like fire. But like fire, the thought of him consumed me. It devoured my mind until there was nothing of me left.

But Dalton was strong, too, in a solid-like-stone sense-of-being type of way. You could build on stone. You could make a life on stone. Stone did not destroy all it touched. It didn't leave you burned and broken, with nothing to show for your time and passion but ash scattered on the floor.

With Dalton, there was no bull, no drama, no chained-up girls, and no magical excuses or beastly traits. And he wanted me.

But did I want him?

I snuggled as close as I could, trying to come up with the answer. But it wasn't long before I realized what I was actually doing was trying to convince my heart to want something it didn't.

I knew what was good for me. Any idiot could see that this man, so wonderful, so kind, was the right choice. But Abram was different. There was something about him that drew me in like a moth to flame. Questions and concerns aside, I knew without a shadow of a doubt that I would go to that flame again.

I was cold without him—isn't that how it is with fire? Whether or not it was foolish to do so, I would keep going back to him, just like all the other times I vowed never to see him again.

Fact was, I trusted Abram. Conduits and beasts be damned, I believed every freaking word of it. How could I not? To deny it would be to deny things I had seen with my own eyes, experienced with my own body. No man, no matter how strong, could throw a woman like that.

What I had told Abram before, about not ever wanting to see him again, was all bluster. If I'd meant that, I would have called the cops by now—would have alerted the one sitting right beside me. Sure, no one would believe any of that magic nonsense, but they would listen if I told them a missing girl was chained up in the woods.

The only reason I hadn't said something was because, deep down, I believed that girl was who Abram said she was. A witch in woman's clothing.

God, I was just a much as a liar as he was. Perhaps worse. He had kept things from me, true, but anyone could see why. But me? I hid things, too, and I lied. Mostly to myself, but still. Maybe we deserved each other. I certainly didn't deserve Dalton. That was for sure.

Jimmy Fallon was halfway through a lip sync battle when I made my decision, or rather, accepted what I already knew.

First, I needed to break things off with Dalton. And that was true regardless of whether I wanted more with Abram. And second, if I needed to move on from Abram—and I wasn't sure I did—I wouldn't be able to until I had answers. And there was only one place where those could be found.

I would have to go back into those damn woods.

CHAPTER 17

I may have been in a rush to get answers, but I'd had enough nighttime treks into dangerous territory for one lifetime. I waited until the next morning, after Ester came to relieve me of my babysitting duties, to head back into the woods.

The path was almost second nature to me now. Unlike the last few times I hiked into these woods, though, I was prepared, and as such, the heels I usually wore had been replaced with sneakers. Underneath were thick socks to cushion the impact of walking on my still sore and battered feet.

And yes, the sneakers were still Coach, but who says a girl can't rough it in style?

As I neared the old house, my heart raced. I thought about turning around, considered writing the events of the last few days off as nothing more than a fevered dream, of going on about my life as usual. Whatever that even was anymore. But what was the use? I had tried that already. I had attempted to do the quiet thing with Dalton, and all it did was make me feel even more out of place.

I needed this. I needed answers to my questions. Hell, I probably needed answers to questions I hadn't even asked yet. I couldn't ignore it any longer. My life was at risk, and if I didn't find out how to fight back, anyone who even remotely resembled me would be in danger until I was found.

And Abram. *Sigh*.

I needed to make my peace with him as well. As much as I hated to admit it, in light of all that had happened, he and I had a connection. And it was more than physical. I found myself thinking about him all the time now. And that wasn't okay. Not when there were still so many secrets between us.

The house loomed into view more quickly than it had the last few times, as if it was coming out to meet me. The building looked somehow colder and more haunting during the day beneath the overcast sky. As if daylight couldn't reach this place if it tried.

The front door might as well have been a beckoning hand as it swung open of its own accord, and a lump rose in my throat. Did this house *want* me to come inside? Could houses want things?

Well, maybe this house could.

I fought back the urge to turn tail and run, and instead resolved to put on my big girl panties and get this over with. Either he would come off his lies and tell me the truth about what was going on, or he would hold firm to his ridiculous stories and prove how crazy he was.

But I think what I feared most of all was possible outcome number three: that all the lunacy Abram told me about actually *was* the truth.

I marched up to the open door with the same mixture of intensity and nervousness that a newbie model would display looking down her first cat walk.

As I crossed the threshold, the floorboards creaked under me. This was the third time I had entered this God-forsaken place, and with any luck, it would be the last.

"I didn't expect to see you here," a voice groaned from beside me.

I turned to the voice. Abram hunched over on the floor, his

face unshaven and his shirt a mess of careless stains. There was a bottle in his left hand, and the look on his face spoke of equal parts defeat and disgust.

"I'm nothing if not surprising," I muttered, noticing how much he looked like he did that day I found him after The Castle had been ransacked. And where had that led us? I swallowed around the lump forming in my throat and tried to push the images from my mind. I'd come here for answers. Nothing more.

"I didn't say you surprised me," Abram answered, taking a swig from the bottle. "I caught your scent when you were a half a mile out. I just said I didn't expect to see you, not after that performance yesterday."

"It wasn't a performance," I said, leaning against the far wall.

Something about seeing him like this, obviously broken, made me want to go to him. And I was afraid that if I moved even an inch, I wouldn't be able to stop myself.

So I stayed plastered against the wall, as far away from him as the confines of the room would allow. "You said a lot of garbage yesterday, as if you actually expected me to believe it. How was I supposed to react?"

"With a little grace," he answered, taking another swig and actually belching as he lowered the bottle.

"Grace personified, I see."

He waved me off and set the bottle aside. "And I told you those things because they were true."

"True?" I scoffed. "You expect me to believe that poor girl is a witch, or a Conduit, or whatever you called her? And that I'm one, too?"

He stood, wiping the moisture from his lips. "You're afraid of me."

"I'M NOT AFRAID OF ANYTHING," I ANSWERED, AND FOR JUST A moment, it was true. I was too upset to be scared. This man had lied to me. He had screwed with my mind, screwed with my heart. I had let him into me physically, mentally, and emotionally. And the truth was, I had no idea who he was. So no, I wasn't afraid. I was angry, goddamn it. "I'm pissed, and I want answers."

"You already got answers. You just didn't like them."

"You've got a lot of nerve," I said through clenched teeth.

"I've got a lot of a lot of things," he answered, still moving closer. "Call it the unintended spoils of a very long life." His eyebrows arched. "And I never said you were a Conduit."

"What?" I asked, half stunned and half exasperated. If he changed his story now, I might really snap. Forget claiming to never see him again, I might kill him on the spot.

"A Conduit. I never called you one."

He couldn't be serious. A part of me had actually considered this, had actually held onto that shred of trust in him. And now he was saying he didn't say those things?

"You did!" I yelled, stepping toward him before remembering my resolve to stay as far away as possible. "Not that it matters," I cut out, "since you're batshit crazy. But you did."

"I most certainly did not." He'd taken a few steps of his own— or rather, more than a few—and was almost on me now.

His chest heaved as he neared, as if he was becoming increasingly short of breath. I wondered about the change, about the monster he became, and about how difficult he said it was to control himself once it took him over. Was that what was happening now? Was I about to be torn apart?

He stopped, his body language softening as though he sensed that fear I had just moments ago denied feeling.

"I didn't say you were a Conduit," he repeated, more lightly this time.

"Then what did you call me?" I asked, my voice quivering as much as the rest of me did.

"Other than a beautiful pain in my ass?" he asked. "You're a Supplicant."

"I'm also a Virgo," I said. "Doesn't mean anything to me, since I don't believe in that stuff."

"You wouldn't be here unless some part of you did," he countered, and he was right. "And as much as you want answers, I want to give them to you."

I let out a shaky breath I didn't realize I had been holding. He was standing too close to me now, and my stupid heart was fumbling around in my chest like a teenage girl's moments before her first kiss.

"Then give them to me," I said, trying to exert confidence with my voice.

His head tilted to one side, and his gaze bore into my own. "Conduits perform magic. Supplicants, Charisse...Supplicants *are* magic."

He ran his forefinger lightly down my arm, causing every cell to stand at attention. I should have been afraid. I should have slapped his hand away. But I was frozen, consumed by a desire for him to keep touching me.

"There's a limited source of mystical energy in this world, Charisse." His finger traced my palm, sending sparks through me. "Increasingly limited, as it turns out. Nowadays, it's only found in ancient relics and specific geographical hotspots."

His finger moved from my palm and rested across my cheek, flirting dangerously with my lips.

"And in people like you," he added. "I told you there was magic in your blood, and there is. Resting inside of you, Charisse, is the essence of everything in this world that's worth having." He moved his finger and cupped the back of my neck with his huge hand. "All beauty, all wonder, everything that poets write about and painters try to capture with a brush—it's all because of you. It's all inside of you."

I swallowed hard, cursing the way heat was spreading through my body, the way my skin tingled beneath his touch.

"You..." I started, my voice a whisper. "You look like shit."

It wasn't true, of course, though he was disheveled—a shell of the dapper old-school gentleman I had come to know. He was still him: magnetic, intense, and quite possibly completely irresistible.

Of course, I didn't want him to know that.

"I do," he conceded, running his fingers down the nape of my neck. "I thought I was never going to see you again." His eyes darted to the floor and then back to me. "The prospect took its toll." His lips pursed. "I don't want you to worry, Charisse. I protected your father for as long as he allowed me. And I'll protect you, too. I swear it on my—"

"My father?" I asked, my eyes glazing over. He had mentioned him the other night, but I'd been too angry to consider it. But it would explain the picture I'd found in Abram's study. "My father's a—"

"He was a Supplicant as well. Yes."

"Was?" I asked, my voice quivering.

I hadn't thought about whether my father was alive or dead for a long time. Sometimes I would pretend he was dead. It made things easier. He was the bastard who left me. Who cared if he died?

But I was beginning to think there might be more to my father's story than what I knew, and being confronted with the possibility of his death now wasn't making anything easier.

The look that passed through Abram's eyes told me all I needed to about my father's fate. But he continued anyway.

"He was a good man, Charisse. One of the best friends I ever had. I know it must be hard for you to entertain the thought that he loved you, but—"

I shook my head so hard it cut Abram off, and the stream of hot tears that drove their way down my cheeks took me by surprise..

"Charisse, things were complicated," Abram started again, wiping my tears away with his massive and powerful thumb. "There were factors involved that none of us could see coming, least of all him. I told him that I could keep you both safe. That nothing would ever harm you. I promised him that. But he couldn't bear the thought of putting you in danger. It was all for you, Charisse."

"Then he should have stayed!" I yelled, batting Abram's hand away. "You have no idea how hard things were for me and my mom. She worked herself to death—literally to death! And all because my dad didn't have the balls to stand up to the people who were after him?"

"They aren't just people, Charisse. And you should know, he *did* stand up to those Conduits. That's how he wound up dead."

My mind revolted the idea. I couldn't let go of being angry at my father. It was my only line of defense at not falling completely apart at the idea I had lost him.

"So Conduits killed him," I said. "Is that what you're saying?"

"They're monsters, Charisse," Abram said. "Just. Like. Me."

Looking at Abram, knowing everything I knew now, and despite him being a beast, I couldn't help but disagree.

"You're not a monster," I said instinctively.

And I meant it. In that moment, looking in Abram's repentant eyes, I realized that not only did I believe everything he said to be true, but I always had. Ever since the first words came tumbling out of his mouth, I knew that my life would never be the same. I had run away because I was afraid—afraid of what he was saying, afraid of what I was feeling for him.

"Charisse, I was a monster before I ever became a beast," Abram said, the weight heavy in his tone. "That is why Satina cursed me. And I am every bit the monsters they are."

"You aren't a monster where it counts," I said, my fingers tracing over his chest, across his heart. My face flushed hot, and I quickly dropped my hand away. "But that doesn't excuse anything you've done. And it doesn't excuse my father for leaving me in this world not knowing the truth."

"He had your best interests at heart," Abram answered. "If he were here—"

"If he were here, he would be alive," I said with a sudden outburst. I tried to calm myself before I continued. "But he isn't.

I'm sure things were complicated. Things always are. But you don't leave the people you care about, Abram. Love doesn't run away."

"It doesn't?" he asked, his voice suddenly strained. Abram blinked hard, and his expression said everything he didn't. *Love doesn't run.* But that was what I had been doing every step of the way.

I opened my mouth, but before I could speak, Abram continued.

"You have every right to be upset," he said, taking an uncharacteristic step back as if to give me space. "But not at your father. He only wanted to keep you out of harm's way." He folded his arms over his hulking chest. "Part of my curse, a piece of what Satina did to me, was penance. She had found me lacking in life, heartless, and without even the slightest compassion for humanity. To that end, she compelled me to help people who were in need. I doubt she had in mind that I would be protecting Supplicants, but I made that my mission. And that is how I came to know your father. The people who came after him, looking to use his blood to power horrible spells, they were vicious. We both knew they would stop at nothing to drain every drop of blood from his body. And, because you were like him, from your body, too."

"Bullshit," I said, narrowing my eyes. "Blood replenishes. Why kill a never-ending source?"

Abram stepped in closer, intimidating in his stature. His face hard, his eyebrows lifted as though to question me challenging him. My heart skipped a beat, and my body betrayed me with the complete wrong reaction—arousal.

I swallowed around the tightness in my thought. "Well?" I asked, the confidence in my tone wilting. "Explain that."

Abram's nostrils flared. "Greed. Not only do these... creatures...lack self-control, but the bigger the spell, the more blood they need to perform it. *Fresh* blood, Charisse. And yes, they will bleed you dry and take your life for *one* spell. They'll take a dozen lives for one spell if they need to. Then they'll move on to the next Supplicant—which is why your father left you.

They had found him, and though they hadn't tracked him back to his home yet, it was only a matter of time. He had hoped to take them out and return to you when everything was said and done."

I shook my head, not understanding.

"He left you to keep you safe, Charisse. To stop them. To attempt to accomplish what I could not." His jaw tensed. "Had I done my job—had I been able to keep both of you safe..." His hands balled into large fists at his side. "If you're looking to blame someone for the way your life turned out, for all that you're lacking, look no farther than the man who stands before you."

I wanted to scream, to rear back and slap him. How dare he rob me of this? My father left me, and now I was just supposed to forgive him? Now I was just supposed to place the blame on this man—this man who I couldn't have hated no matter how hard I tried?

My whole body was trembling now in my effort to resist the emotional hurt ravaging my body, but I steeled myself against the tears. "So what? They got him before he could get them? They used my dad's blood, and that's all he was good for? They ran out, and now they want me?"

Abram shook his head. "Conduits do use people for their blood. That's all they care about, that is all the value a Supplicant has to them. But no, they are not after you because your father's blood ran out. They have always wanted you. They just don't know it yet."

"What does *that* mean?"

Abram sighed. "A while ago, rumors began in our world about a Supplicant girl—one who was an extremely potent being of magical origin. They didn't know it was you. Of course, if they had known you were a Supplicant at all, they would have gone after you anyway. But now they are hunting you *specifically*."

"Something must have changed, then," I mused under my breath.

Abram nodded. "It was not long before you returned here that the rumors took shape. A location—this town. A woman—fitting your description."

"That's why those women were killed..." I said. "Monsters want to bleed me out to make a voodoo cocktail. But couldn't they tell those girls weren't Supplicants?"

Abram titled his head back slowly. "That is the ever-concerning mystery. Whoever is after them, they aren't a true Conduit. If they were, they would have known those women were not Supplicants. They would have been able to find you by your nature alone. Though I suspect there's more to it than that as well."

"More than that? I'd say that's more than enough."

"I should have sensed you in town before we ever crossed paths," Abram said, leveling his gaze at me. "But there's something...masking you. Something that's been keeping you hidden."

"Something that made other women more of a target than me," I said, shuddering. "Those poor girls."

"More people I couldn't save." Abram's voice dropped to a bitter growl. "But I won't make that mistake with you. I'm here *because* of you, to keep you safe. I made a promise to your father, and I intend to keep it."

"What are you going to do then?" I asked breathlessly.

"I'm going to find that creature who's after you, the one who chased you into this house that night, and I'm going to relieve him of his head."

* * *

Abram had gone to clean up, leaving me standing in the foyer, reliving the craziness that had just unfolded around me. My mind was spinning, which might as well be its new default for all the times it had happened lately.

That was when I heard her voice.

Chaaariiiisssssseeee.

It was the girl. I shook my head, remembering what Abram had said. She wasn't a girl. That was Satina, the woman who had cursed him. The Conduit was calling to me, just like she had the other day.

I didn't want to, but I found myself moving closer to her room. She sang my name again.

Chaaariiissseeeeeee.

It was a siren song, a call that pulled me toward it without need of my cooperation. And somehow both the room here and the room at the club called me in the same way. But how could that be? She was here.

I crossed the threshold to the room before I realized where I was. She sat on the floor, still chained to the wall.

"Are you here to help me?" she asked in the same 'poor me' voice she had used the first time I saw her.

Suddenly, I snapped out of my fog. "Stop," I growled. "I know what you are."

"Do you?" Her face dropped all pretense of innocence, and she snarled at me so viciously, she barely looked human anymore. "And do you know what you are, *Supplicant?*" When she said the word, her voice dripped venomously, so much so that I stumbled a step back. "Do you really know?"

Her mouth twisted into a haunting grin, and her tongue flickered between her lips.

"Stay away from me," I said, taking another step back, this one more determined. "*Satina.*"

"Oh, someone's been brushing up on their ancient history, I see. Did he tell you the rest?" The Conduit arched the dead woman's eyebrows. "Did he tell you what happened the night I died?"

"Of course." My back knocked into the far wall. "And if you think I'm going to listen to some idiot girl who gets herself so twisted up over a man that she throws herself off a building, then you've got another thing coming."

For the first time in my life, I heard an honest-to-God cackle. It escaped her lips as she threw her head back gleefully.

"Is that what he told you?" She shook her head. "I must not be the only one who's found herself in the throes of that man's charms."

I narrowed my eyes.

"If you're willing to accept that pile of horse manure, then you're in deeper than I imagined." She leaned in closer, so close that the shackles pulled tight. "I didn't throw myself, Supplicant." She smiled again. "*I was pushed.*"

CHAPTER 18

"Pushed?" I asked, crossing my arms. "That's not what Abram said."

"Of course it's not," Satina spat back. "He's the one who pushed me! Did you expect him to offer that up?"

This was too much. I wanted—no, I *needed*—to be done with this back and forth. Abram was good. Abram was evil. The whole thing was enough to give me whiplash.

"You're a liar," I ground out, "and I won't fall for it again."

It was one thing to finally make my peace with the existence of magic, Conduits, Supplicants, enchanted beasts, and leprechauns. Okay, so I might be winging it with the last one. But it was something else altogether to put my trust in someone the way I had just done with Abram. And standing here, watching this ridiculous creature threaten the stability of that trust with some horrible lie, wasn't something I was prepared to do.

Even if, somewhere in the back of my mind, I still wondered if it was true.

Satina sighed. "You know, I don't see what he sees in you." She eyed me up and down with a sneer. "You're not his type. He's never been with a chunky girl before."

"Curvy," I corrected, then I waved my arm at her. "No different than you."

"This?" she asked, looking down at her own body. "This is nothing more than a borrowed opportunity. I was waif-like and beautiful in my time...back before your boyfriend killed me."

"You killed yourself," I said, finding it suddenly easy to not feel bad over the loss of her life. "I know that's probably hard for you to deal with, but that doesn't make it any less true."

Satina leaned back, letting her chains hang loosely in the air. The look on her borrowed face was cool and collected. She eyed me up and down as if I was a slab of beef and she was picking the choicest parts to chop off.

A shudder ran through me. This woman...well, first of all, she wasn't a woman at all, at least not the one I was looking at. She was a creature, some sort of spirit who had slung on a poor girl's corpse and was wearing it around the same way I'd have worn a pair of Louboutins.

She was a walking obituary. Or, more aptly, a sitting, chained-up obituary. And she wanted something from me.

"You better hope you're right, Supplicant. Otherwise, I think it's safe to say that you're in over your pretty little head." A disgusting smile parted her dry, cracked lips. "He was good, wasn't he?" She rolled her eyes, seeming to relish some unspoken memory. "He was amazing back then. Not good enough to make up for the murder, mind you, but I can only imagine what a dozen decades of experience has brought to the table. Let me ask you, is he still a moaner?"

I shuddered again, thoughts of Abram and I in the Castle, thoughts of Satina and Abram all those years ago.

God, he *was* a moaner.

"Shut up!" I yelled. "He didn't murder you. He's not that kind of person."

The smile fell from her face, replaced with hard lines that the girl Satina inhabited hadn't lived long enough to earn. "Are you willing to bet your life on that, Supplicant? Because that's exactly what you're doing." Her eyes flickered to the door and then back to me. "I was just like you back then. A little less thick around the waist, but we shared other qualities. I, too, was kind and naïve. I gave people more credit than they were due, and lent my trust to the wrong men."

"Sweetie, you don't know anything about me." Now I stepped closer to her, a little bit of my hard-earned edge creeping in. "I cut my teeth on the mean streets of New York City. And I realize that, since you're about as relevant as socks with sandals, that doesn't mean much to you. But suffice to say, it chews up and spits out scarier people than you on a daily basis." I sneered at her, leaning in even closer. "But it didn't get me, and you won't either. You see, you might have been some stupid little girl who couldn't get past the fact that the guy who screwed you didn't love you, but that's not me. I'm a grown ass woman, bitch, and you don't scare me."

She lunged at me with a growl, the chains clanking as she pulled at them to get her face closer to mine, but I held steady, not letting my body or expression reveal my lingering fear.

When I didn't flinch, she flopped back against the wall, sighing. "I'm tired of this."

Good. So am I.

But I was wrong to think she was done trying to intimidate me.

She pulled against her chains again, this time so hard that one of them snapped. Before I could react, she flicked her hand, throwing the loose chain at me. It struck me, wrapping around my neck like a noose. I grappled at it, but she jerked with more strength than I'd have ever imagined that body to be capable of.

I fell to the ground as she pulled me closer. I tried to scream, but the chain cut off my airway. I couldn't breathe. Panic shot through me, electric and terrifying. My heart thundered in my chest as I struggled against the witch.

Clawing at the floor, I tried to slow my journey toward Satina, but it was no use. She jerked the chain again, and with each pull, the chain got tighter around my neck. Pressure pounded in my head. I could feel the blood settling there, all my brain cells dying.

Spots started to ping at my field of vision, and the edges of the world blurred. Somehow, from the corner of my eye, I spied a shard of something.

A piece of glass from the broken picture frame. Abram hadn't cleaned it up yet.

Using a tiny bit of my quickly dwindling energy, I swiped it up, hiding it inside my clenched fist. Now all I had to do was wait until she pulled me toward her, and I would slash the bitch.

If I didn't suffocate first.

As she pulled the last bit of the chain's slack, I sprung (or rather, inched) into action. Arching my hand, I drove the shard toward her neck.

She grabbed my arm, stopping me in my tracks. I wasn't giving up now. Since she had to use one hand to grab me, that meant she let go of her vice grip on the chain.

Instinctively, I whipped the chain off my neck, gasping as a rush of cool air replenished my dry and sore throat.

The relief was short lived. I was still in danger. Looking up, I saw Satina had swiped the shard from my hand. I looked at my feet. Stupid shoes. If I had been wearing my heels, I could have flicked one off and drove a red-heeled point into this witch's ugly eye.

My agent was right. Women shouldn't wear sneakers. And to think I had thought he was just being sexist. However, he also said that no woman who cared about proper nail care should ever throw a punch. I was going to have to prove him wrong on that one.

I swung at her. A bit of me felt guilty and squicked out as I realized it was a dead girl's head I was connecting with. She pulled back as I clocked her across the face, but she didn't let go of my hand.

"You stupid cow!" she spit out. "I'm just trying to show you the truth."

She sliced the shard down my arm, breaking the skin. My eyes widened as a thick red mark appeared along my forearm.

Abram's words rang out in my head.

There's magic in your blood.

Uh-oh.

"Abram!" I screamed as the Conduit ran her finger along my arm, soaking up the blood.

She shuddered as a faint golden glimmer danced its way through her eyes.

"You truly are special." She sighed. "Now sit back and enjoy the show."

She slapped her palm hard against my forehead. I shook as I felt it—sparks and electricity running through my body. I tried to scream again, but my voice was gone. Then my eyes were gone.

Then everything was gone.

CHAPTER 19

Suddenly, I wasn't lying on the floor in Abram's upstairs dungeon anymore. I was in a different house, standing in the corner of a bedroom lit by candles and hanging lanterns.

It was dark outside, and as I tried to move toward the open window to better gauge my new surroundings, I realized I couldn't move. I was, once again, not in control of my body.

How refreshing.

A giggle shot through the orange-hazed room, followed by a fuller chuckle and then a shushing sound. Without my consent, my gaze flashed to the direction of the noise. A couple moved through the doorway, tangled up in each other and kissing.

The blonde woman was thin and unassuming. Her milky white skin was almost completely covered by a plain navy burlap sack of a dress, save for her arms and neck.

The man, wasting no time, was already halfway out of his shirt, whipping the puffy white fabric off and letting it fall to the floor. He had a hat on, swooping and bulky. As he pulled it off, letting dark curls fall down his shoulders, I instinctively knew a few things to be true.

First, I was in the past. That much was clear from the lantern light and ridiculously dated clothing.

Second, the man I was looking at was Abram. I knew that sculpted chest. I knew those strong arms.

And Abram, given the tremble in the girl's voice, was clearly about to get lucky.

But why was Satina showing me this? I knew Abram had a past. He told me he was a cad (or whatever grandpa language he used to let me know he used to sleep around). Did this stupid witch really think that giving me front row tickets to a time Abram made a girl regret her choice of bed buddy would be enough to make me turn on him?

"What if Father hears us?" The girl gasped as Abram slipped the dress off of her shoulders. It fell the way you would expect something large enough to hide every curve might—completely and all at once.

The girl was left standing in only a white slip, which was still more clothing than you would see in Milan this season. But I could tell that, for her, this was a line she had never crossed before.

"Father should be the furthest thing from your mind right now," he said, kissing her neck. He moved down her untouched skin, his lips wrapping around the softness of where her shoulder met her neck.

His fingers, as skillful as a surgeon's, pulled at the lace of her slip, loosening the fabric.

The girl shook all over as her breasts were exposed. Her eyes filled, and instantly I recognized something in them. I had been a girl who had never been naked in front of a man once. And the feeling that overtakes you when you finally are, that mix of regret and excitement, is something you never forget.

"Do you have any idea how much trouble we'll get into if—"

Her words stopped as Abram's moved down to her breasts, his mouth circling her nipples. She bit her lip, feeling the warmth overtake one of her most sensitive areas.

Oh God, I could *feel* it. I could feel everything he was doing to her, every sensation and emotion coursing through Satina's body.

I felt his lips on me, his tongue flicking at my hardening nipples. Satina wasn't satisfied to make me a voyeur to whatever was about to happen. She wanted me to be an inactive participant as well.

His hand ran up her back, and I shuddered. His palm, steadying her back, steadying her insecurities. It was more than just the physical sensation I was indulging in. I felt all of her anxiety, all of her excitement. All the trembling, worry, regret, fear, longing, and connection; it all belonged to me somehow, too.

It felt—it felt like the first time all over again.

"Father will—"

With his free hand, Abram ripped the rest of her slip away, revealing the entirety of her supple body to the open air. She was cool and trembling, afraid of what he was about to do, and desperate for him to continue.

His fingers searched her thighs as his mouth explored her abdomen. I stifled a breath as his tongue ran across her naval. Slowly, her inhibitions were falling away. Everything she had been taught, all the truths about what a proper lady was supposed to be, melted away under the heat of his touch.

The strangeness subsided for me as well. Her feelings were my feelings. Her sensations were my sensations. And it would be a lie to say I wasn't starting to let myself get swept up in them. Abram had a way of doing that to people—apparently even through the memories of times past.

My chest tightened as his fingers found their way into her. The moisture that came with her excitement pooled around his touch, and if I would have been able to moan in my current state, I sure as hell would have. Every sex dream I had ever had paled by comparison.

Even now, seemingly before his lifetimes of experience, Abram was skilled in the art of pleasure. Though he wasn't touching me, I felt him deep within myself. His hands were a symphony of sensations, each one more precise and exhilarating than the last.

I tried to remind myself that this was a spell, that the creature responsible for this may very well have been bleeding me dry and that this was nothing more than a magical ruse to keep me occupied.

But if it was a ruse, it was a damn good one. I felt myself lunge as Abram kissed the girl, letting his tongue slide where his fingers had just been.

She threw her head back, and her pleasure coursed through me, stealing away what little resolve either of us had left. If Satina was going to kill me like this, hopefully she would at least have the common courtesy to wait until he was finished.

Yet I couldn't live in the moment—not this one. No, not with Satina's stream of conscious rushing over my own. Thoughts of her family—all powerful Conduits—and how in a few short days, on her eighteenth birthday, she would shift into the form of a beast herself. All she wanted was to escape, to live a normal life. And here was Abram, charming, handsome, and strong. If anyone could help her, it was him.

Suddenly, the door flew open. The girl pulled away, covering herself with her hands and leaving Abram on his knees, shirtless and smiling.

"Father!" she yelled, tears pooling in her eyes.

But the man on the other end of the door wasn't her father. At least, not the sort I expected. He was a priest, complete with collar and rosary.

It was then that I realized what was going on. The emptiness of the room, the way the girl was so apprehensive. She was a nun. He was actually screwing a nun.

"Again, brother?" the priest said, looking down at Abram.

Heaven help me. Satina wasn't a nun...

Abram was a priest.

"I suppose asking for forgiveness wouldn't help my cause?" he asked with a fiendish glimmer in his eyes.

The priest's frown carved deep lines around his mouth. "Not this time."

"I'm not even the first," the naked woman muttered, and I felt the shame, regret, and anxiety slam back into her.

"Not even close," the priest said. "But you will be the last."

The girl scampered to dress while keeping her body shielded from the other priest, but he had already turned his attention to Abram.

"You're a disgrace to all who would give themselves to the Lord," the priest said. "And I, for one, am done covering up your sins. I'm reporting you to Father Jacobs with the sunrise. You'll be arrested within a fortnight. Let's see you break your vows within a prison cell."

"You wouldn't," Abram cut out, the lightness leaving his voice. "You know of the demons I struggle with, brother."

"Enough of your excuses and lies!" The priest raised his hand. "I will not let you make a mockery of this house, of these women, or of your own body. Not any longer. You *will* be brought out into the light of day, brother. Nothing short of divine intervention will stop me this time."

Suddenly, I wasn't in the room anymore. I stood on a crowded dirt road, watching a building as it was devoured in flames. People stood around it, gawking and praying. Most of them were priests as well.

The building I had just been standing in...it was on fire.

My head snapped to the right. Abram stood beside me, a hood pulled low over his face. His grin had returned.

"I suppose not all intervention has to be divine," he muttered.

"You burned it!" I yelled, but I wasn't there any longer. I was back in the old house, lying on the floor with a faded ceiling above me.

"What have you done?" Abram's voice boomed. Satina's throat was in his hands. She was pressed against the wall, rope binding her hands where the chains had failed. "Where is she?"

"I-I'm here," I said hoarsely, trying to stand.

Turning to me, Abram's eyes widened. He released the Conduit and rushed over to me, helping me up.

"Are you all right, Charisse? Where did she send you?"

I pulled away from him, squirming at his touch.

Satina laughed. "I suppose you know the truth now, don't you, Supplicant? You see the type of man he is."

"Quiet!" Abram growled. "Before I silence you myself!"

"All monster, no magic," she taunted. "Such a waste."

He spun around on her. "And whose fault is that?"

She glowered at him. "Yours, you idiot! I offered to protect you. My family could have kept you safe after what you'd done!"

He clenched his jaw. "I told you then, and I will tell you now: *I don't need you or your family.*"

"Actually," she said, tipping her head to the side. "You do need me. If you didn't, I wouldn't be here, now would I? You could have had it all, Abram. You could have shared this magic with me. But you made your choice—your stupid, idiotic choice! Look where it got you. And still you try to deny me."

Now it made sense. She hadn't wanted him to save her from becoming a beast. She'd wanted him to join her. For him to marry into her powerful Conduit family so she wouldn't be alone. She'd given a piece of herself to him in that bedroom, and when he betrayed her, she'd given a piece of herself to him in her death as well. The piece of her that would become a beast, making Abram a monster with none of the Conduit power to fight her back.

Was that why she couldn't turn into a beast now? It would explain why she hadn't broken from her chains sooner. By reanimating herself in that poor dead girl's body, Satina had found a way to be a Conduit without the curse of being a beast.

Well, if she thought that was going to make me side with her, she was dead wrong. I would have chained her up, too.

Abram turned to me hesitantly. "She told you I murdered her, didn't she?"

"Did you?" I asked.

"Of course not. Everything I told you was the truth."

"You were a priest," I said, shaking my head.

His jaw set. "I was in training, but I never completed the

process," he said. "Is that what she showed you? You need to understand, I was a different—"

"What happened to them?" I asked, backing away from him. "To all the people in the building you set fire to?"

His gaze lowered. Quietly, he said, "They were awake and outside when I set that fire. Working. I did horrible things, Charisse, but I wasn't a murderer. I have never been a murderer."

"And what about the girl you slept with? That was Satina? That must have ruined her life!" As much as I hated the witch, I had to admit I felt bad for the girl she was before all that happened.

"I ruined a lot of lives," Abram conceded. "I was selfish and more than a little irresponsible. But I'm not that man anymore, and I wouldn't do that to you."

"Are you really this stupid, Supplicant?" Satina asked, eyeing the way Abram's hand hung expectantly in the air, waiting for me to take it. "He has broken every promise he has ever made. He turned his back on God himself. What makes you think you'll be any different?"

I glared at the witch. "For such a crystal clear vision, you didn't take the opportunity to show your supposed murder. Not that I could trust anything you show me anyway." I turned to Abram. "Could I?"

He pressed his lips together. "She can't show you a memory that hasn't happened. Even Conduits have limits, though not enough of them," he added, glaring at her. He returned his gaze to me, and he frowned. "She had to show you a horrible truth, and I've certainly given her enough to choose from." He reached for my hand. "And she's right about one thing. I've broken a lot of promises in my long life. But not with you," he said, his voice cracking. "Never with you."

"He lies." Satina scowled. "We're all the same to him. What makes your relationship with him any different?"

I looked at him for a long moment, studying his dark eyes, watching the lines on his face, considering his strong hand, still outstretched and reaching for my own. I knew him—maybe not the man he was then, but certainly the man he was now. And I would make this choice. I would trust him.

Because I already did.

"It's different now," I said, taking his hand, "because *he's* different."

CHAPTER 20

Something about the small act of taking Abram's hand changed everything. It was then, with my fingers knotted in his, that I let go of all my doubts and fears. Everything that had been holding me back since that day in The Castle...it all melted away in the heat of his touch.

All the nonsense that had been and still was swirling around me lost its potency. Abram was here. He was mine. There was some evil force trying its best to bleed me dry and discard me like last year's spring line, and it didn't matter. Abram would keep me safe. I trusted him. I really, honest-to-God, without a shadow of a doubt, trusted him. And that made the world a brighter place.

Of course, it didn't change the fact that, googly eyes aside, there was still work that needed to be done.

As we walked through the forest, still hand in hand, my body trembled as everything I had learned came rushing in at me. Suddenly, it wasn't a wild story. It wasn't crazy talk. This was my new reality, and as much as I was ready to accept that, it wasn't any easier to come to terms with.

Abram gave my hand a gentle squeeze. "Are you all right, Charisse?"

I chewed my lip. "To tell you the truth, it's a lot to take in."

"Of course it is," he said, his voice just as steady as his resolve. "You've had only days to take in what I've had decades to learn and accept."

As if I needed the reminder.

The path where our feet fell was well worn, and I imagined Abram walking it ten, fifty, one hundred years ago. The idea that it was possible, that he had been this breathtaking man even then, was enough to spin my head around.

It made me uneasy. He had lived so long. He had seen so much. And maybe, my grand gesture notwithstanding, I *was* no different than the rest of them. How could I compete with a hundred and fifty years of life experience?

No, that wasn't true. Those were Satina's words, her insecurities, and I wasn't about to let them become mine. Besides, I was Charisse Bellamy. I had been on the cover of Seventeen, Cosmo, *and* Maxim magazine. I was third runner up to the 2007 Miss Plus Size Manhattan. A hundred and fifty years of life experience couldn't compete with *me*. And that was just the way I liked it.

"I'm just not sure how I can help when I still don't have the first clue what any of it *means*," I said finally.

"Don't worry about that right now," he said. "The only thing you need to know is that I will protect you. On my life, I'll keep you safe. The rest will fall into place with time."

I sighed and pulled my hand away from his as we continued down the path. We were almost back at the house now, and the fresh air had done little to calm my nerves.

Abram stopped in his tracks, and the wind picked up, sending strands of dark hair blowing across his night-black eyes. Some people might have seen those eyes as menacing, as capable of horrible things. And honestly, I might have been one of those people if things had turned out differently. But that couldn't have been further from the truth now. To me, those eyes were kind and beautiful.

He had tried so hard to explain away the mistakes of his youth.

Though he always took responsibility for what he had done, he must have thought me knowing about those things would make me think less of him.

He couldn't have been more wrong.

To me, that only made him stronger. My own mistakes in life might not have been as grand, but I'd lived enough to know everyone was guilty of something. Knowing that he had been that boy and then came out the other side of the man he was now...I was in awe.

When I didn't say anything, Abram's eyebrows arched. "Did I misspeak?"

"No," I answered, running my hands through my hair. "Yes. I don't know." I shook my head. "Look, I get that you want to take care of all this. And that's sweet. It really is. Lord knows there are probably a billion girls out there who want nothing more than some gorgeous man to swoop in and save them from their problems, no questions asked. But I'm not one of those girls. I ask questions, Abram." I pointed to myself. "This is my problem, *my* fight. You said it yourself—those girls are dying because of me."

"You can't blame yourself for that," he snapped, though, despite the anger in his voice, his body language told of a man who wanted to comfort me.

I raised a hand to stop him. "I don't blame myself. I blame the son of a bitch who's killing people. But that doesn't absolve me of my responsibility here. This monster might have been the one to kill these girls, but that doesn't change that they died because I moved back to New Haven."

It had been weighing on my mind, and it had to be said.

As the sun behind Abram's head began its descent westward, we finished our stroll and stepped into the living room. We had little time left before his change, but somehow I sensed that wasn't going to stop him from arguing with me.

"It started before you came back," he said, locking the door behind us and waving arm toward to the couch for me to sit.

I flopped down on a soft but dusty cushion and clutched my purse in my lap. "I visited Lulu weeks before I moved back. I couldn't ask her a favor as big as moving in over the phone, so I'd come by. I'd been here, Abram. Probably around the same time that first girl went missing. If I hadn't come then—if I hadn't moved here—those girls might still be alive."

Abram, seating himself beside me, pressed his lips together into a defeated frown. "You couldn't have known coming back would start this."

"That's just it, Abram. I don't know anything." I turned my body toward him, grasping my purse even tighter, as though if I held on tight enough I wouldn't been thrown from this world that was spinning too fast for me to keep my balance. "Maybe if I knew who this person was, or even if I knew what they wanted, then maybe I could make sense of all this. At least then I'd be able to put reasoning behind why all of this is happening. At least then I might feel like all these people didn't die for no—"

"I know," he said firmly.

"You know what?" I scoffed, ready for him to tell me that he knew exactly how I felt so that I could tear into him and assure him that he didn't.

"I might not know who the person is," he said, "but I'm fairly certain I know what he wants."

I blinked hard. "And you didn't say anything?"

"I didn't want to tell you anything." Abram huffed. "If I had my way, you would be mixing drinks for your over-privileged friends or helping Lulu with the baby. The fact that this has touched you even this much is a testament to how much I've failed you already."

Lulu. God, I hadn't even thought about her. Some friend I was. I would have to call her later and check up on things. Of course, if she was still in labor (very possible given the seventy-two hours it took for her to squeeze out the first one), that would mean I would have to call Dalton...which was a completely different can of worms I didn't have time to open right now.

"Your father wanted you to have a normal life, Charisse," Abram finished.

"Well, that ship has sailed, don't you think?" I arched my perfectly plucked eyebrows at him. "I get that you're old world, that you think a man is supposed to take care of everything and a woman is just supposed to be barefoot and in the kitchen. But I'm not Donna Reed, Abram."

"My sentimentalities are actually much older than that, I assure you."

"Whatever. The point is, this is the twenty-first century, and even if it wasn't, I'm not the type of girl who'll just let you make everything better. This is *my* life—not my father's, not yours, and certainly not whatever outdated gender roles you subscribe to. I want to know everything you know. I *deserve* to know everything you know."

For a long moment, he stared at me. I couldn't be sure, but he seemed impressed.

"Fair enough," he said. "I brought Satina back."

"What?" I narrowed my eyes. "Why would you do that? She's horrible. And that poor girl..."

"The girl was dead. But I knew something was coming, and Satina was right. 'All the monster, none of the magic.' I was outgunned. I needed a Conduit to help me through this."

"So you brought back the worst woman you've ever known? How did you even *do* that without magic?"

"A mystic owed me a favor. He brought her back. But I couldn't trust him for what was coming. You're a very potent Supplicant, Charisse. I had to be careful who I exposed you to."

"Something tells me you made a bad call." I chewed the inside of my lip, shaking my head. "She tried to kill me."

"She was trying to get you to turn on me, and that's the least of what would happen if a full blown Conduit ever got their hands on you. Satina's powers are diminished while she's trapped in that body. It's why even the simplest of memory projections required your blood—a skill that, in her past life, would have required no blood sacrifice at all I can control her this way, Charisse. And she has no choice but to give me the guidance I need."

"What guidance?" I gave Abram a proper glare. "You still haven't told me anything."

The sun dipped well below Abram's head now. We only had so much time, and I needed to make sure we put it to good use.

"Satina thinks she knows what the other beast is after." Abram folded his arms over his chest, making him look twice as hulking. "He's not an actual Conduit, not a born one anyway. They give off certain energies, and Satina was able to pull a sort of psionic fingerprint off of the body she's inhabiting. The only thing we don't know is why its energy changed the night it followed you into my home—that night it was certainly more of a Conduit and less of...whatever it was when it killed Satina's host."

I shook my head slowly. Back in New York, I wouldn't have been caught dead marching around the woods in sneakers. And I never imagined I would be in a position where I would have to listen to a sentence with the words 'psionic fingerprint' in them. But here I was.

Guess you can't fight fate.

"You said I was born a Sassafrass," I muttered.

"Supplicant," he corrected. "And you were."

"And Conduits are born, too?"

"Traditionally," he answered. "But there is another way—a much more gruesome way entirely. "

"You have to kill one, don't you? That's the other way?"

Abram nodded, giving more weight to Highlander than I ever thought truly possible.

"Unbelievable!" I threw my hands in the air. "Everything is about killing with you people. Why does life always have to be about death?"

He moved toward me and, this time, I didn't stop him. "I wish I had the answer to that question, Charisse. But they're not my people. I'm a bastardized monster—a product of a curse, not a beast by birth or by murder."

"Are you sure they killed a Conduit, though? Maybe they were cursed like you were."

Abram shook his head. "They wouldn't be after you if that was the case. Your blood would be no good to them then. A Conduit without the magic is a beast and nothing more. And you must understand—this is actually more *your* world than mine. It's because of that that this monster can use you."

"To what end?" I asked as he neared me.

"This other beast—he has some of the powers of a Conduit, but not all of them. That is why his visions of you are unclear. Any other Conduit hunting you would have found you by now—would not have killed the wrong people in error. But Satina believes he is after something much more potent, something only your blood could give him, due to your bloodline being one of the strongest Supplicant bloodlines in history."

"And what is that? What is it that my extra special blood has to offer that is worth this blind killing spree?"

Abram looked down at me guiltily, as though he was somehow to blame for this. "Eternal life."

"What?" I gasped. "That's ridiculous. I don't have the power to make someone live forever."

Abram just stared at me.

"Do I?"

He continued to stare.

"But I thought you beasts already had that?"

"I do, but only because it's part of my curse. Someone who has stolen the life of a Conduit, however, would have to keep replenishing their state of being with fresh Supplicant blood... unless they could find a permanent solution. You could be that solution."

"Oh my god," I said, and I started pacing. "Oh my God."

"It's all right," Abram said, wrapping his arms around me and stopping me. "It's a lot of power, but it doesn't change who you are. You're still you. You're still—"

I rested my head against his chest, listening to the steady beat of his heart. "If we can't stop him—if he *does* get to me—then he'll never die. Think of all the people he could hurt, all the people he could kill. *Forever.*"

Tears burned behind my eyes.

"I—I mean, *we*—won't let that happen," Abram answered. "I promise."

"How do we stop it then?"

Abram rubbed his hand up and down my back and let out a long, soft breath. "For now, just try not to hurt yourself. No falling down steps or running through the woods with cut up feet. The blood will only draw him to you."

I shuddered, pulling away. "So my blood acts like a beacon for demon monsters? Geeze, better hope I don't knick myself shaving."

Abram leveled his gaze at me. "This is no laughing matter, Ms. Bellamy. I've already chased it off several times thanks to your...injuries."

"Then let's do something about it," I said. "I'm not going to wait for some accident to send this thing hurtling at me while I'm unprepared. I rather see it coming."

"No, Charisse," Abram said firmly. "This man killed a Conduit —something most would consider a suicide mission. That he actually accomplished that only speaks to how dangerous he is."

"Which is all the more reason for us to stop him," I said. "And it sounds like there's only one way to call out something so single-minded."

"Please, don't." Abram placed his hands on either of my shoulders. "I shudder to think of whatever it is you are considering."

"There's nothing to think about, Abram. I'm going to give him what he wants." I slid his hands from my shoulders and scooted back. "I'm going to give him me."

CHAPTER 21

The look on Abram's face told me that I may as well have shot him as suggested what I had.

"Are you out of your mind?" He huffed, staring at me with bewildered eyes. "I've spent all of this time trying to keep you safe, keep you hidden, and now you just want to dangle yourself out there like a worm on a line?"

"A worm, Abram? I think as far as prey are concerned, I could at least pass for a rabbit in a fox's den, or something less...slimy."

"I'm being serious," he responded without even a shadow of a smile. "This is deadly business."

"I know that." I spread my hands. "And I'm not the only one. I bet all those girls that bastard massacred knew it, too. I bet that was the last thought that went through any of their minds." I looked down at my feet, suddenly ashamed that I'd ever thought the sort of shoe adorning them was in any way important. "I won't let their deaths be for nothing, Abram."

"God, you're amazing," he mumbled under his breath, and I couldn't tell whether he was exasperated or impressed. "Don't you see, Charisse? If you die, then all of it really *would* have been for nothing. He'll get what he wants, and those girls will never be avenged."

I shook my head. "That won't happen."

"How do you know that?"

"Because you're here," I said. I stuck my finger into his hard chest and let it sit there. At first, I'd only intended the gesture to hammer home my point, but soon, I found myself taking comfort in this small connection. Touching him, even like this, seemed to quiet my mind and steady my stance. "You'd never let anything happen to me."

His voice had dropped to nearly a whisper: "Not in a hundred lifetimes."

His hand traveled upward and encompassed mine. Sparks shot through me and, for an instant, I forgot about everything else. I wasn't a Supplicant. He wasn't some Conduit's pet science project. He was just a man, and I was a woman. There was no danger, no pile of lookalike corpses for me to hang my guilt on. There was only this tenderness between us. Tenderness and heat.

He cleared his throat, and I realized he was feeling it, too.

"That doesn't mean I want you to go spearheading into danger, though," he said. "We need to go about this in an intelligent manner."

"Does intelligent mean slow, Abram? Because I don't think the next poor sap who looks like me has that kind of time to waste." My hand was still his to hold. My heart was still his to break. But I couldn't fold on this.

"I know you want to save them, and that's admirable. But you have no idea what we're up against. I was dealing with Conduits while your grandfather was still in diapers. They're dangerous creatures, and I doubt you have the foresight to fully understand that."

I narrowed my eyes. "So I don't understand anything?" I wrestled my hand from his. "I'm just some child then?"

He sighed, his expression forlorn. "That's not what I meant."

"That's exactly what you meant," I answered, grinding my teeth. "You think that because you're older than sand, you have some kind of immaculate perspective on this."

"I think my situation affords me a unique advantage, and if you weren't so close to the situation, I'm sure you would agree."

"You're sure?" I asked indignantly. "And I suppose you're sure because I'm so infantile and predictable."

His eyebrows shot up quizzically, which was just what I was going for, and he blew out a thin stream of breath. "Why are you acting like this?"

"Acting like what? Childish? Well, I suppose I'm acting this way because that's how you see me. Like a child!"

I wasn't, of course. I knew better than that and, even if I didn't, I wasn't the type to go off on some poor guy just because he said the wrong thing. That was way too 'How to Lose a Guy in Ten Days' for my taste.

I had slipped into mega-bitch mode only to create a distraction. And I was trying to create a distraction because I didn't want Abram, with his heightened beast senses, to realize that I was—at this very moment—fumbling for the nail file in my purse.

And he wouldn't like what I was about to do with it.

"Why on Earth would you think that?" he asked, raking his hand through his hair.

Turned out that, magical or not, *all* guys fell apart into confused messes when the girls they liked got emotional.

"Because it's the truth!" I yelled way too loudly. "You know it's the truth! And what about my clothes? I know you don't like the way I dress!"

"I—What?" Poor Abram. He was as lost as a socialite at a NASCAR race.

"You know you do! All you ever do is judge me!"

"Charisse, I—I don't understand where this is all coming from. I just—"

I pulled the file out quickly and ran it across my palm, breaking the skin.

"Goddamn it!" Abram yelled, rushing toward me. He pulled my palm toward him, sandwiching it between his and effectively stopping any of my blood from hitting the ground. "What the hell are you doing?"

"What I have to," I said, dropping the charade of the easily offended psycho girlfriend. "I have to do this. I have to save those girls."

"What about *this* girl?" he asked, eyes wide, motioning toward me. "What about *my* girl?"

A touch of guilt pinged at the back of my mind. Dalton had called me his girl not two days ago. And he meant it.

I pushed that aside and let myself drown in the other, more pleasurable sensations that Abram's proclamation brought about.

I was his, something that belonged to him. He was saving me. He was prioritizing me. He was taking me.

And I wanted nothing more in that moment than to be taken. My inner feminist was appalled by my reaction, but I didn't care. All I wanted in that moment was his hands on my body, his mouth on my lips.

Too bad he wasn't done scolding me.

"You can't be this foolish, Charisse," he said sternly. "Not when so much is at stake."

He looked at me, his dark eyes bearing clear down into my soul. And I realized that the thing at stake—the thing he was putting so much emphasis on protecting—was me.

"I just wanted to—"

"I know," he said, leaning in close and shutting me up with his nearness. "But the only way to keep everyone safe is to keep our wits about us."

He opened his hands, revealing that he had soaked up most of my blood with his palm. It shimmered, gold and sparkling against his tan skin.

"My God..." I murmured. "I've cut myself before. It never—"

"It wouldn't, not unless your blood came in contact with someone of a supernatural persuasion." It was then I noticed just how hard Abram was trying to keep his hand from shaking. "Just one drop of your blood," he said, biting his lip. "You have no idea how much—"

"Oh God, are you in pain? Is this hurting you?" I asked, pulling my hand away. "Am *I* hurting you?"

"Not you," he answered, closing his eyes. "The magic. I'm an abomination—all beast, no magic, remember? The magic doesn't take to me very well."

"Well, wipe it off!" I yelled, reaching for him.

"No!" He pulled his hand away. "It's a beacon. Conduits can track it. If this touches anything, it'll send the person after you right to us."

"That was the point," I said.

He glowered at me, but his scowl soon turned to a wince.

"Okay, so maybe this wasn't my best idea."

He shook his head. "Oh, no. I'm not playing that game with you again. But could you please stop with the blood luring?"

My hand was still bleeding, but I hadn't touched anything. That was all I had to do, and the trap would be set. As I chewed at my lip, contemplating, his hand shot out to cover my wound again, his face twisting into deeper pain.

"Charisse, *please.*"

God, his voice was so strained. But what other choice did we have? "We can't do nothing."

"I promise we'll do something," he said. He barely got the words out. "Something. Not this. Please."

Seeing Abram beg twisted up my insides. I couldn't do it. I couldn't see him like this.

"Okay," I whispered. "I won't, okay?"

He nodded and released my hand again, then stumbled back to sit on the floor, leaning back against the wall clutching his hand against his chest.

"I didn't mean for you to get hurt," I said, overcome by guilt.

He balled his hand into a fist. "I'll be fine, Charisse. This is far from the worst pain I've been in."

"Uh-uh," I said. I dug in my purse for a bottle of Evian. "At least let me help fix it."

I kneeled beside him, opened the water, and pulled his fist apart before splashing the liquid onto his hand. The blood dispersed, as if by magic. Just...gone. When Abram's hand was clean, I noticed his palm had been scorched.

"God," I said, staring at his palm. "If that's from me, then maybe I'm the monster."

"You're a miracle. I'm the monster," he answered, visibly relaxing. "But that's all right. If a monster is what it takes to keep you safe, then I wouldn't have it any other way."

And there it was, the miracle and the monster. But even if Abram was okay with being a monster, as he called himself, I wasn't. He *wasn't* this horrible thing. Hell, even in his beast form, he had done everything he could to keep me safe.

But that didn't change the fact that, once the sun went down, he would lose control of himself. He would be forced to take a shape that wasn't his own, to live a life that wasn't of his choosing. And he had done it every day for well over a century.

"Satina," I muttered, looking at him and seeing not just the man I adored or the monster that intrigued me, but also the naughty roguish boy who had gotten himself into a hundred and fifty years' worth of trouble. "You said something about breaking the curse."

"I said no such thing." He wouldn't look at me.

"No more lies, Abram," I said, grabbing his chin and turning his face toward me. "And no more secrets. You said Satina's spirit is connected to you until you die...or until the curse is broken. How do you break it?"

"Why don't you ask her?" he grumbled.

"Well, for one, because I want to hear it from you. For two, we both know damn well she's a liar."

His gaze swung toward me. "And who do you think told me how to break the curse?"

"Right," I said, feeling the sinking of defeat in my stomach. "Satina."

Which meant anything he might know about breaking the curse was a moot point. For all we know, if he even tried to do what she said, it would only make matters worse.

"I don't want to get either of our hopes up, Charisse," he said quietly. "I'm not keeping secrets, and I'm not lying to you. I'm just not sure what the truth is."

"I see. But there has to be a way," I said, "And my hopes are getting up regardless, Abram. It's a little something called *faith* that my Grandma taught me."

"Hope you have enough for both of us," he muttered.

I smiled. "At least I got you hoping for something."

Abram didn't respond. Instead, he straightened where he sat and tore the sleeve from this shirt. "Give me your hand."

"Um, okay," I said, stretching my hand out to him. He tore the fabric sleeve in half, making a scrap of cotton that he began to wrap around my wound.

As I watched him, I tried to think what our next move should be. My blood was magical—the sort of magic that was no less than poisonous to the touch, at least for Abram. If we were going to see our way out of this, we were going to need guidance—the same sort of guidance Abram sought out when this whole thing started.

"We need her help, Abram," I said, though I couldn't believe the words were coming out of my mouth.

"Whose help?" he muttered as he finished tying off the fabric. He looked up to me, and his expression shifted from blank curiosity to sheer disbelief. "You can't be serious, Charisse."

"I am."

"Satina's not going to help us. Never, not in a million years. Just get that idea out of your head right now."

I placed my uninjured hand over his and gentled my voice. "If we're going to have even a chance of surviving this, we need her on her side. You must have had that thought at some point, too— that's why you brought her back here."

"And we see how well that went."

"Abram," I said, steeling my voice. "You need to set her free."

He nearly choked on the air. "That's a little unfair, don't you think? *She's* the one who needs to set *me* free."

I knew why I needed Abram. Having him in my life meant it was safe for me to have moments of weakness. After years of staying strong while my mom fought cancer, I needed that. I needed for it to be okay to not be strong all the time.

But now I knew why Abram needed me. He needed someone to help him move past all his anger and bitterness, his self-loathing and regret.

"Maybe she *will* set you free," I said. "Or maybe she won't. But do you think she'll even consider it while you're keeping her captive?"

He swallowed and looked toward the staircase leading up to the room where Satina sat locked away and chained to a wall.

"We'll try it," he said slowly. "But if she tries to hurt you, I really will be the one to kill her this time."

CHAPTER 22

"I don't like this idea," Abram said, standing beside me in front of the enchanted room that held Satina. "I know I agreed, and since I'm a man of my word, I'll do it. But I think it should be noted that I don't like it."

"Noted," I answered drolly, arms folded. "And your word, is that the only reason you consented?" I arched my eyebrows at him.

A grin spread across his face. This was a dark time. That much was true. But, if being there for my mother through her painful last days taught me anything, it was that darkness without a touch of light was too unbearable to get through.

"It was either that or your lips," he answered.

I felt my eyebrows pull together, surely forming a future wrinkle on my forehead. "My lips?"

"They curl up when you get angry. Would you find it demeaning if I said it was arousing?"

A spike of warmth leaked out from my heart, filling my chest. "No," I admitted. "Not if *you* said it."

A long moment passed between us with him looking at me. Clearly he was as lost in me as I was in him, sinking gleefully into the possibility of what we might be to each other. Soon though, his expression sobered. We didn't have time for this, and we certainly didn't have the luxury of forgetting what we were here for.

He turned his attention back to the door. "I don't think this is going to work," he said. "Satina isn't going to help us."

"You said you brought her back for the express purpose of helping you. Try to channel some of whatever you were feeling when you did that."

"That's probably not a good idea," Abram said, running a skillful hand through his hair. "And you saw how much good that did. If you didn't have your father's eyes, who knows if I would have even made the connection. I might have still been scouring that stupid club, combing through beautiful women."

The idea of Abram combing through beautiful women didn't sit well with me, regardless of how pure his intentions were. But that wasn't the only thing about his sentence that I took offense with.

"Don't call The Castle stupid. It's where we met. It's your work."

"You're my work," he answered. "The club was just a vessel to facilitate that."

"Well, I like it." I smiled, nudging his shoulder. "Ridiculous ice maker and all."

His hand trailed down my side and rested at my hip for a brief moment before he pulled away. "Maybe I'll give it to you one day."

"The ice maker?" I asked.

"Whatever you want," he answered quietly.

The proclamation made me flush. I cleared my throat and swiftly shifted the conversation. "You just have to tell her what the other beast did. Tell her he killed a Conduit to get his powers. She'll hate that. Conduit solidarity and all."

"They're not the Girl Scouts, Charisse. She already knows about that, and she doesn't care. And if you remember, she didn't even want to be a Conduit in the first place. Besides, I was under the impression you were going to speak with her."

"Me?" I balked. "Why would you think that?"

"Because this was your idea," he answered, eyeing the door. "And because Satina still hates me for what I did to her when she was alive."

"Have you tried apologizing?" I asked, leaning in.

A quizzical look came over Abram's sculpted face. "You're not serious."

"Dead serious."

"No," he said firmly. "I will not lower myself to apologize to a woman of that nature."

"Of that nature?" I asked, scoffing. "I get that you're from another time and you were raised with outdated values, but I don't think I'm comfortable with the idea of slut-shaming Satina, even if she is a psychotic witch."

"They don't like that word," he scolded. "Conduits aren't witches." He shook his head. "And I'm not some out-of-date fossil. I might have been born in a different time, but I grew up alongside this world. I'm just as contemporary as anyone."

"Really?" I asked. "What's a Kindle?"

"A bundle of sticks one uses for a fire. And it's pronounced kindling," he answered proudly.

"Right." I sighed and turned away.

"What?" he said. "You can't be mad at me for telling you how to say it correctly. Is this one of those times where you are pretending to be upset over nothing to distract me?"

"Look," I said, laying a hand on his muscle-corded left arm. "I felt what she felt. I know what she went through that night with you. She was ashamed. She was afraid. She was embarrassed—more so than I've ever been in my life." He tried to look away, but I traced his cheek with my fingers and held his attention. "I know what she did to you was wrong, and nothing could ever excuse that. But the healing has to start somewhere. And I know you can be the bigger person here."

As he stared at me, I could see his resolve softening.

"My lips are curling again, aren't they?" I asked.

"Every time," he said, a smile breaking through his mask. "It's uncanny."

I knew I had him, so I nudged him toward the door. "So get in there, big boy." I slapped his ass, surprised both at how firm it was and how this little gesture caused him to jump.

His eyes slid over to me. "I'm going to make you pay for that later."

"So long as you make sure there is a later, I just might let you." I winked. "Now go."

I pushed the door open and felt a chill as the room revealed itself to us.

Satina sat in the corner, her chains reset from when she had broken one earlier. Her eyes darted toward us and, inexplicably, her tongue danced in and out of her mouth.

"I was wondering when you were finally going to come in." Satina groaned, and her body twitched as though she was in pain.

My first instinct was to feel for her, but I quickly remembered who we were dealing with. This very well might have been a ploy to garner my sympathy. Satina was more than capable of that.

"You heard us?" I asked, suddenly hyper-aware of all the flirting.

"I sensed you," she answered. "A residual treat from your blood, Supplicant." She smiled all wide and unearthly. "I wonder if you'd be so kind as to top me off."

"We're not here for that." Abram moved through the doorway and toward Satina. "I need to talk to you, to give you something."

"And what could you possibly have that would interest me, Beast?"

I kept my distance as he neared her. Nothing good would come from taunting Satina with my blood, not when she looked like one of those junkies on 9th Street, desperate for a high.

He settled in front of her. "My apology, Satina," he said. "That's what."

She looked up at him, her eyes licking over every inch of his body. Then, surprisingly, she cackled, shaking the entire room with her boisterous laugh.

"You're desperate? Is that it?" She looked over at me, disdain flickering in her eyes. "You realize you're out of your depth, and you think that some halfhearted apology will soften my heart." She spit, literally spit, at him. "I'm not the weak-willed girl you knew, Beast, ready to spread her legs with little more incentive that a roguish brute telling her she's pretty."

"You were pretty," he answered, wiping the spittle from his cheek. "And you're right. I'm desperate. We won't survive without your help, but that doesn't change that I wronged you once. And it's past time that I take ownership for that."

Her eyes went wide. For a second, I thought she was actually going to accept the apology. But then she scowled, twisting the dead girl's mouth downward.

"This is about her." She motioned toward me with her head. "About making yourself out to be the chivalrous hero to some chunky damsel in distress."

She said that as if my curves were a bad thing, but I bit my tongue.

Abram's posture stiffened. "That's not what—"

"You still think you can trust him, don't you?" she asked, looking past him to me. "I ask you, Supplicant, has he given himself to you entirely, the way I'm sure you've given yourself to him? Or are there still places he withholds from you, say a particular room in his Castle?"

I balked. She was talking about the strange marked door in the Castle, the one I still had never set foot in. But we hadn't been back there yet, and I hadn't asked him about it. There had been more pressing matters.

"And has he told you of the price he paid in order to bring me here?"

"Enough, Satina!" Abram yelled.

"You don't think I see it?" Satina matched his yelling with her own. "The way she looks at you, the way you look back! It's everything it should be—every required ingredient. But it would ruin everything, wouldn't it?" She cackled again. "God, that is delicious."

I stepped closer to them, eying Abram carefully. "What's she talking about?"

"Forget it," he ground out. "She's trying to distract you."

I could sense the anger coming off him in waves. He wanted to go, to turn away from this and find another solution. But that anger only lasted for a moment. As he stared at me, his emotions took a different turn. He sighed, clearly resolved to do what he had to in order to keep me safe, no matter what that meant.

Just like he said he would.

Crouching down, his elbows pressed against his knees, he settled himself face to face with Satina.

"Satina," he started, looking her directly in the eyes. "I know you think this is about Charisse or about me using you. And I can't blame you for that. I did use you. I used you in a way that was completely and utterly wrong. You were a beautiful girl. You were kind and warm. You trusted people, and all you wanted was to be accepted, to be loved. I took advantage of that. I twisted it and used it for my own perverse pleasure. I broke that light inside of you. I turned it into something else. I drove you to do what you did, and I didn't realize that before. Even standing outside that door just now, I didn't fully understand how much I hurt you. And I suppose that's because I never let anyone in. When you knew me, I had a wall up. My parents, they weren't good people. They didn't trust anyone, least of all each other. And they led me by example. I learned how to treat women by watching the way my father treated my mother. And while that isn't an excuse, I think I at least owe you the explanation."

He bit his lip and held his gaze steady on Satina. "I didn't deserve you. I didn't deserve to be looked at the way you looked at me. I was unworthy. But I didn't realize what it meant to open yourself up to someone. No one had ever been behind the walls I built up around my heart." He blinked hard and peeked over at me.

"Now someone has. Now I do understand. Now I realize you are right. In a sense, I am the one who killed you. In a sense, I *did* push you, even if not literally. And for that, I am truly and deeply sorry."

"You're serious, aren't you?" Satina asked, eyeing him again. Her face seemed to light up. Her body seemed to loosen, as though it had been freed of a weight it had carried for far too long. "God above, you're really serious. You *have* changed." She looked over at me. "I suppose the Supplicant was right...it *is* different this time."

An uneasy sensation started in the pit of my stomach. I had hoped she would come around...but that was too easy. She was up to something.

She touched Abram's cheek with a shackled hand and stared softly into his eyes. "I will help you. I'll do everything I can. The mystery beast was in the room adjacent to us. Bring me something he touched. I can use that to identify his energy signature and track it."

Abram stood.

Satina grabbed his leg. "This is a complicated spell, Abram. It requires much magic, much energy. I need—"

"I know what you need," he said sternly, and they both looked at me again. "I'm not comfortable with—"

"No," I answered, realizing what they were talking about. Regardless of my distrust for her, this was our only chance. We would just have to be careful. "If my blood is what it takes, then that's what she'll get."

My eyes darted from one of them to the other. They looked different to me now. They weren't the strapping supernatural monster and the suicidal witch who made him that way. They were a man and a woman with a complicated history. They made mistakes, and now they were trying to make it right. Maybe she really was being sincere...

Walking toward her, I ran my nail file over my palm again, irritating the cut enough to draw blood again.

Satina gasped, shuddering just a little. Lord, my homemade heart juice must really be powerful stuff. The blood pool in my hand as I moved toward the Conduit. This was a calculated risk. Hesitantly, I glanced back at Abram.

He gave a firm nod. "The chains will hold, and I'm not unchaining her until this is over."

She scowled a bit. "Still don't trust me?"

He frowned. "Do *you* trust *me*?"

She nodded slowly. "Fair enough." She tilted her head to one side. "Maybe in time," she added. "Let's just get this done so we can all move on."

Trying to step carefully, I somehow managed to trip over my own feet. Leave it to a former model to traipse around in five inch heels like a pro but turn into a world class klutz once you get her in a pair of sneakers.

I fumbled, stopping myself from falling.

But the blood...

The blood in my hand spilled into the open air. I couldn't stop it before it splattered into the ground.

"Oh God..." I muttered, remembering what Abram said.

If just a drop of my blood was akin to a beacon meant to lead my killer to me, then I had just sent out a signal flare.

CHAPTER 23

"You have to leave now," Abram said, already taking my hand.

The instant my blood touched the floor, he changed. It wasn't fear as much as determination. He had made a promise to my father. He had likely made a promise to himself. And judging by the way he now pulled me toward the door, he clearly intended to keep this promise.

But I was intent on something else. I pulled my hand free. "No, Abram."

He turned to me, panic reaching his eyes, sighing too loudly for me to miss his clear exasperation. "I understand your penchant for being infuriatingly contrary might be hard to control, Charisse, but now is not the time to disagree with me. That blood you just spilled will act as—"

"A beacon. I know. It'll draw that monster here." I shrugged. "Isn't that what we wanted? To draw the bastard out?"

Abram narrowed his eyes at me, his hands clenching into fists. "That was what *you* wanted. I thought we agreed to go about things another way. Or were we giving your blood to Satina for the hell of it?"

"What's done is done, Abram. That monster is going to come here now, and there's nothing we can do to change that."

"I understand that, but ideally you would be out of harm's way when that 'bastard' got here."

I pulled my hand away from his grasp. "What good would that do?"

"It would go a long way in not getting you killed." His nostrils flared.

"That won't be a problem," I quipped, pointing to him. "You already told me you won't let that happen."

"I did," he conceded, as irritated as I had ever seen him. "Now you need to let me do what I need to keep you safe."

"There's a cost in keeping me safe." I glanced back to Satina, remembering what she said about costs. Maybe there was a cost for everything in this new world I had stumbled into. "The girls who look like me—"

"Are already dead," Abram said. "Joining them won't help anything."

"And what about the others?" I asked. "If I leave now, and that monster—" I found myself choking up. "More girls will be in danger. Every curvy brunette in a fifty mile radius will be fair game to this son-of-a-bitch, including my best friend." I swallowed around the knot tightening in my throat. "People always used to think Lulu and I were sisters. That's how similar we are. How much longer before this monster targets her? She has a family. I won't put her in danger like that. This ends right here, right now."

He stared at me, his eyes narrowing even further. "I won't lose."

"Then we don't have anything to worry about," I said, moving closer to him and making sure he knew that I could be every bit as hardheaded as him.

"I don't understand you," he said glumly. "You've been trying to sacrifice yourself ever since you learned about all of this."

"You're one to talk."

"That's different," he said. "I'm different. My life doesn't matter."

"It matters to me," I said, surprised to feel tears burning behind my eyes. "Do you really need me to spell this out for you?" I asked. When he didn't answer, I knew he did. Damn him. "I don't want to leave you, you jackass. I will *not* leave you here to fight this thing alone. And if you pull me out of this house, I'll come marching back." I stuck my finger into his chest. "You're not in this alone, Abram, no matter how much you want to be. So suck it up, big boy. I'm here to stay."

"You're unbelievable," he answered, but his tone said he was just as impressed as he was concerned.

"As touching as all of this is, it's unnecessary," Satina's voice, stronger than it had been before, echoed from the background.

Abram whipped around. "What are you talking about?"

"I can shield us. All of us," she answered. "Wasn't that the whole point of enlisting my help? The spell is complicated, and I'll need a bit more of your blood and one of my hands to be unshackled. But I can scramble the draw that's leading the other monster here. It will buy us some time. Though, if I'm being honest, I wouldn't mind seeing him. His form is a trademark of mine, and I'd like to see what changes he's made to it." Her eyes flickered over to me. "If you would be so kind."

I marched over and extended my hand. Running a dead, cold palm across mine, she soaked what blood remained on my skin. Like it had with Abram, the blood glowed and turned a bright golden color. Though, unlike with Abram, it seemed to invigorate Satina, lighting her up rather than causing her paid.

"And my hand," the Conduit said, rattling the shackles on one side.

"Just one?" I asked, half-skeptical and half-concerned. If she was really going to help us, had the roles reversed? Were *we* the bad guys now, keeping her chained up for no reason? Or was this a ploy of hers to make me wonder just that? I would rather be a fool than an asshole, though. "What if there's danger? Don't you want to be able to run?"

"Supplicant, I have no interest in this body or in the life that it would tether me to. I've moved on from this world. Being brought back to it was an unwelcome intrusion." She looked over to Abram. "One hand will be sufficient."

He moved toward her. With one quick, jarring motion, Abram ripped the chain binding Satina's hand from the wall.

"There," he said as dust and plywood splinters flew through the air.

"One more thing," Satina added.

"What's that?" Abram asked warily.

"This spell takes concentration. I'll need privacy. I'm sure the two of you can find some way to keep yourselves...occupied."

Abram narrowed his eyes at her, but after a moment, he quietly mumbled some agreement and led me toward the door. As we descended the staircase, I saw the sun had set. It was dark outside, which meant Abram should have turned by now.

"I don't get it," I said as we stepped into the foyer. "Why aren't you the beast? The sun has already set."

"That's not how it works, Charisse." He placed his hand on my hip and guided me into the living room. "The curse is tied to the moon, but I can control it until midnight. That's when the magic is the strongest. After dark, though, it becomes increasingly difficult to maintain control. The monster begins to creep in, and it takes huge amounts of willpower to keep it at bay." He ran a hand through his hair. "It also becomes harder to control my other...impulses."

A spark lit in my chest and spread to the rest of my body. "You want to eat me or something?" I chuckled nervously.

"Among other things," he muttered.

It was then that I noticed the sheen of sweat glistening on his forehead. He was fighting against something, and the small voice in my head told me he would win.

It also said that I didn't want him to.

"Charisse." Abram reached out to take my hand. "I believe I promised I would make you pay for what you did earlier, and I can think of no better time to handle your misgivings than the present. I know how much you love a man of his word."

I grinned, remembering how he jumped at that playful smack on his rear. "Why, Abram, I have no idea what you're talking about."

"I think you do," he said. "But I don't think you realize how disrespectful your actions were."

He seemed actually upset now. Was it really that big of a deal?

"It was just a smack on your butt," I said. "It was meant to be playful."

"In my time, it would be considered completely unacceptable."

I motioned around us. "In case you haven't noticed, this isn't 'your time' anymore."

He stepped in closer. "But it is my house."

I bit my lip, and his hand slid up to caress a tendril of my hair. "How would you like it if I had done that to you?" he asked. "You would probably be ranting at me this very second about how degrading it is for a man to do that to a woman."

There was no denying the red hot blush that fired up in my cheeks. "Some people enjoy that kind of thing."

His eyebrows rose. "Well, I don't." He spun me around and pulled my body against his, his pelvis pressed against my back side. His hands held my arms crossed against my body, pinning my wrists at my hips. "Perhaps *you* are one of those people, though."

"I don't really know much about that whole BDSM thing, to be honest," I said, trying to keep my voice even. But my heart was thundering in my chest, and there was no way he didn't sense that.

"I am not familiar with that. Is it new age?"

I tried not to laugh. "To you, maybe."

"I'm not laughing, Charisse," he said sternly. It was hot the way he said it, though I couldn't be sure if that was what he was going for. I wished I could see his expression, get a better read on him. "It wasn't long ago that it was considered acceptable for a man to spank his woman for her misdeeds."

My inner modern-day woman bristled. "But not for a woman to spank her man?" I countered. "You don't think that's biased?"

"On the one hand, what's fair is fair. You got a good swat at me." He breathed against my scalp, and his hips shifted behind mine, shooting a pleasurable tingle between my thighs. "On the other hand, I still think I ought to teach you a lesson."

Now there was some playfulness in his voice; meanwhile, I was appalled by the way my body was reacting to this conversation.

"Do you know what that tells me, Charisse?"

I shook my head.

"Answer me."

"No," I whispered.

"It tells me I ought to spank you with both my hands." He released me and turned me back to face him. "But I'm not going to."

"You're not?" I asked, surprised by his words as well as my disappointment.

"No," he said, sliding his hand down my arm. "You taught me something important today."

"I did?"

He nodded, a smirk playing at the corner of his lips. "You taught me the importance of apologizing. Now it's your turn. You are to show me how sorry you are."

"I'm—uh—what?"

He kissed me hard on the mouth, backing me up against the wall and pressing his body against mine. Then he pulled back. My body shot into overdrive, and my hands slid over his hard chest and chiseled biceps. There was just so...much of him.

"Show me, Charisse."

My entire body trembled. "Show you how?"

Raising his eyebrows, he leaned back against the arm of the couch beside us. "Use your imagination."

I swallowed around the lump forming in my throat and stepped closer to him. I'd never been ordered around like this in the bedroom...or living room...before. I was turned on and shutting down all at once.

I ran my fingertips along his collarbone and then down the

length of his arm, trying to work up the courage to do something
—or rather, the one thing I knew drove most men crazy.

His eyes blazed, and my heart thudded wildly. But he just stood
there, stone still and hard as a rock...in more ways than one. Gosh,
I felt like I virgin all over again. Like some prude idiot. My hand
finally found the way to his erection, gliding over it through his
rough jeans. His body stiffened, and his jaw flexed. He wanted me,
I knew that much.

I fumbled with his belt, unbuckled his pants, and carefully
undid his zipper before tugging on his pants just a little. They
hugged his thighs, and as I pulled the jeans lower, his erection
sprung out. I caressed it with my fingertips, careful not to upset
anything with my perfectly manicured fingernails. Then I slipped
both my hands up under his shirt to push it off over his head.

Suddenly I felt the weight of all his experience against my own.
It wasn't that I was at all inexperienced, but when we'd had sex the
first time, I hadn't realized that he literally had centuries of
conquests before me. Now here I was, trying to—I don't know—
impress him? Show him, somehow, that I was sorry I smacked that
fine ass of his? Because, well, that wasn't true at all. I would do it
again in a heartbeat.

His hand slid to my shoulder, and his thumb caressed the side
of my neck as I kissed his chest. Slowly I trailed my kisses down
his stomach, across his waist, inside his thighs. His erection
pulsed, and a small burst of triumph coursed through me. I was
driving him as crazy as he drove me.

I stole a glance at him, and immediately regretted it. Looking
up at him from my knees, with his intense gaze bearing down on
me, was nothing short of intimidating. He was watching my every
move.

I quickly averted my attention to focus on the task at hand.
Moving my kisses to his cock, I covered the length first in soft
rubs of my lips, then twirled my tongue around the head before
taking him into my mouth. I'd forgotten how large he was—and

not just his body. *Everywhere*. It made this sexual offering a little...difficult.

My fingernails scraped down the tops of his thighs as I worked him with my mouth, and he responded instantly with a low moan. His skillful fingers tangled in my hair, encouraging me to continue. Finally I felt like he was really getting into it, his hips giving small thrusts to get more from me, but then he nudged me away.

"Enough," he said breathlessly. He pulled me to my feet. "God, you're amazing."

"I don't think God wants anything to do with what we're up to right now," I said cheekily.

He grinned, his hands possessing me at the hips. "You're probably right."

"So you forgive me?" I asked. This little 'game' was proving to be the perfect escape from everything that lay ahead, and I was ready to submerge myself into every moment of it.

"Not yet," he said, starting to slowly strip me of my clothes. "I don't think you're actually feeling very sorry for what you did."

Guilty as charged. Sorry was not the word I would use to describe how I felt right now at all.

"You know, Charisse, you are a powerful woman. And I don't just mean because of your Supplicant blood." My shirt and bra were already on the floor by this point, and now my pants joined them. "It's who you are. It's in your nature."

"I suppose then you've met your match."

He tilted his head to the side, his expression thoughtful. "Maybe."

I did not like that word one bit. Not in response to what I just said. I started to pull back, but Abram held me firm.

"It wouldn't be a bad thing for you to surrender sometimes. To let someone else make decisions. It's not a weakness to let someone else take control for a little bit now and then."

"Someone?" I asked. "Or you?"

He spun me around again, this time bending me over the arm of the couch and tugging down my underwear. My whole body went hot. His hands slid lower on my hips, the heels of his palms grazing my ass.

"You're right. Just me. You want all of me, Charisse?"

I opened my mouth, but no words came out. He did not just ask me that!

"Heaven help us, you have a dirty mind, Miss Bellamy," he said, slipping into his old name for me like it had become a kinky afterthought. He pressed closer to me, his cock nudging against my intimate folds. "I mean, you want me, body, mind, soul. Correct?"

"Oh," I said breathlessly. "I think you know that already."

"I do," he said. "And that's why you should understand that I want you in the same way. I want you to belong to me."

The head of his cock pressed into me, but he did not push any farther. He trailed a finger down my spine, stopping just below the small of my back to trace small circles as he throbbed inside of me. Some part of me was telling me I had to argue with his choice of words—"belong to me"—but the other part of me just wanted him to fuck me and tell me I'm pretty.

My arousal was making it hard to think, and my body squirmed. I pressed my hips back, wanting to take more of him, overwhelmed by how impossibly hard he was, but he firmed his grip to hold me still.

"Not yet, Charisse." He paused, and the heat radiating off of him alone was enough to set me on fire.

I took a slow, deep breath. I wasn't sure if he was doing this to drive me crazy or to control his own impulses, but I think he was accomplishing both either way.

"You're your own woman," he said, sliding in a smidge deeper, stretching me and making me feel empty all at once. "So you do realize it would still be your decision, even if your choice was to be my woman? To surrender every now and then? It may be more empowering than you think."

I could fight it all I wanted, but there could be only one authority in this relationship, and Abram claimed that role long ago, despite any resistance on my end. And deep down, I liked it that way.

"You already have me, Abram," I whispered.

With that, he leaned over me, pressing his lips against my ear. "I know."

I gasped at the feeling of fullness as his erection pushed the rest of the way inside of me. Abram was larger than life, in more ways than one. And in that moment, I felt more full than I ever had before. My heart, my body. My undeniable love for him. The lusting ache that begged for release. This new freedom to stop worrying about being a Modern Day Woman and just let this man ravish me. He was right. It was much more empowering than being the boss of our relationship.

That is, until I was about to climax, and Abram pulled away.

I turned around. "Why did you stop?"

He pulled me to him and cradled body against his chest.

"Your lesson," he said, kissing my temple.

He released me to gather my clothes from the floor and toss them to the other side of the room, then dressed himself.

"My lesson?" I asked, stumbling over the words. "What are you talking about?"

Why was he pulling on his clothes? I'd met men who didn't care if a woman got off or not, but Abram wasn't one of them...and he hadn't even taken care of his own needs yet.

Abram dressed himself and then scooped me up in his arms and laid me out on chaise lounge. "Your lesson, Charisse. To respect me in my home—and everywhere else. That is how you will get what you want from me."

"Don't you want the same thing I do?"

He nodded, kneeling between my legs and rubbing his thumbs over my nipples. My body shuddered, every nerve cell alight with need

"Of course," he said. "But I also want to see you beg for forgiveness."

"For slapping your ass, Abram? Really?"

My sentiment was cut off by a gasp as he leaned over and flicked his tongue against my nipple. He stopped and let me finish.

"You're can't be serious," I breathed.

"You saw me grovel to Satina today," he said, his hand slipping between my legs. "You're so wet," he added, sliding a finger inside of me, and then another. "When you can convince me you are sorry as well as I convinced Satina that I was, I'm going to give you the biggest orgasm of your life."

I didn't doubt for a second he could, but I wasn't sure how to convince him I was sorry, though the way his fingers were so skillfully pumping into me was a great motivator.

"I am sorry," I tried.

Abram chuckled. "No, you're not."

His fingers worked inside of me, and my body writhed against the crushed velvet of his chaise lounge. His thumb grazed at my clit with each movement of his hand, sending me into the depths of erotic insanity. My fingers splayed through his hair, and my back arched as a moan escaped my lips. Again he stopped. By the third time he put me through this unique brand of torture, bringing me to that brink only to withdraw his attention again, I was equally infuriated and desperately sorry.

This must have been how he felt apologizing to Satina, sans the arousal.

I gasped, reaching down to grab his hands and stop him from starting again. "I'm sorry, Abram. I swear. I MEAN IT, OKAY?"

He brushed me away, smirking, ready to start again, but I snatched his hand once more. I had become desperate. I couldn't take any more. I needed release.

"I swear on every Gucci dress I own, I will never smack your butt again. *Please*, Abram."

He sat back and pressed his lips together triumphantly. "Well, that wouldn't be much fun..."

His coy grin nearly sent me over the edge, and I grabbed him by his shirt and pulled his body on top of mine until his lips crushed against my own. He could have resisted—he was only infinitely stronger than me—but he fell between my legs with ease. I bucked my hips against him, and he ground his pelvis in return, his jeans rough against my skin. But I didn't care.

He pulled back, just enough that I could make out the strong lines of his face. "Well, I suppose if you're truly sorry..."

"I am," I said breathless and desperate. "Now, will you please fuck me proper?"

"Of course, Miss Bellamy. I love it when you're proper."

And not to my surprise, Abram delivered the orgasm of my life, just as he promised.

It was only moments after every muscle in my body contracted and relaxed in the most exquisite of respites, however, that the door burst open.

I threw myself back, covering myself with my hands. My clothes were in a pile on the other side of the room, and standing here, in the middle of Abram's living room, was the one person we weren't prepared to face.

Dalton.

Dalton, and several other police officers along with him. All wearing bulletproof vests, their guns drawn.

"Charisse, are you..." His voice trailed off as he looked up. "Jesus Christ."

Following his eyes, I found the source of his astonishment wasn't finding me here naked. It was who—or rather *what*—I was with.

Where Abram had only moments ago been lying beside me now resided a hulking, fanged, and feral beast.

CHAPTER 24

My heart ground to a halt. I had seen the beast before. I had trembled as it stood over me and marveled at his familiar eyes as they bore down on me. But I didn't know it was Abram then. I couldn't look and see all the clues I had missed before.

Now, with it literally inches from my naked body, I could see how much of the beast *was* Abram. It wasn't something that took him over and made him an imprisoned bystander in his own body. It was *him*.

The creature's long arms were covered in thick black fur but also corded in the same muscle Abram's had been. The creature's face, while pulled into an elongated snout, still retained some of Abram's more striking features.

Even his chest, that chest I longed to lay my head against while drifting to sleep against the drumming of his beating heart, was recognizable behind the alterations.

It was like looking at a model after her first trip to Europe. He was the same, but somehow very different.

"Charisse, get away from it!" Dalton's gun was pointed straight at Abram, as were the guns of the officers who flanked him.

His sudden voice pulled me from my reverie, and I grabbed a

nearby throw blanket to cover myself. Sure, I'd done some nude art modeling in college, but that didn't mean the entire N.H.P.D. needed to see my charms.

"I have a shot!" said the officer to Dalton's left.

"No!" Dalton yelled. "Stand down. Nobody discharges anything until that woman gets to safety."

That woman.

Was he angry with me? Was that why he called me that instead of my name? He certainly had the right to be. Though I hadn't meant to, I had strung him along. I kept him in the—what do they call that baseball thing?—the bullpen. And all the while I pretended, especially to myself, to be confused about my feelings. But that was never the case. Since the first moment I laid eyes on Abram, since he literally swept me off my feet, deep down I knew there was no one else for me.

And I had lied to Dalton as much as I'd been lying to myself.

So maybe this was Dalton finally realizing that I wronged him. Or maybe it was just him reacting to seeing my boss transform into a giant wolf-monster.

Either way.

"Char, move away," Dalton said, his teeth clenched. His gun was still fixed on Abram's head, and I wondered how in control my lover was at this moment. The last thing anybody needed was for him to go all 'disgruntled werewolf' on the New Haven Police Department. None of us could explain that.

"You don't understand," I said as quietly as I could manage. "He's not going to hurt me."

But could I be sure of that? The beast huffed beside me, and hot breath and moisture pushing against my neck as its muscles tensed beside me.

Fighting the urge to dart to the other side of the room for my clothes, I tried to remind myself that this was Abram. He would never hurt me. Even in this form. He had proven as much. He fought off that other beast tooth and nail when it wanted to make a Supplicant energy drink out of me, and he would do the same now if need be.

Except, in this particular moment, I wasn't the one who was in danger.

Would bullets hurt Abram in his beast form? Would anything? There was so much I still didn't know, and there was no way of denying (to myself or anyone else) that I was in this. All the way. So I hung onto the things I did know. Abram was a good man. Beast or not, I was safe with him. Dalton was a good man, too. He would listen to reason. I just had to make sure he saw it.

"I promise you he's not going to hurt me," I repeated. Clutching the throw blanket tighter around my body, I ran my free hand along the length of Abram's forearm.

It was strange, but not completely unpleasant. In fact, it was surprising how right it felt.

A low growl escaped Abram's mouth. I thought about pulling my hand away, but there was no need. Abram wouldn't hurt me. I knew that as well as I knew my own name.

"Get away from that thing, Char," Dalton said, his hands and voice steady.

He was less of a boy now, less of the snot-nosed kid that used to tag along behind Lulu and me. There wasn't even a shadow of the easygoing guy I had once flirted with. This was Dalton the detective—Dalton the grown man who was exceedingly good at his job.

Unfortunately, at this particular moment, his job very likely entailed firing live ammo at my boyfriend.

"Don't shoot him, Dalton," I said, standing my ground, shifting my body farther in front of Abram's.

Abram's growl grew louder, and Dalton inched toward me.

"If you're not going to move, then I'm going to move you," he said quietly.

"You'll shoot him if I move," I answered.

"You're damn right I will."

I resolved to stay exactly where I was. I would be a human bulletproof vest if necessary. Not because I thought I could stop bullets—nor did I even know if they would harm Abram in this state—but because I knew that Dalton would never take the shot if there was even a chance of hurting me. And if he did start firing, Abram would never forgive himself for what the beast did in retaliation.

It didn't matter, though. In an instant, Abram was on his feet, settling into a human-like stance—all fur, teeth, and trepidation. He slunk away from me, his hands warped into razor sharp claws.

Dalton's pistol followed him, and I realized what he was doing. Abram was moving away in order to keep me safe. All these stupid men were going to get themselves killed to keep me safe. And the funny thing was, in the end, it probably wouldn't be close to enough. Not with that other beast out there.

"Dalton, don't you dare!" I yelled. But Abram's growl got louder, and before I could stop it, shots thundered through the room.

"No!" I screamed.

It was too late. The idiot to Dalton's left had begun firing. And once he started, he didn't stop.

Bullets rocketed toward Abram. He darted around with all the agility one would expect from an animal, but that moron's gun kept firing. Abram skidded along the walls, and I watched as fresh bullet holes appeared closer and closer to his body.

Abram sprung toward the idiot just as I heard the click that signified the officer was out of ammo, and I braced myself to watch Abram tear him in half.

Instead, another gun fired. Dalton's gun.

And he didn't miss.

Abram reared back, howling loudly. It was so strong, so sharp, that I thought my ears might bleed.

"Dalton!" I screamed.

Abram swung at him, knocking the gun out of his hand before

he could fire again. But instead of attacking Dalton, Abram grabbed his gut, charged out of the way, and jumped through the nearby window, shattering the glass.

I ran for the window, still clutching the throw blanket around my body. But by the time I got there, Abram was gone. He had vanished into the woods, save a trail of blood that marked his path.

I spun to find Dalton staring at me, holding his arm and narrowing his eyes.

"Search the house," he said breathlessly to one of his officers. Turning to the other, he motioned to me. "Get her dressed, and put her in the car."

* * *

After getting me out of the house, Dalton gave me a quick look over with his first aid kit, then locked me in the back of his squad car without saying so much as a word to me. Now we were on our way back to New Haven, and the silence was killing me.

"Why am I in the backseat?" I asked.

I expected the silent treatment, but apparently all it took was one of us to break the ice.

"Because I'm not sure it's safe for you to be up here," he answered, eyes on the road.

I pressed my hands against the cage that separated us. "What the hell is that supposed to mean?"

"You're acting irrationally. I think you may have been drugged."

"Drugged?" I asked, scrunching my eyebrows. "Look, you don't know what's going on here, Dalton. And if you did—"

"I understand enough, Char. I understand your boss has some weird cabin in the woods. I understand he was holding Ellie Farmer, the first girl who went missing, like some kind of caged animal. And I understand he turned into something that I definitely *don't* understand." He swallowed hard. "I also understand he might very well have been raping you, and that whatever he's been dosing you with has kept you unaware it was going on."

"He wasn't raping me," I screamed, slapping my hands against the cage. "I told you, you don't understand! It's very dangerous for me to be out here right now, Dalton! You need to bring me back!"

"Is that what he told you?" Dalton took a right onto Main Street. He slid to a halt in front of Town Hall. The sheer amount of cars here shocked me.

"What are you doing?" I asked. "If you think I've been drugged, then shouldn't you bring me to the damn doctor?"

"Dr. Miller is inside. Everyone is," Dalton said, stepping out and rounding the car to open my door. "After you disappeared, I convinced the mayor to declare a state of emergency. Everything is on lockdown."

"How did you find me?" I asked, as he opened the door and helped me out.

"I pinged your cellphone."

"But my location services—"

"Were turned off. I know." He had me by the arm now. It felt strange, as though he had never touched me before, as though no man other than Abram ever had. "That's why it took me so long."

The thought of Abram leapt into my mind. He was hurt. He was bleeding. He might die if I didn't find him. But even if I could manage to get away, I wouldn't know where to start looking for him. But I couldn't just let him die in the woods like an animal.

Even if he was an animal at the moment.

"What are we doing here?" I asked as he pulled me toward Town Hall.

"I told you. We're in a state of emergency. The mayor's called a mandatory town meeting to discuss how to deal with the situation."

"And what situation is that, exactly?"

He pushed open the double doors, and all uncertainty I had about what he meant washed away like suntan oil at Sports Illustrated beach shoot. The hall was jam-packed. The lights were off, and a movie was playing against the wall.

No, it wasn't a movie. That was Abram. He was standing there stark naked with his naughty bits blurred out. It was the scene from just a few minutes ago, only I had been cut out, replaced with a huge blur.

"Officer Evans was wearing a vest cam," Dalton said. "Everything was transmitted to the chief of police. And it's a good thing. I'm not sure I'd have been able to convince them of this."

"I'm going to play this again," the mayor said from a podium at the end of the room. "But I'll repeat my initial warning. This subject matter is intense and frightening. It would be best to shield your children's eyes."

And with that, Abram morphed into the beast right there on the wall-turned-screen. Gasps, whimpers, oohs, and ahhs filled the room. Someone toward the back shrieked.

Dalton marched toward the stage as the lights turned back on, and the two other police officers came up on either side of me. Their stance made their intentions clear. I wasn't going anywhere.

Halfway down the aisle, Dalton started speaking, as though whatever he had to say couldn't wait until he got to the podium.

"We have to keep our wits about us, people," he said, loud enough for his voice to carry over the chatter of the room. "I know this isn't a situation any of us ever thought we'd find ourselves in. But the truth is, we've all known that something has been plaguing New Haven for quite some time."

If it wasn't Abram he had been talking about—if I didn't know all that I knew—I would probably be swooning right now over his amazing leadership skills and bravery. But that timeline could never exist again. Life wasn't that simple.

Dalton settled at the podium, looking particularly comfortable up there. "We've felt the unease. We've sensed the foreboding. We've all held our children a little closer, all locked our doors extra tightly." He pounded his fist on the podium. "And now we know why."

Pointing to the light-drenched image of Abram on the pull-down screen, he continued, "This thing—this *monster*—is very real. It's after our citizens. It's after our women. How many people does it have to hurt, does it have to kill, before we take action?" He hit the podium again. "There is only one course of action. We have to put an end to this before it goes any further."

Applause lit up the room, but Dalton continued, shouting over it. "We have to protect our town, protect our citizens, and protect ourselves by whatever means necessary," he yelled. "We have to fight back," he continued. "We have to kill the beast!"

CHAPTER 25

I stood there in shock as the chants grew louder.

"Kill the beast! Kill the beast!"

It was a living nightmare. New Haven had been whipped into a frenzy, with Dalton at the head. And the object of their misplaced fear and anger was the man I loved.

"Stop," I muttered as people started to clap and raise their hands in solidarity.

This was like a tsunami—destructive and unstoppable. But I had to try. Because if I didn't, then either Abram or a hell of a lot of the people demanding his murder were going to wind up dead.

"Stop!" I said louder. But my voice was lost in the sea of screams, in the fog of rage.

If I could just talk to them, if I could just get them to calm down for a second, I was sure I could make them see reason.

They would have to come to terms with magic, and witches, and monsters, and all of that, which hadn't been the easiest thing in the world for me personally—but I had done it, and they could, too. Heck, if they believed in the beast, most of my hard work had already been done for me.

Though I didn't care for this town, the people in it were generally good. They looked out for each other. They protected their neighbors. This sort of mob mentality wasn't like them. They had their backs against the wall, though, and the same desire to keep their community safe was pushing them toward this bloody agenda. I had to change the course of this conversation, and to do that, I needed to be up at that podium.

I inched forward, eyeing the two police officers on either side of me. Their focus was on the crowd, but I wasn't going to sneak away undetected by walking right into their line of sight.

I chewed my lip and looked around. Okay, I could do this. Just had to channel my inner actress, the same way I had at the Fright Night Runway Show in New York City. Direct my attention at some unseen danger and get the police officers to notice my reaction.

As I looked over my shoulder, one of the officers shifted their gaze to me. Slowly, I shifted my focus past him, at the empty doorway, channeling a sense of sheer terror. I drew my eyebrows together and opened my mouth in a horrified "o" shape, leaning back, inching away. I let out a small gasp.

The officer looked over his shoulder now, too, then back to me.

"What is it?" he asked.

I shook my head as though too afraid to speak and pointed toward the door.

"Wait here," he ordered. He tapped the other officer on the shoulder, put his hand on his gun, and nodded his head toward the door. "I think he's here," he whispered. "Cover me."

As soon as they disappeared into the hall, I zipped myself into the crowd where they would not be able to easily retrieve me. Then I moved toward the front of the room, suddenly aware of how tired I was. It had been like this since almost my first day back in New Haven—one crazy turn after another. And for all my fighting, I ended up here, as desperate and alone as ever.

Abram was hurt. He could already be dead—but I couldn't entertain that. I *wouldn't* entertain that. Abram was strong. But he wouldn't be able to protect himself in the condition he was in now.

The mob would find him, and they would kill him. If, of course, that other beast didn't get to him first.

Suddenly, I realized that my own life had become very secondary. I would give it up easily if that meant I could keep Abram, Lulu, Jack, and Dalton safe. If turning myself over to this monster would be enough to spare New Haven all of this tragedy, then I would happily put on my best pumps and march myself over to him.

But something told me we were past that now. No amount of sacrifice could get us out of this. I could only hope that my words somehow would.

A hand grabbed my shoulder and pulled me back. I spun, jumping back, fearing I had wasted my choice and the other officers had caught up to me.

"Char, it's me," Lulu said. Her face was pale and tired, and she wore loose-fitting black clothes. She threw her arms around me and pulled me closer. Her arms were so weak, though, that it felt as though she was using me to hold herself up. "Thank God you're okay. I thought for sure that you..." She cleared her throat. "Thank God."

"Lulu," I choked out as tears streamed down my cheeks. "The baby..."

"Allison," she answered through tears of her own. "She's fine. She's at the hospital with Jack and her dad."

"You need to be there with her," I said, and I looked her up and down, shaking my head in horror. "You just had a baby! You can't be here, walking around. Lulu—"

She chuckled weakly. "Oh, Char," she said, in that bemused way of hers. "You always worry too much. You do realize the prolonged maternity ward stays are a cultural thing. There are places where women have their baby and immediately go back to work in the field."

She was undermining things. For my sake. And I hated myself for it. "We don't live in one of those places, Lulu. You need to rest."

"Rest?" she said. "My best friend was *missing*. I couldn't just lay there, thinking about that while the baby sleeps all day. I had to do something, even if it was just sit here with the rest of the town and worry."

I squeezed her tightly. This was a detour. I should push her away and start my tirade of crazy sense-making, but I needed this. I needed this respite to remind me of who I was, of what I was fighting for.

"Thank you," I said over the noise of the crowd. "But I'm not missing anymore. Go back. I'll be okay."

"Will you?" she asked, her mouth twisting up. "Did that bastard hurt you?" She studied my face as though the answer might lie in my sunken cheeks or disheveled hair.

"It wasn't like that," I assured her. "Abram's not who you think he is."

Ester's voice screeched in my ears like fingernails on a chalkboard: "Don't you mean he's not *what* you think he is?"

"I don't have time for you," I snapped, looking past Lulu to the epitome of privileged bitchiness that was Ester. Returning my attention to Lulu, I continued, "He's not a monster, Lu."

"The hell he's not." Ester tilted her coiffed head. "We all saw it, and the fact that you're still willing to defend whatever that thing is, after what he did to you, means you're either sick or stupid."

"Ester!" Lulu spun around. "Charisse has been through a horrible ordeal. I can't even imagine—"

"Neither can I," Ester said, folding her arms. "But I don't need to." Ester's eyes traced me, resting on my bosom. "Look, it's no secret that you and I aren't exactly friends. But that doesn't mean I wanted to see you dead, and it sure as sugar doesn't mean I wanted to see you kidnapped and harmed by some strapping man-monster."

"Sure as sugar?" I repeated slowly. "What are you, from Pleasantville?"

"I have children to protect." She pursed her lips. "We all do. This is our home and, unlike a certain washed-up slash never-was supermodel, we actually like it here. So, while I have all the sympathy in the world for you and your plight, if you're insist on being the twenty-first century Patty Hearst, I'm just going to have to write off your plus-sized behind." She looked to Lulu. "And you'd be smart to do the same. You've got as much to lose as any of us."

"You're right," Lulu said, and my heart sank. Was it possible that she was turning on me, that one of my worst fears was coming to pass, and Lulu had finally realized that she had outgrown me? "I do have a lot of things to lose, Ester. But a friend won't be one of them. Certainly not my best friend."

She took my hand and, in some small part, that was enough. It certainly helped to see Ester's face fall in recognition.

"I hope you know what you're doing then," Ester said, glaring at me. "Putting your friend in danger like this." She clicked her tongue and narrowed her eyes as she leaned in closer. "But I'll say this much, Charisse. You have brought nothing but trouble to our town since the minute you slunk in here. Death after death. One strange occurrence after the next." Ester shook her head, then turned her attention back to my best friend. "Don't come crawling to me when she gets you killed, Lulu."

I would have told her dead people don't come crawling back, but then I thought of Satina. Besides, Ester wasn't worth the time spend arguing with her.

Lulu squeezed my hand as Ester turned and walked away.

"She's kind of a bitch, isn't she?" Lulu asked, smiling.

"A little bit," I answered.

Looking to her, I felt a wash of emotions. She had just had a baby—a baby I hadn't even seen. And what if Ester was right? This *was*, in some way, my fault. What if knowing me, if choosing me, was enough to get Lulu killed? I couldn't live with myself if that happened. But there was Abram to think about, too. He was out there somewhere, injured. If he died...

I couldn't even think about that.

"You believe me then?" I asked.

"I believe that you believe," she answered, her face placid. "But

I also believe that you've been through a lot, much more than anyone should have to go through." She squeezed my hand again. "And maybe you're not seeing things very clearly right now."

Oh, Lulu. She meant well.

I felt hands on my back. I didn't have to turn to know they were Dalton's. I knew his hands, and though they had never been as rough with me as they were now, planted firmly against my shoulders, I recognized them.

"We need to go, Char," he said softly. Looking ahead, I realized that the crowd was dispersing, funneling out the front of the building, undoubtedly on their way to 'take care' of Abram. And Dalton wanted me to go with them.

"I won't help you!" I spun around. "I won't lead you to him! I can't!"

"I wouldn't ask you to," he said, narrowing his eyes. "You need to rest now, and the doctor wants to run some tests on you."

"No!" I shrieked. That was the last thing I needed. Being in the hospital, strapped to machines and surrounded by orderlies, would make it impossible for me to find Abram.

I turned on my heel and bolted for the podium. I needed to tell everyone the truth. I needed to stop them before they left and did something that couldn't be undone.

I stumbled up the stage steps, nearly tripping, but I caught myself on my hands and clambered the rest of the way up. I darted to the podium. My hands fumbled on the microphone.

"Everybody! Attention, everybody."

I stared at the microphone in disbelief. It wasn't on.

"Everyone," I shouted, louder.

Dalton came up behind me and wrapped his arms around me. "Stop this, Char."

No one could hear me. I needed them to hear me. "Everyone, please!"

As Dalton pulled me back, I gripped the podium, but he was too strong. My fingers slipped. He tugged me aside, set me down, and put his hands firmly on my shoulders.

His face was inches from mine. "Enough, Char! Pull yourself together."

If I couldn't get them to listen, I needed to stop them, or find Abram and warn him. Help him. Somehow. I pushed Dalton off of me.

"I have to go!" I yelled, and I spun on my heel to run.

It was crazy, the sheer amount of running I had done since all of this started, and something told me this was far from the end of it. I just needed to find Abram, though. I needed to save him the way he had saved me. After that, we would figure the rest out. So long as we were together—

Hands latched onto me again, driving me to the ground.

"Let me go!" I yelled, struggling against Dalton's weight.

"Doctor!" he yelled, pinning me down at my shoulders. "Doctor, I need your help! She's not well!"

"No!" I screamed, struggling futilely to get up. I pounded my hands against his chest, but he was not fazed. Steps settled near me, and I saw brown shoes.

"Stay still," a stranger's voice said calmly. "It'll all be better soon."

Something pricked my arm and sent a burning sting through my veins. The world darkened. My body got heavy, and my eyes struggled to stay open.

God, they had drugged me. Could they do that?

I struggled to hold on to my consciousness. They were doing all kinds of things they shouldn't do. None of this was right. Nothing in my world made sense anymore.

I was going to pass out. This was it. Abram would die out there without me, and I would lay helpless in some hospital until the other beast found me and drained every drop of blood from my body.

This shit never would have happened in New York.

CHAPTER 26

I woke slowly, aching and with the worst headache I had ever experienced. The lights on the ceiling, bright and white, buzzed the way only hospital or school lights ever did.

I knew where I was. I could feel it in the uncomfortable bed and paper thin gown that scraped against my skin. I could hear it in the steady rhythm of a heart monitor. I could see it in the plain white walls and the dry erase board that displayed my name and condition.

Charisse Bellamy: Shock
The patient is confined to bed rest
and to remain under constant supervision.

Looking forward, I saw that 'constant supervision' took the form of an officer standing guard outside of the door. At least he didn't seem to be very attentive. His head was slouched forward at an awkward angle.

I sighed as loudly as my sore throat would allow. Lulu was slouched over and sleeping on the chair adjacent to my bed. We were in the hospital. Her newborn was probably a unit or two away, and here she was with me. Guilt clawed its way up my chest.

"They're all asleep."

The voice startled me. Jumping, I turned back. I didn't see her before, but Satina—still trapped in the body of the first missing girl—stood at the foot of the bed, flipping through my chart nonchalantly.

"It's amazing what they've done with parchment in the last two hundred years," Satina mused. "This would have all been done by quill in my day, and without near the penmanship. I'll tell you that much."

"You have to help me," I said. "You have to get me out of here."

"Do I?" she asked, arching her borrowed eyebrows.

"Abram is in trouble," I said quietly. "He's hurt, and the entire town is looking for him, not to mention that other beast. Have you told them the truth about yourself, about who you are? Maybe that would help them understand."

"And why would I do that?" She shook her head. "So that I can spend the rest of this shell's life beating against padded walls? No, thank you. It was hard enough dodging the police without a scene. I'd rather ride it out. I hear something called 'spring break' is right around the corner."

"But Abram!" I said with tears in my eyes.

"Is halfway to whatever country now borders this one, if he has the sense God gave a common house flea."

"N-no," I stammered. "He wouldn't leave me." I knew this was true, even though deep down, I wished what she said was true.

"Perhaps not," Satina conceded. "But that doesn't mean he shouldn't. There is no 'win' in this game, Charisse. Not for him, not for you, and certainly not for the both of you together. I know you think he loves you, and perhaps he does. But have you ever considered the idea that love, at least this love, isn't what either of you need?"

"He's here!" I said, much too loudly. "And he's hurt, and I need you to help me get out of this hospital! If you want to leave after that, then so be it. But I won't give up on him. He doesn't deserve that."

"When has what someone deserves ever mattered for people like us?" she shot back. "Listen to me, Supplicant. You need to leave, and not with a beast in tow. You need to run somewhere where you can fit in. Become a waitress, dye your hair. Blend in. Just don't stick out, certainly not the way being in a league with someone like Abram would force you to."

"Don't you get it?" I asked. "They know now. They all know. They have it on camera. It's all out in the open. It's never going to be like it was again. There's no disappearing, not for any of us."

"To be so young." She chuckled. "They always do this, Supplicant, and it never lasts. They don't *want* to believe. They can't handle believing. So yes, they see and they know. And then, after a while, they convince themselves that it was all conjecture or imagination or special effects. It's in their nature. But it isn't in yours. You need to run."

"No..." I said through gritted teeth.

"Your funeral." She shrugged. "I hope he's worth it."

She turned and began toward the door.

"Wait!" I said. "I still need your help to get out of here."

"You already have it." She smiled, looking over her shoulder and holding up a vial of blood—*my* blood, no doubt. "I said they were all asleep, and they will be for the next ten minutes."

"All?" I asked, my eyes narrowed. "Everyone in the hospital?"

"Everyone in the town," she answered flatly. "Now run. Ten minutes isn't much of a head start."

And with that, she walked out without another look back.

I pulled the electrical wire stickums off of myself, wincing as the machine they attached me to made a long flat-lining beep. As soon as my bare feet hit the cold tiled floor, I scurried to find my clothes. Ten minutes, that was all Satina had given me. Perhaps it was all she *could* give me. I had no idea how magic worked, but sending an entire town's worth of people off to sleepy town didn't seem like an easy job. And she only had a singular vial of my blood.

Or did she?

For all I knew, she had pumped me like a farmhouse well before I woke up. That would account for the dizziness. But why? Abram had said Supplicant blood had a shelf life. Was she planning on using it all soon?

Whatever the case was, I was still alive, and that put her one up on what that horrid mystery monster wanted to do to me and what the town wanted to do to Abram.

My shoes were in the corner, scuffed and practically screaming with wear. As I moved closer, I saw the sole was coming off of one of them, an absolute abomination of a thing that, on any other day, would have sent me screaming back to bed. But at the moment, I was in a tender situation. Shoe integrity would have to take a backseat, even if the sight of it made me want to heave.

Lulu was still asleep in the chair at my bedside, and I crept over to her. "Sorry, Lu," I said, leaning down and untying her laces.

I really did not want to steal her shoes, and it wasn't because she had bad taste. On the contrary. She was stylish, and there were more than a few times when I'd shipped her an extra pair or two of whatever I was gifted on a particular photoshoot. She had just had a baby, though, and her low top sneakers spoke to that.

It was a good thing, though. My feet (along with the rest of my body) were killing me. I wasn't worried about style today. I was worried about function.

I slipped Lulu's shoes off her feet and placed them on mine. They felt like heaven, all cushioned and relaxed. For all of our similarities, Lulu had a slightly larger foot than me. I slid around a little as I stood, but they would do. I tied them extra tight before I scanned the room, lips pursed.

I still didn't see my clothes. Shit. Where did they put them? I didn't have time to think, so I started throwing open cabinets and doors, much like I had that time I lost Jack. Never in a million years would I have guessed that day would lead to here.

When all the cabinets came up empty, I raked my hands through my hair. I didn't have time for this! I spun in a slow circle, begging for a solution. Clothes, Satina! Why didn't you leave me *clothes?* My throat was closing off, making it harder to breath.

Calm down, Char.

I ran into the next room and looked around. The sleeping beauty in this room was apparently allowed to have clothes, because a pair of sweat pants and a large shirt were folded neatly on the chair next to her bed. Thankfully she was on the curvier side like me, even if she didn't have the best fashion sense.

Knowing I wouldn't have time to put them on, I scooped them up and decided I would get dressed after Satina's magical timeout wore off.

Running through what signs now told me was the third floor was just about the creepiest thing I had ever seen. Halloween 2 had taught me to be distrustful of hospitals, especially empty hospitals. And watching it now, devoid of any conscious movement, sent my heart racing.

People littered the floor, having fallen where they presumably stood just minutes before. A nurse at the desk had knocked her coffee over, effectively destroying a desktop computer. Another nurse had fallen with her head just inches away from her soup bowl. I wondered what would happen if she hadn't missed it. Would she wake up, or would Satina's spell stay in effect, drowning her in clam chowder?

And what about the poor bastards in surgery? Were they bleeding out on some operating room table, unable to wake up? And what if that were true? What could I do about it? I couldn't undo the choices Satina had made.

The sickness in my stomach would not settle, though. Whatever she had done, she had used *my* blood to do it. I had to know. So as I slipped past one of the operating rooms, I stole a moment to peer inside.

Frozen. *Everything* was frozen—even the blood.

I let out a breath I didn't know I'd been holding and ran back into the hall, trying to make up for wasted time—trying to orient myself which way to go. I trained my eyes forward, doing my best to block out the sights along with the thoughts. My steps came faster, softened by Lulu's comfortable shoes.

I pushed through the doors and onto the streets. The first thing I felt was warmth. There was a fire. A car had crashed into a nearby telephone pole, and the engine had ignited.

"Damnit," I muttered.

Clearly Satina had not thought of *everything*.

How much damage had this spell, had my blood, caused? Guilt, as familiar as an old friend, sprung up inside of me. The man in the car, old and balding, lay snoring against the steering wheel. He was unaware that he had destroyed his Lexus and was about to burn to death because of it.

"Goddammit!" I yelled, knowing what I had to do.

Ten minutes wasn't long enough. As it was, I would have been lucky to get out of the Town Square mere minutes before the angry mob woke. I could have hid in the woods and done my best to find Abram after they passed. Maybe my super magic blood would draw me to him or something. That was a thing. Right?

But I couldn't do that now. I couldn't leave this man to die because of me, even if I wasn't the one who cast this stupid sleeping spell. Dropping the stolen clothes, I sprinted over to the car. Warmth washed over me, making me even more lightheaded than before. Almost woozy, I swallowed hard and pushed on. Passing out wouldn't help anything now, and the clock was ticking.

The door creaked as I pulled it open. That meant it must have been damaged in the crash, because I had been in enough luxury automobiles to know that the doors on cars like these didn't creak.

Whipping off the old guy's seatbelt, I groaned.

"It's gonna be okay," I told him as I pulled.

The bastard was heavy—like, *really* heavy. The flames grew higher. They got closer. And still this old guy wasn't moving.

"What do you eat, Cream of Lead?" I huffed, pivoted my right leg against the door for leverage, and gave one last tug. The old man jarred out of the car, barreling toward me like some sleeping, geriatric cannonball.

He landed on top of me, knocking the wind out of me and shuffling back into a comfortable (for him, anyway) position.

I was trapped, pinned beneath this slobbering fool.

And that's when I heard the footsteps.

My body went ridged. It hadn't been ten minutes, not even close. If it had been, then this old guy would be awake right now instead of having his wrinkly unconscious palm placed firmly against second base.

No, these steps belonged to someone else, someone supernatural in nature.

"Abram..." I muttered, pushing at the old guy futilely. He was heavy, and I wasn't able to get him off me. "Abram, please tell me that's you."

The only answer though was continued and closer footsteps.

"Abram," I called again.

A huff answered me this time. Paws—not feet—settled in front of me. I traced the beast upward. Full hair-laden thighs, a massive chest, and shoulders that would have blocked out the sun if it wasn't the middle of the night. As I got to his face, the worst fate was confirmed. Those weren't Abram's eyes. This wasn't Abram's face.

This was the other beast.

The beast who wanted me dead.

And here I was, trapped and helpless to stop it.

The beast growled at me, teeth bared and eyes glaring hungrily. Its jaw snapped at me before it licked its snout.

"Get away from me!" I said, pushing wildly against the old man's body. Of course, he didn't move.

The monster knelt toward me, and the scent of burning flesh wafted through the air.

"Get away!" I repeated. But what could I do? I was meat, literal meat, waiting to be consumed and drained of everything that made me, me.

I pushed against the man again, but this time I felt a stiff mass pressed against the waistband of his pants.

Well, this is awkward.

No. It wasn't that, I realized. This wasn't New York, and that hard mass wasn't an old man's excitement. It was a gun!

God bless this town.

I whipped the pistol out of his pants and aimed it toward the monster. Without flinching, I pulled the trigger. The barrel pushed back, knocking me in the chest. But the blast did its job. Opening my eyes, I saw that the monster was gone.

Adrenaline pulsed through me, sweet and freeing. After placing the gun beside me, I pushed hard. I pushed like I should have the first time—like my life depended it—and finally he budged enough from gravity to help tip him off of me.

I jumped to my feet and bolted. I needed to get out of here, get away before the beast returned.

I rounded the corner, desperate to get back to the woods which had ironically become my safe haven. Unfortunately, I wasn't the only one who had that idea.

I ran smack dab into someone. Panicking, I starting clawing at the body instantly.

"Hey," a familiar voice said. "Stop. It's me! Char, it's me."

Looking up, I saw Dalton standing in front of me. His hair was disheveled, and his face was pale.

"I'm sorry," I stammered. "I thought you were—"

And then it hit me. Everyone else was still unconscious. Even now the streets were littered with sleeping citizens. The fact that Dalton was awake right now, that he was standing in front of me—

I shook my head and swallowed hard, cautiously stepping back. "No, Dalton. Please, no. Not you."

"Oh, Char," he said, and he grabbed my arm, his expression darkening. His hands turned to claws, digging into me, breaking the skin. His eyes flickered red as my blood touched him.

It was him. Dalton was the other beast.

"I should have known. I was so frantic, hoping that my sister wasn't the Supplicant. I looked right past the most obvious candidate." He grinned wide and manically. "It was you. It was always you."

"No," I said, shaking my head in disbelief. "No, it can't be. You knew I was in the woods that night. You would have known it was me."

"Oh, Char. How limited your scope of this earth really is. Of course I wasn't the one who attacked you in the woods that night. I had been...preoccupied."

My mind flashed to the woman who had been found dead that same night—the one who had been walking her dog. I shook my head, the horror piercing every inch of my skin like a thousand needles. But how—

"I admit, I should have figured it out when your blood lured me to Abram's home," Dalton continued. "But then Ellie Farmer was there. I thought I'd left her for dead, but there she was, taunting me, and I thought for sure she was the Supplicant, that somehow I'd missed it the first time. But then she skipped off again, right out of protective custody, and who should I find when I go to look for her? You. You walking around when the rest of the town is trapped in some frozen spell."

As terrified as I was, my mind just wouldn't let go of one thought: Dalton was the beast who had killed those women. Dalton was the beast we were looking for. But Dalton was *not* the beast who attacked me in Abram's home. Which meant...

I didn't want to say it. I didn't want to admit that there could be more...that there could a third beast in New Haven. With everything I knew, it made sense, but admitting it made this situation feel even more hopeless.

Finally, I whispered what I already knew to be true. "It's not just you, is it, Dalton? There are others. Aren't there?"

"It's a good thing you're pretty, isn't it, Char? You wouldn't have gotten far in life if you had to rely on your mind." He titled his head, a smirk playing at the corners of his lips. "Of course there are others. You escaped, after all. And my victims never escape."

It was true. Ellie Farmer had died eventually, even if Abram had reanimated her with Satina's spirit. But where did that leave me now? I finally had all the answers I wanted, but I wouldn't live to tell about it.

With a low and deep growl, Dalton pulled me closer with one arm and punched me hard in the face with the other. I whipped back, but he wouldn't let me go.

"Sorry, Char, but I'm going to have to make you bleed."

CHAPTER 27

Blood poured from my nose, and Dalton looked at it hungrily. This didn't make any sense. This man, the one standing before me now, wasn't anything like the person I had come to know since returning to New Haven, much less the boy I grew up with.

Dalton's mouth twisted into a determined, but sullen, smirk. Still, he held my arm tightly.

"This isn't how I wanted it to end. You should know that." His voice was light and apologetic. "Even if it wouldn't have been you, even if it had been one of those random girls who looked like you, I still didn't want it to come to this."

"It doesn't have to," I said, trying to tug free of him. But he was supernaturally strong; I would've had a better chance of pulling off white after Labor Day than breaking free of his grip. "You don't have to do this."

"I do." He ground his teeth together. "I don't have a choice." His bright eyes filled with tears. "Do you think I wanted to be this? Do you think this is what I envisioned for my life?" He stomped hard against the ground, causing a crack in the pavement.

Damn, he *was* strong.

"I had a good life, Char. I had ambitions. I had dreams. I had a fiancé. And do you know what she did when she found out?" Tears tripped down his cheeks now. "She just left. Said she couldn't handle it, that she didn't think she had the constitution to care for a sick person."

"Sick?" I muttered, my face tensing as my eyebrows drew together.

"Cancer." The word left him like a breath.

Images of my mother flooded my mind the way they always did when that horrible word was uttered. I always figured time would change that. But I was wrong. Even now—in the most dangerous situation of my life—her face was the first thing I saw.

"Stage four," he continued. "There was nothing the doctors could do. There was nothing anyone could do. They just expected me to rot away, to lie around and wait to die." He shook his head. "And do you know the worst part? By the time it's finished, what they bury won't even look like me." He stared past me for a moment, then shifted his gaze to the ground, but his hand never left my arm. "And I've tried, Char. I found as much blood as I could after that old man came to me. But it wasn't enough. The magic always wore off, just like he said it would."

"What old man?" I asked, wincing as his hand tightened around my arm, his nails digging into my skin.

"That doesn't matter!" He yanked me closer. "None of it matters, because it wasn't enough." He blinked hard. "But he showed me what I needed to do. I had to kill that stupid Conduit and change myself." He shook his head, slowly lifting his gaze back to me as he gentled his tone. "Have you ever killed someone, Char?"

"You don't have to do this, Dalton," I said emphatically. "It doesn't have to be this way. Maybe we can help you...somehow..."

"It changes you," he said. "It digs deep down into you and steals things away." His Adam's apple bobbed. "Things you didn't even know could be stolen."

"Dalton—"

"I had to," he said, as if begging me to understand.

And the scary part was, some small part of me could. Some

small part of me wondered how far I would have gone to save my mom from the same fate Dalton had faced.

But I wouldn't have gone this far.

"I couldn't die like that," he continued. "I had come too far. I had done too much to let it all end like some chump, connected to machines and living off applesauce and medication."

His eyes filled with some dreadful emotion I could not pinpoint. Desperation? Determination? Or was it agony and regret?

"And that's still true," he said. "I hate to do this, but I can't just give up on life. I'm sorry, Char. I can't. Why should it be me who dies? Why does fate get to decide?"

I shook my head. I didn't know what to say. That was just the way it was. He couldn't play God. It wasn't right. "So—so what are you going to do?"

He let out a slow sigh. "I need more Supplicant blood. All of a Supplicant's blood. The *right* Supplicant's blood," he added. "And this was the only clue the old man gave me. A description, matching my sister's. I knew there had to be someone else. And there way, and I finally found her. Found you." His cracked his knuckles in front of him, then slanted his gaze toward me. "I really wish it wasn't you. Please don't make this harder for me."

"Harder for *you?*" A new wave of anger came rushing through me. "What are you expecting, Dalton? That I'm going to willingly sacrifice myself for you? Clearly you would not do the same for me."

He bit down on his lip and shook his head. "Sorry it has to be this way."

Then he swung at me again, striking me hard against my right cheek with a sickening crack. I slumped in his grasp. Now that I was limp and defenseless, he finally let go of my arm, and I crumpled to the ground.

"I wondered if you could use it, the magic in your blood." He kicked me hard in the gut, knocking the wind out of me. I lurched to my side, holding my stomach. "Guess not."

My eyes scanned the ground. Of course I would leave the stupid gun over there. Of course I would.

"D-Dalton..." I said, my voice nothing more than a thin rasp. "P-Please..."

"I wish I could stop, Char." He advanced, his fists morphing into sharpened claws. "I'll make it quick."

This was it. He was going for the finishing blow.

"You *can* stop," I murmured. "You can."

He raised his right hand over his head, readying to bring it down on me. "Pleading won't save you. Nothing can save you now. I'll make it quick."

A blur whizzed across my line of sight. In a blink, Dalton was on the ground, gasping for air with scratches across his face.

Looking up, I saw Abram standing there in his human form, bare-chested and glistening in the moonlight. "I think I'd like to test that theory."

My heart leapt. The rest of me would have followed, but I was as bruised and battered as the honorees of Mr. Blackwell's 'What Not to Wear' list, and my heart was the only part of me capable of doing any leaping.

Abram glared at Dalton with enough animosity to break glass. His chest huffed up and down like waves crashing against a gorgeous shore. He was obviously pained. Panicking, I scanned his torso, searching for the bullet wound. All I found was dried blood. It seemed the injury had closed itself. I should have known better than to worry. It would take more than a bullet to stop Abram.

Of course, the same could be said for Dalton.

But what did that mean? If Abram wasn't injured any longer, then why was he in so much obvious pain? The answer came to me almost immediately. It was after midnight. He was trying to maintain his human form, probably so that I would recognize him.

"Are you okay?" he asked, speaking to me but never removing his gaze from Dalton.

"I think he broke something," I answered, already feeling how much my jaw was swelling up.

Abram growled. "I'm about to break *him*."

Dalton smiled from the pavement. His wounds were stitching themselves together, too. This wouldn't be an easily won fight. The only thing clearer than that was the fact that *I* seemed to the only person around who couldn't heal her own wounds, which put me at a distinct disadvantage.

"This doesn't have anything to do with you, Abram," Dalton said, getting to his feet much quicker than he should have been able to. "Run along like a good dog, and you just might survive this."

Abram leaned toward Dalton, not a wrinkle of fear to be found anywhere on him. "I would say the same about you, but I'm not going to afford you that luxury."

As they circled each other, Abram's eyes flashed down to me.

"Run," he said, his worried voice gravelly with warning.

Then he sprung forward, morphing into full-on beast mode as he came down on Dalton. His elongated jaw went right for Dalton's throat. He was obviously not wasting any time, freeing up of whatever energy it took him to remain human and going right for the kill shot.

Dalton ducked out of the way, and Abram landed, spinning around on his paws. Deep claw marks gashed into the pavement.

I darted off, heading right for the woods. But Dalton appeared in front of me.

"Stick around," he said. "I don't want you to miss this."

Grabbing my arm, he flung me hard. I stumbled back and crashed against a parked car. The impact dropped me to my knees, and I curled up, spikes of pain shuddering up my back.

Abram's howl pierced the night air. It was, at once, terrible and wonderful. He looked over at me, his beast form lean and muscular. His eyes traced me, taking ownership of all they saw. He lunged toward Dalton, but this time Dalton wasn't lucky enough to get out of the way.

Abram collided with him, a mass of fur and teeth. Soon, Abram had eclipsed him, and all I could see from where I slumped against the car was Abram's massive form huddling over what surely by now was Dalton's bloodied corpse.

Astonishingly, though, Abram's form lifted from the ground—Dalton held him over his head. He flung Abram through the air. The beast hit hard against a nearby building and yelped.

I shivered, realizing what Dalton could have done to *me*. But he wanted me alive—at least until he was ready to drain all my blood for himself. If I died before then, I would be no good to him.

Dalton started toward me. "Let's go, sweet thing. I don't exactly have an endless amount of time."

Another howl danced across my eardrums, and Abram raced between us. He was on all fours now, growling with bared fangs and raised fur. The two beasts pounced toward each other, claws connecting with bodies midair, slicing gashes into each other as they tumbled back to the ground. They rolled closer to me. A spray of blood—I hoped not Abram's—splashed onto my hospital gown.

With so much blood streaking and matting their fur, I could not fathom how either of them continued to brawl. Abram swiped at Dalton's face, his nails slicing through his snout, and Dalton howled. He whacked Abram hard, sending him flying back, then barreled toward me again. His dirty claws tore right through the hospital gown, into my thigh, and I screeched.

Though my mind went numb with terror, my whole body shook from the pain. Dalton raised his paw again. But Abram towered behind him, pulling Dalton back by his beastly shoulder and sending him hurtling through the air.

Oh, Abram. This is a disaster.

Abram's eyes, even in beast form, looked so human. So anguished. He made a small mewling sound, tilting his head as he looked over my wound. He ripped off a piece of my hospital gown and tied it around the large gash in my thigh, then tried to lift me.

Before he could get me off the ground, Dalton pounced on his back, wrapping his beast-arms around Abram's neck and digging claws into his shoulders to hold tight. Abram's grip on me slipped, and fell back, my head knocking into the car. There was just...so much blood. My stomach lurched, and I squeezed my eyes shut.

Please, God, do something.

A shot rang across my field of vision, nearly striking Abram in the head. Turning to the left, I saw Mr. McKenzie, gun pointed toward the beast. They were waking up—the entire town. And that meant that, once again, the game had changed.

"It's back!" Dalton screamed. "The monster is back!"

I spun my gaze toward him, only to find Dalton had already morphed back into human form, his clothes hanging in tatters off his body. *The devil.* He'd created the perfect scene to further incite the mob: a battered detective hero, the bleeding damsel in distress, and the hulking beast waging war on this sleepy, peaceful town.

One by one, the people of the town encroached on this tableau, an entire town, readying themselves for the kill.

"Abram..." I murmured, reaching out helplessly toward him.

He pounded his clawed-fists against the ground, getting onto all fours. He looked at me and then shook his head forward, snorting. I knew what he wanted. With what little strength I had remaining, I thrust myself onto his back and grabbed two handfuls of fur.

Abram took off, driving a path through the terrified townspeople. The muscles in his back flexed as the wind picked up around me. It was almost like flying, moving through Main Street quicker than I had ever gone before. But where were we going? Where *could* we go? There was no escaping this.

When Abram's paws hit hard against the pavement to take an all-too-familiar left, I knew where he was headed, even before he descended the staircase—the very one I fell down the day we met.

Abram burst through the locked doors of The Castle and darted down the hall, huffing as he settled in front of the strangely marked door.

He lowered his back, and I climbed off. Chanting and clanging and thundering from the streets poured in. The mob was legion. And they were coming.

The beast stood and, slowly but surely, morphed back into Abram. His shape returned before my very eyes, naked, muscular, and mouthwatering.

"How are you doing this?" I asked.

"The room," he said as his voice returned. "This room is letting me do it."

"How?" I asked, my voice shaking.

A loud crash echoed from down the hall. From here I could just barely make out what it was: someone had thrown a lit bottle through the window. A table caught fire, and it quickly spread to the drapes.

"My God," I said.

He took my arm gently. "We have to go inside. You're losing a lot of blood."

I'd nearly forgotten my own wounds; I'd been staring at Abram, whose body was unmarred, no evidence of his injuries remaining. I hadn't noticed the blood streaming past the cloth Abram had used to tie off my wound. I was dripping blood all over the floor.

I gasped and stumbled back, about to faint at the sight of all the blood—worse, somehow, coming from my body. A body I knew would not heal itself and was a beacon for any beast that might be seeking me.

Abram caught me and pulled me against him. "The room will protect us. Get inside."

But I just stood there, frozen, unable to pull my gaze from the fire. The flames licked up the walls the same as fear burned in my core. Abram pushed the previously unmovable door open and swept me inside.

A soft light—like moonlight—swelled around us, so pale it was nearly blinding. He pushed the door closed behind us and, slowly, my eyes adjusted to the light.

But my mind could not comprehend what I saw.

CHAPTER 28

No sooner had my feet crossed the secret room's threshold than something flared inside of me. Some pieces of myself, parts that I didn't even fully realize existed, started lighting up and falling into place. The light here shimmered in flecks of gold, sort of like the way my blood looked when it came in contact with someone magical.

As the light washed over me, all my pain subsided, all my wounds tingled into a glorious numbness. Once my eyes adjusted from the burst of light, I began to take stock of the room. It was quaint, nearly empty. Nothing inside betrayed whatever importance existed within these walls. Why had keeping me out of here been so important? And why was this barren space able to keep us safe now when all other areas came up lacking?

Something was wrong about all of this. I couldn't pinpoint what, but unease was seeping through my bloodstream, rapidly replacing that brief moment of peace the light had afforded me.

I turned to Abram, my heart nearly stopping in my chest at the sight of him. While I'd ventured farther into the room, he'd waited just by the door. He was stunningly handsome, of course, but that's not why my heart stopped. His eyes were so full of sorrow, and yet his expression was calm, his body language confident. I could only explain it as a quiet resolve. But it made me more concerned.

"Abram..." I said, watching his face carefully. He was scared about something. "The place is on fire Abram. There's a mob building outside the door. Shouldn't we be running?"

"It'll be okay," Abram said. But there was too much apology in his voice.

"Please, no more secrets." I shook my head and splayed my hands. "How can anything be okay? How, Abram?"

His Adam's apple bobbed, and his jaw tensed. His chest puffed up a little as he took a deep breath, and I expected him to approach me, but he didn't. I wished he would.

"There's something you should know about this room," he said finally. "About this town actually."

Oh, no. Here is it. More things I don't want to know.

But they were things I needed to know. I turned away, blinking back tears as anxiety throttled in my chest. "We don't have much time, do we?"

"No," he said. "We don't. But it's not what you think."

My gaze landed on a crucifix on the wall and a stained glass window that sat under it. That window, with its red moon almost completely colored in—I had seen it before. I had seen this entire room before. But where?

"Oh, God," I muttered as the answer came to me, as soft as the last whispers of a peaceful dream. "Satina. This is the room where it happened."

"This is the genesis point," he said, his voice gravelly. "The origin of the curse that, even now, still envelopes me."

"That was here?" I asked, moving closer to the window. I turned to face him. "But it was a monastery. You said you burned it down."

"I attempted to burn it down," he said, eyes plastered on the floor. Even now, it seemed, the incident still brought about shame in him. "They don't make buildings like they used to. The fire destroyed most of the interior, but the structure remained intact. And this room was completely untouched."

"I don't suppose that's coincidence," I answered, running my finger across the colored-in moon.

"Sometimes, if the magic is strong enough during a certain event or occurrence, it leaves something of an imprint on the area affected." I felt him behind me, the heat of his human form radiating against my skin. "The magic that envelopes this room was made for me. To *curse* me. But part of that curse is also what keeps me alive."

"Well, what good is a curse if you're not alive to suffer through it?" I asked as he ran his fingers down my arm.

"That's the idea," he answered. His lips traced my hair, settling along my ear. "It's stopped me from being able to end my life during my darker moments of the last century."

My throat tightened at the thought of that, and although I knew emotions came from the mind and not the heart, I still felt that honest-to-God heartache in my chest. "You tried to...to what?"

"Shh," he breathed into my ear. "It was a long time ago, before I had something to live for. Before you."

My heart fluttered. I felt myself dancing close to a cliff that would drop me right off into ecstasy. It was strong. The way it always was with Abram. His musk, his lips—they all joined to form the sweetest and most seductive song I had ever heard. But I couldn't allow myself to be seduced, not right now.

"Abram, they're right outside."

"And that's where they'll stay," he answered, hands wrapping my waist.

"The fire," I breathed.

"Won't cross into this room. I promise you," he said low into my ear. "The magic here is strong, Charisse. You need to trust it, to trust *me*. We don't have much time."

"I do trust you," I answered wholeheartedly, looking into his eyes that were dark and mysterious pools. "But you're also scaring me. What do you mean we don't have much time? If this room will protect us—"

I cut myself short as my gaze fell back onto the painted moon. That was it. The stained glass moon was much fuller than the one on the door—less of a crescent, more of a waxing moon—nearly full, in fact.

"What does this mean?" I asked, waving my hand at the symbol. "People don't just have empty rooms with moon symbols on the door and stained glass displays with moons to match inside."

"You're right," he said.

I narrowed my eyes at me. "It means something, though, doesn't it? It has something to do with your curse."

He shook his head, but something in his eyes told me I was right.

"Tell me."

"Please don't, Charisse. I've told you many things. I don't want to—" He nearly choked on the word. Anger clouded his expression, and he jutted his finger toward the painted glass moon. "I don't want to talk about *that*."

I looked from him to the moon and back again. "Abram, if you don't tell me what it means, I'm going to walk out that door."

When he didn't stay anything, I started to storm past him, ready to play this game of chicken, fire and all. But he grabbed me by the wrist and pulled my body against his. His hands were firm, but his expression was gentle.

"Tell me," I demanded quietly.

He wrapped his arms around me and rested his cheek against my forehead. "This is my last full moon. After tonight, the curse will be permanent. Every night, for the rest of eternity, this will be my life, with no hope of ever changing that. I'll be this... this...*thing*...forever."

"But there's a way to break it," I said. "There has to be. Just do whatever Satina said it was. What's the worst that could happen, Abram?"

"The worst?" he whispered, his voice nearly cracking. "Losing you."

I pulled back and shook my head. "You won't lose me, Abram."

"You don't know that."

I balled my hands in fists at my side. "Well, neither do you."

His finger came up to my lips. "Please don't argue with me right now."

I smacked his hand away. "I don't want to argue with you. But I'm not the one who cares if you are a beast. *You are*. I'm trying to help you. Why won't you just let me help you?"

"If you want to help me, then be with me. Please, just be with me and let me do what I'm meant to do. I promised I would protect you, and I will."

Something rumbled in the room, and a voice echoed through the chamber. "I'm not sure how seriously I would take *that* promise."

I knew that voice. It was the same one that kept me up at night, and when it did allow me sleep, it was the same voice that haunted my dreams.

But it couldn't be. It wasn't possible. He was dead.

And yet, the voice of my father continued, "Given that he gave the same promise to me. And we all know how well that turned out."

I jerked away from Abram's touch and spun around. My father stood behind Abram, arms folded and staring at me with those eyes that I had come to both miss and vilify. My entire body went rigid. How was this happening?

Well, that was a stupid question. I knew *how* it was happening. It was this magic, the kind surrounding us, the king we were—even now—breathing in.

My face must have been a horrible thing to behold, because Abram took my hand and squeezed it tightly.

"What do you see?" he asked.

He knew. Somehow, he knew the magic was showing me something. And now I knew he couldn't see it, too.

"My father," I whispered, my voice sounding weak and small, the way it did when I was a child.

My father moved around Abram, almost floating toward me with his lightness. It wasn't like him, to move this way, to have a look on his face that screamed of mischievous glee. Or maybe it did. I hadn't seen my father since I was a kid, and even the man I knew then was a lie. That much was obvious.

Why was I even thinking this way? My father loved me. Abram being here was proof of that. Why was I forgetting everything I had learned about the man?

"You need to run, Charisse. You can't trust this thing." My father looked Abram over with disgust darkening his eyes. "He'll use you up, even more than he already has. He'll destroy you. He lies. Everything he says is a lie." My father moved closer, and my entire body trembled. "But that's what you like, isn't it? That's what you want from your men." He shook his head. "Is that what I did to you? Did I ruin my little girl?"

"What?" I balked, backing away. "Of course not."

Abram's hand squeezed mine. "It's not real, Charisse. It comes from the curse, and the curse wants me to suffer. It doesn't want to be broken."

Abram's comforting grip did little to steady me. All I could see was my father's eyes, weighing me, judging me, finding me lacking. And all of this to keep some curse going. But how would me suffering keep the century-old punishment that Satina leveled onto Abram running strong?

"You need to run, Charisse!" My father's voice was panicked now.

No. *Not* my father.

I leaned toward the apparition. "Go away," I said firmly. "You're not gonna win this one."

"Get away from this monster!" my 'father' demanded, a cloud of anger storming across his face. His face twisted and darkened, and his eyes disappeared as he bent disgustingly into a dark, shadowy creature. It was the magic. It was the curse. "I've healed your wounds so you can run, not so you could stand here staring like a fool! Now go away, and leave him to suffer on his own!"

It was greedy, this curse. It wanted to strip away all light from Abram's life, as though it fed on the darkness, as though it needed it to survive.

"It's me, isn't it?" I asked, turning to Abram and connecting the pieces. All the strange things Satina said, the way she looked at me...and now the way this room was attacking my devotion to Abram. It all made sense now. "I can break the curse, can't I?"

"Don't ask me that," Abram said.

"You have to tell me the truth." I took his unshaven face in my hands. "You have to trust me, too, you know."

He stared at me, parting his lips and then closing them again.

"Abram! I mean it!"

"You can, in a sense..." he said, closing his eyes. "When Satina placed the curse on me, she did so because she realized I didn't love her. She said I wasn't capable of love. She said if I could love someone, really love someone, and have that love returned, then the curse would be broken."

"Oh, God," I murmured, stroking his face. "I do," I said, shaking my head. My eyes welled up with tears. "I do love you." And it was the truth. I knew it as clearly as I knew Betsy Johnson's Spring 2002 Collection. "I love you, Abram."

But then a sickening realization came to me. I did love him. I had loved him for a long time now. But he was still this monster, still this beast. And that could only mean one thing.

"You don't love me..." I muttered.

It wasn't a question. My heart sank so hard and fast I felt it slam into my toes. I stepped back, almost stumbling. It couldn't be. The rules of the curse only left room for one answer.

"Charisse..." He stared at me apologetically. "I can't—"

But I didn't want an apology. What good would it do? What he'd said leveled more pain than all the punches Dalton had thrown at me.

"Charisse, you don't under—"

"Don't bother," the shadow magic said. Judging from Abram's reaction, the way he stiffened and clenched, he could now see it, too. "I've tired of you, and I've tired of this." The magic raised something that looked like a misshapen hand. "And this is what I'm doing about it."

CHAPTER 29

Within moments, we found out exactly what the shadow magic intended to do. The light in the room burst in a thousand little echoes of darkness, and the cool of the room was replaced with immediate intense heat.

We were no longer untouchable. The fire was coming for us, and so was the mob. I could hear it in the screams and bangs that were now evident outside the club's entrance.

The door to the room that had once been a force now lay in shambles on the floor, a victim of the curse's fickle temperament.

"Get behind me," Abram growled, but before I could move, he thrust me against his back. His skin was warm and, even pressed against the wrong end, I could feel his heart racing like a jackhammer.

The stomping and banging and chanting of the mob grew louder. Could I even blame them at this point? They thought they were putting an end to the danger that had been tormenting their town for months now. They were out to a kill a murderer, a monster.

"We need to run," I murmured.

Abram nodded, but he didn't move. His gaze swept down the hall, and I knew he could see the same thing I could. We needed to run, yes. But there was no place to run *to*. We were cornered. And the club's front door was splintering inward. It wouldn't be long before—

The door caved, and the first of the mob poured in. Five, ten, twenty. It seemed the entire town was after us, all rushing in toward this small, sacred, and (until now) secret room. Everyone but Dalton. He was mysteriously absent in the midst of the fervor he had been so busy whipping up.

Abram held one arm out in front of him while the other circled my bicep. He stepped back, leading me into the doorless room, then turned to me and held his finger to his lips. I chewed on the inside of my cheek, shaking my head and holding back a whimper. What good was this? It wouldn't be long before they found us. All he was doing was buying time.

As though sensing my distress, he slipped his hand down to mine, wrapping his fingers around my palm possessively. His touch steadied me. The even nature of his breathing brought an ounce of comfort to an otherwise unbearable situation, though I still couldn't explain why. He didn't love me. It had been magically incontestable, deemed truth by the highest and most unexplainable of vouchers.

And yet, I still sensed something was wrong about that. Looking at his hand, still human as it entwined with mine, I could not help but wonder how he was resisting the pull of the moon that should have changed him into a beast by now. If love wasn't the driving force for his resistance, then what was?

"Hey," a young man yelled. "There's some rooms down here!"

My whole body stiffened, bracing for the inevitable—not even sure what the inevitable was. Soon the young man was in the doorway, staring us down. He trembled, though, not so brave when faced with Abram...not until the others were at his back.

Dozens of people clogged the hallway, and some of the bigger men of the town forced their way to the front. My heart dropped as I recognized some of the faces in the crowd. Faces I grew up with.

Mrs. Adler, who had tended my cut that time I scraped my knee following Lulu on our brand new roller blades, was nearly foaming at the mouth with a pick axe in her hand. She had been so gentle then, so kind as she washed and bandaged my leg. Seeing the fear and anger in her eyes now was almost surreal.

And there was Douglas Feathersby—my first kiss. He gave me a nickel under Hopkin's Bridge and planted a wet one right on my lips. He told me he would always love me. I probably shouldn't have expected him to keep his word, given that we were seven and all. Of course, I also never would have imaged a reality where he was running toward me with a pitchfork.

But now that they had us cornered, it seemed everything slowed down, each man and woman assessing the best way to kill the beast—or rather, the man with the beast within him.

"Char," Douglas said, "get away from him." He reached his hand out to me, as though I would go running to his protection, as if the mob were here to save me. Maybe they were. "Hurry, before it's too late!"

I took a step back, shaking my head. If I left Abram's side, he was as good as dead. If I stayed here, eventually they would go after Abram anyway, and they would kill us both. But, at least for now, this was buying us time.

"I don't want to kill them," Abram said to me quietly. He hadn't so much as flinched this entire time.

"Then don't," I said.

And I meant it. These people didn't know what they were doing. They were pawns, just like me—chess pieces in a game none of us understood. Killing them would be as useless as wearing socks with designer heels.

But as the first man lunged at Abram, swiping a torch in a large arc meant to set him on fire, I didn't know what to want anymore. If Abram didn't fight back, they would kill him. If he did, these men and women would die—none of them bad people, just misled and afraid.

Abram pounced, even in his human form so clearly animalistic with his grace and fluidity. But before he landed, the pull of the moon finally had its way with him. His hands twisted into something sharper as he reared back.

I flinched for what would be bloody impact. But instead of shredding the townsfolk, Abram's claw drug across the light fixture, blanketing the room in darkness.

I felt hands grab at me hard. I struggled against them, sure that Douglas Feathersby was either going to drag me away or demand his nickel back. But then I felt a breath on my neck, and I knew it was Abram.

His now much hairier, beastly arms pushed me westward, and the last thing I saw was the glint of shattering glass against my face.

I spun around to throw my arms around Abram's neck as a rush of cool invaded my nostrils and filled my lungs. He swept me around onto his back as we flew through the air, falling toward the hard concrete of Main Street.

But I wasn't afraid. Abram was with me and, our current predicament aside, I knew enough to know my best shot was in his arms—or in this case, on his back.

"I've got you," he called over his shoulder to me as the ground rushed up to greet us. "I've always got you."

His feet hit hard against the ground, but he didn't falter. I slid down from his back, and he turned to face me, once again a man. He was really fighting the beast thing, and while he wasn't entirely successful, I was impressed.

"Are you all right, Charisse?" he murmured, brushing the stray hairs from my face.

Of course I wasn't all right. I was running for my life—running away from people I grew up with. "We have to hurry," I said breathlessly. "They're still coming."

Looking behind us, I saw that the moon window, the window he had just jumped through, was still intact. But how could that be? I'd felt it shatter against my skin. I heard the crunch as

Abram's boot landed against shards of it. Now it was there again, the red moon almost completely colored in.

"The window..." I said.

"I know," Abram answered. In one swift motion, he threw me over his shoulder. "Wouldn't be much of a curse if all it took was a couple of warm bodies to break it."

As he sprinted forward, a cold gust of wind cascaded over my back. He was moving too fast for me to tell where we were heading. All I knew was that the sounds of the mob, as well as the lights of Main Street, were fading away.

He skidded to a stop. Leaves rustled around us. After he helped me slide off of his back again, I saw we were back in the woods, only feet away from the old house.

It was strange how much time we had spent in these woods together. Along with the Castle, it sort of felt like 'our place'... aside from how we almost got ourselves killed every time we came here.

"What is it?" I asked, spying the way he grabbed his shoulder.

"It's nothing," he answered. "I just need a moment."

I brushed his hand away, revealing his shoulder as a mess of red gashes, and I gasped. "My God! Look at all that blood!"

"One of them nicked me with something. I'll be fine. Self-healing, remember?" His face shifted, nearly changing back into that of the beast. His mouth closed hard, and he reverted to his old—and quite stunning—features. "We need to move."

"To where?"

"Inside," he said, nodding toward the house, the hand of his good arm clutching his wound once more. "I've set up some fail safes, just in case something like this happened."

"But you won't be you," I answered, grazing his arm with my fingers. "How much longer can you keep the beast at bay?"

"Not as long as I need to." He grimaced. "I think I'm out of time."

And the way he said that, the finality of it, sparked something inside of me. I narrowed my eyes at him. "What do you mean by that?"

He brushed past me to head toward the house, growling under his breath. "Nothing you need to concern yourself with."

"Hell no!" I said, grabbing his arm and spinning him back toward me. "I'm about ten miles past ready to hear that, Abram." My hand tightened around his arm. "You're gonna be straight with me. You're gonna stop treating me with kid gloves. Or this is where you and me part ways. Got it?"

He glared at me. "That would be a death sentence for you, Char."

I tilted my chin up. "Like you care."

The expression in his face was so pained it felt like razors in my own heart. "I do," he said, his voice shifting lower. "Damn it, Charisse. You're making this harder than it already is."

"Trust me, at this point, the truth would be a lot easier."

"It's the damn moon," he said finally. "And what I did to it."

"*What* did you do to it, Abram?" I asked.

"Magic is about balance and energy. When Satina was on the other side, keeping the curse fed wasn't an issue. There's unlimited energy in the afterlife. But when I brought her back, all that changed. The curse began to sputter out. With Satina cut off from the energy that powered it, the curse began a sort of countdown. And, because the moon is what she tied the curse to, the next full moon became the anchor for it."

"Speak English," I said with a growl of my own. "And do it quickly. I doubt Dalton and his mob are going to take long to figure out we came back here."

"The reason the moon on the window phased into waxing is because I brought Satina back. With every moon, we took one step closer to stripping all the magic from the curse."

"That's a good thing," I said. "It's almost colored in now. Your curse will end. So what's the issue?"

"Yes, the moon is almost colored in now," Abram conceded, but he didn't have the same joy I had. "This is the last night. This is the last moon of the curse that's plagued me for over a hundred years."

"That's great," I answered. What was his problem? Was this like Stockholm syndrome? "You can be a man again. You can have another chance. Isn't that what you want?"

"More than anything," he answered. "Well, more than *almost* anything. But I don't think you understand, Char. I never broke the curse. The curse isn't breaking. It's...ending."

My eyebrows pulled together. "What's the difference? What does that *mean?*"

He looked past me, to the sky above, to the moon with only but a sliver away from complete. "When the moon is full, Charisse, I will remain a beast. Forever."

CHAPTER 30

Abram's words literally clanged against my ears, screeching like nails against a chalkboard. Instantly, they exhausted me. It seemed it would never end, the constant twists and turns of fate. Every revelation seemed to dig us deeper into this hopeless pit. And this was no different.

We were hours away from sunrise, hours away from his curse becoming a permanent, unbreakable thing. And I could do nothing to save him.

He had to love and be loved in return. How does one accomplish that in the span of a single night?

Hurt engraved itself into my heart. The truth was, I did love Abram. I loved him more than I had every loved anyone in that way. And he...just didn't feel the same way.

It was then that a sickening truth leveled itself onto me. Is that why Abram had gotten so close to me? Had he wormed his way into my heart hoping that I might be the person he could fall in love with? Had he used me in some halfhearted attempt to break an age-old curse? And, worse than that, had he found me lacking?

Still, it wasn't as though I could fault him for his feelings, or for trying to love me, or for wanting to break his curse.

The fact was, I would fight for him until the end. And, even though he didn't love me, I knew he would fight for me, too. He had proven that much. He had risked his life for me time and time again. Even now, in our darkest hour, he didn't flinch once as he faced the incredible odds to keep me safe. But why?

"Are you sure about this, Abram? If you don't break the curse tonight, it can really never be broken?"

He gave a solemn nod. "I would still have the days, same as now. But that would be it for me. The hopes of reclaiming nights as a man will be gone forever. All chance for redemption will be lost." He looked down at his clawed hands and let out a sound between a growl and a sigh. "But that doesn't matter now."

"Of course it matters," I said, determined not to let his lack of feelings for me alter my feelings for him. I took his hands in my own, claws be damned. "There has to be something we can do. Anything. Just tell me what."

"You shouldn't concern yourself with this, Charisse. There's too much going on, too much at stake. The curse is the least of my concerns."

"Well, it shouldn't be," I said. "And you shouldn't have started whatever mystical clock you did by bringing Satina back."

"I don't want to fight with you right now," he answered quietly.

"Too bad." I ran hands through my hair, shaking out my natural curls and trying to reset my tired brain. "I'd rather not be running from a Frankenstien's monster-esque mob, but we are where we are." My voice was lower now, more sincere. "I didn't ask for this."

"I understand that. And I also understand that you didn't do anything to deserve it. You were born into this life." He was barely able to keep his human form now, struggling as he was against his beastly nature. "But I will keep you safe," he said. "I swear it."

"That's not what I'm talking about," I said, my voice breaking. "I know you'll do everything you can to keep me safe. But I didn't ask you to. And I certainly didn't ask you to give away your one chance at happiness to get it done."

"Charisse—"

"No." I threw my hands in front of me, no longer willing to let the elephant in the room remain unseen. "I get that you don't love me and, if you give me a little time to process that, I might even be able to understand it. But what I don't understand—what I'm not sure I'll ever understand—is why you would do something like this for someone you don't even care about."

His eyes shot open. The entirety of his morphing body tensed. "Why would you say something like that?" He moved closer to me. "Why the hell would you even think something like that?"

I bristled as he neared me. It was strange. Hours ago, his body felt like home to me—that safe place I had spent my entire life looking for but had never found. And now, with this newest revelation, I couldn't think of anything more ludicrous.

"You know why," I said. Anger started to pool in my gut and bubble up like venom through my throat and out my mouth. "I scoffed at Satina when she compared me to all your other conquests. I actually thought there was something different about me, about us. But I was wrong. I didn't think someone could touch someone the way you touched me and not feel anything behind it."

His mouth, almost completely a snout now, clenched shut. With pain etched in his face, he transformed his face back into human form. "I know you think you know everything. God knows you're stubborn enough to think you can see every piece on this chess board. But there are some things, Charisse, that are even above that beautiful, hard head of yours."

"You either love me or you don't, Abram. Love isn't a complicated thing. It's there or it's not."

A loud shuffling sounded from far off.

"They're coming," Abram said, crouching into a feral position. "We need to get into the house."

"Why?" I asked.

"There's no time for arguing." He leaned over, motioning for me to climb on his back. "Get on."

I didn't move.

"Damn it, Charisse! Get on my goddamn back!"

Again, I didn't move.

"Do you want me to beg to save you?"

Still, I didn't answer. The rustling just got louder, signifying that the mob, or at least part of it, was getting closer.

"Fine," he growled. "Get on my back, *please*."

Hiding a smirk, I climbed on. He let go of all his resistance and shifted completely from man to beast as he darted off toward the house. My heart sped in tempo with his thundering footsteps, and my hair whipped behind me. Something about being carted around by Abram made me feel alive in a way I really never had before. Or maybe that was just Abram himself.

We burst through the doorway like a pair of twin bullets. He shrugged me off of his back, placing me gently on the floor and nudging the door closed behind him with his snout.

He was all beast now—all strong hind legs, massive thighs, and thick, luscious fur. He glared at me for a moment with those familiar eyes, perhaps expecting me to be disgusted at the sight of him. But if that's what he was looking for, he was going to be sadly disappointed.

The beast was Abram, and Abram was the beast. They were interchangeable to me now, one as much a part of the man I loved as the other.

Looking away from me, he padded up the staircase on all fours. His paws hit heavy as he neared the top.

I followed him, settling in front of the room that once held Satina.

As soon as we stopped in front of it, Abram began to morph back into the man I knew.

"Magic," I answered, putting it together. "This room is magic, too?"

He stretched, brushing off the last bit of monster as the man fully emerged. "I told you that magic is about balance. Even curses like the one that affects me has to be equal parts light and dark. The room in the Castle held the darker magic that fueled the curse. It wanted me to suffer. When it believed keeping me alive would accomplish that, it was happy to accommodate, but when it realized...when it realized how you felt, it wanted you to die so that I would live on in agony. That's why it dispersed when it saw that the mob was its best chance to see you dead."

His eyes flickered to the floor.

"Which of course means that this room holds the light side of the magic. It stands to reason that this aspect of the curse yearns to see my redemption. To that end, it'll do everything in its power to keep you safe."

"Should have brought us here first then," I mumbled.

"It wasn't clear then," he said, and he sounded sort of...hopeful.

Please don't let him be guessing all this.

"So now it's clear?" I asked skeptically.

"Aspects of the curse only reveal themselves when the curse is at its most powerful, which only happens when—"

"When the bitch who cast it comes back from the dead and starts a magical timer?" I asked.

He grinned, pushing the wooden door open. "You learn quickly."

"Mm-hmm," I said, thinking of all the things I hadn't learned quickly enough.

Abram gestured for me to enter the room, and as soon as I crossed the threshold, I felt the magic pouring into me. It comforted me, made me feel whole, made me feel at peace.

But was this true peace, or was this an illusion like the last time?

It was then, in the midst of that clarity, that a question filtered its way into my mind. "Why did the curse want me to die?" I asked. After all, my love alone clearly wasn't enough. "You said the outcome is already in stone, isn't it? What does the curse know that I don't?"

I turned to Abram. He was still on the other side of the doorway. The look on his face both troubled and soothed me. It was clear and full of the sort of stoic and tempered joy that only existed when you realized you had found the best the world has to offer...and that you were sure that you were never going to see it again.

"I wish I could answer that," he answered. "More than anything, I wish I could tell you."

In that moment, I could sense the truth of his feelings burning under my skin. I knew him as I knew myself. It was mystical, cellular, beyond bone deep. And I knew that he loved me. I just knew it. It was in the way he spoke to me, in the way he drove my passion and allowed me to stoke his own. It was in his voice, in his gaze. It was as singular and real as my own name.

There was something about all of this that I didn't know, something that would make sense of this whole thing.

"Please, Abram," I said, shaking my head. "Just say it. Whatever it is, just say tell me, and we'll figure something out. We'll fix it somehow."

He swallowed, and his head shook a fraction of an inch. "I am fixing it, Charisse."

The tone of his voice and the expression on his face sent a panic into my chest that I couldn't explain. I started back toward the door, back toward him. "Abram, what are you doing?"

"What I have to," he said.

Then he slammed the door shut.

I rushed toward it, but I already knew what I would find. The door wouldn't budge. Like before, I was trapped inside, protected by magic that I knew nothing about.

"Abram!" I screamed. "Abram, open this door!"

He was going to do it. He was going to keep me safe by any means necessary, even if that meant facing that mob by himself.

"Abram!" I screamed, beating so hard against the door that I thought I heard something in my hand snap. "Abram! Would you listen to me damn it? For once, just listen to me!"

Tears streamed hot down my cheeks. My heart shattered into so many pieces it might as well have been dust.

"Abram!"

No answer. He was gone. And I knew where he was going.

I rushed toward the window, wiping my eyes and looking past the nearly full red moon that graced it, a perfect match to the one back at The Castle.

The mob had gathered outside. All of them. The entire town littered the ground, armed with pitchforks, rifles, and other weaponry.

Blinking through fresh tears, I saw Abram walk out the door and into the yard, already morphing into the beast.

The crowd reared back, but soon overcame their fears and pushed forward. Shots fired at Abram, and I beat against the window. Maybe I could jump through it, the way Abram had back at the Castle.

But I knew better.

I wasn't as strong as him, and the truth was, if this room didn't want me to get out, then I wouldn't.

All I could do was watch. Watch the man I love fight. Watch the people I grew up with try to kill him.

"Stop!" I screamed. But no one listened. Did they hear me? Could anyone even see me?

I slapped my hand over and over again on the glass pane, but no one so much as looked up at me. The glass rattled and my palm stung, but it was useless.

Bullets collided with Abram, and his body stumbled backward.

"No!" I screamed.

Howling loudly, he lunged forward, but he didn't attack. Didn't defend himself. Didn't even try to run. A swing with a baseball bat to his hind leg hit so hard that the crack could be heard over the cries and shouts of the mob. Another person—this time someone I didn't recognize—swiped at him with a kitchen knife, but the man kept too far a distance to make contact.

But the more people who braved their assault on him, the more people who found the courage to do the same. Soon the town had swallowed him up. My fingernails dug into the old window frame, splintering against the soft wood. Pain cut off the air to my lungs as they kicked him, punched him, stabbed him.

Seeing the blood matting his fur did something to me—changed me. This was a nightmare. I couldn't cope.

I ran back to the door and tried it again, rattling the doorknob and banging on the wood. "Please, please," I shouted. "Open."

My voice was strained and cracked, my body weak, my mind a swirl of confusion and hurt and anger. I stumbled back to the window, falling to my knees at the sight of him. They had backed off now to observe their damage. He staggered sideways. Someone threw a stone at him, and he yelped.

No one wanted to go through with it. No one wanted murder on their hands, even with such a beast as they believed him to be. For a moment, hope bubbled up through my heartache. But through the blur of my tears, I saw the one person who could shatter all that hope in an instant.

Ester.

Ester, with a gun in her hand, marching up to Abram with the barrel already pointed down and finger on the trigger. She didn't even look like herself. My body tensed.

Ester, please. Don't.

I shook my head as though I could will her to stop. This couldn't be happening. Why couldn't she just leave him alone? He was already a heap on the ground, bloody, broken, barely able to move.

But Ester didn't stop her advance—didn't even flinch—as she fluidly approached the beast.

With a swift, almost graceful motion, she took aim at his head and pulled the trigger.

CHAPTER 31

I watched Abram's body fall lifeless to the ground and, as it did, reality twisted into a dark and unsettling thing.

Things would never be the same.

My body shut down. The pain in my chest was so strong that I couldn't feel if my heart was still beating, but if it were, each beat would be hopeless anyway. My soul had been shattered, and I felt the pieces of myself scattering away from my body, leaving behind only the sinking feeling of dread that weighed my every limb.

My hearing went out. Could a gunshot do that, or was I in shock?

The crowd dispersed—Ester with her horrible gun and the rest of the townspeople behind her, ambling away as though they had awoken from a spell. They had done what Dalton implored them to. They had killed the beast. Their nightmare was over, and mine was just beginning.

I stared in trembling, core-quaking silence as they filtered back into the woods, so much more ceremoniously than they had come. Marching victoriously back to the safety of their beds and leaving Abram to rot in the night air.

Bile rose in my throat. They had won. It was over.

Except that it wasn't.

Dalton was still out there, hiding somewhere, waiting for me to appear. It was only a matter of time. He would find me, kill me, drain me, and then live forever, enjoying the spoils of his victory. But only if the third beast didn't get to me first.

And the thing was, I didn't care. I was already dead. Everyone I had ever loved was dead, save for Lulu, and if my track record were any indication, it would only be a matter of time before she was killed, too. Because death followed me, wherever I went, and there was no denying that now.

The yard was empty. Only one piece of evidence remained to indicate what had happened here. I bit down on my lip to brace myself as I turned to face it. To face...him.

I swallowed hard as my gaze drank him in. He was still a beast. Was he not going to transform back? Would this be how he would spend his eternity—in the body of an animal, afforded no more dignity than a dog who had been hit by a passing car and pulled off the side of the road to die? Body battered. Limbs bent at impossible angles. Blood everywhere. All the signs that life had been present but was not anymore.

I stared hard, willing him to breathe, praying to see that rise and fall of his chest, clinging hopelessly to that thread of hope, knowing if anyone could survive this, Abram could. And yet knowing no one could survive this.

Everything was still. The yard. The leaves in the trees. And worst of all, Abram. So peacefully, painfully still. The realization of how true his death was rocketed into me like a missile.

I turned my back against the window and slid to the floor, by body plastered against the damn wall.

This can't be happening.

I repeated the thought like a mantra, over and over, again and again. And nothing changed. I was so crippled with emotion that even my tears escaped me. There was nothing left. My entire being was evaporating around me, my mind and emotions at war, pulling me in every direction.

All the fire that blazed within me while Abram was fighting for his life was now extinguished. He was dead, and he was taking my will to live with him.

Let Dalton come. Let all the beasts this world had to offer come for all I cared. What more harm could they do to me now? In less than five minutes, everything had changed. All hope had been erased. All of my worst fears had been realized.

Just five minutes ago, Abram had been standing before me, his chest heaving with determined breaths. How could those breaths be his last?

My senses started to return. First with the sound of my pulse in my ear—a rushing, shushing sound. An agonizing reminder of life. I dug my nails into the wood floor beneath me and pressed the back of my head hard against the wall.

Abram, no.

I squeezed my eyes shut, and the burning tears that had been floating in my subconscious came streaming out, reminding me I was still alive to cry. To feel. Alone.

The more I wanted the pain to end, the harder I cried. I was hyperventilating, and this was even worse than when cancer stole my mother from me. I choked on life's air as I gasped for breath.

I had the fleeting thought of getting up. Of pulling myself together. Of just stopping crying long enough to breathe. But those thoughts only made me hurt more, made my cries flood faster, made the ache spread farther in my chest.

Like an insult, the door clicked and creaked open, releasing me from my prison. I didn't bother to open my eyes. I wasn't ready to see life beyond that door. I just shook my head and curled into myself.

"I know you must be disheartened."

The voice tore through my mind. Whipping my eyes open, I looked toward the source of the noise.

Satina stood at the doorway, still wearing the dead girl's body and looking every bit as refreshed as a girl coming off a week-long Daytona vacay.

I licked my dry lips, trying to find the will to speak. "How long have you been standing there?"

She titled her chin up. "Charisse, you have to understand—"

I lifted my hand to stop her. "Don't," I ground out, anger bubbling up inside me. "Don't fucking say another word, I swear to God, Satina."

She had been right outside this door the entire time, I just knew it. She could have helped. Could have used her Conduit magic and saved his life. Could have freed me and allowed me to at least try to protect him. Could have done *something*. But she'd just stood there. Stood there and let him die. Left me in here to watch hopelessly as his life was stolen from him. From *me*.

"I did what I had to do," she said firmly, not wavering an inch from where she stood.

Indignation swelled in my heart. "You *bitch!*"

I darted to the far wall to grab an ancient-looking sword in a scabbard that hung there as one of the few adornments in the room, but as soon as I touched it, I realized it was fake. I could still give that bitch a hell of a swat nonetheless.

"This was all some plan of yours, wasn't it? You pretended to help us so we'd let you free. And then you just did nothing while they killed him!"

Satina rolled her eyes. "If you recall, it was your other boyfriend who freed me. The cutie in the police uniform."

"In case you didn't know—and I'm *sure* you did—he's the beast that's after me. But you probably knew that all along."

I marched toward her, costume arsenal in hand. To her credit, Satina didn't look worried. Given the fact that she was a one hundred and fifty year old witch, had already died once, and was being threatened by a woman who had never swung a golf club much less a sword, that shouldn't have surprised me.

She just remained where she stood, leaning against the doorframe with her arms crossed. "Calm yourself, Supplicant."

"I'm as fucking calm as it gets," I said through clenched teeth, choking up my grip on the sword's hilt.

"You're blaming the wrong people." Satina cocked her head curiously to the side. "It isn't I who is responsible for the death of your love, nor the mob who assailed him."

"You could have helped him!" I yelled, lunging toward her.

"I *did*," she said, a tinge of annoyance in her voice. "I helped him achieve what *he* wanted. To keep *you* safe!"

"That wasn't his call." I had settled in front of her, sword still in hard, but it hung limply at my side now. Fresh tears swelled on the cusps of my eyelids. "That wasn't your call." I wiped my eyes with the back of wrist. "Damn it, fuck you both! It's *my* life!"

"And his life was his," she said, her eyes flickering past me. "And I'd dictated more than enough of it. He at least deserved to die with the honor he sought." She shook her head. "Alas, I am afraid rest doesn't always come so easily."

I deflated at her words. Beating Satina to a pulp wouldn't bring Abram back, and it wouldn't stop Dalton's crusade. It was over. I dropped the sword, letting it clatter to the ground.

"You're not worth my time." I shoved her out of the way and moved past her through the threshold.

My empty shell of a body glided downstairs and out the front door. The night air punished me as I stepped outside, lighting up my skin and reminding me that it would never again feel the touch it yearned for.

As I neared the dark mass that was Abram's body, my entire body shook. It was a death march, the quickly vanishing line that led to my last moments of happiness—perhaps my last moments ever. Death was coming for me next, and I couldn't think of a better place to die than by Abram's side, where I should have been all along.

Dalton would be here soon, but damned if I wouldn't say goodbye first.

I couldn't stop the tears from falling as I settled over his large, rippling body. His blood-soaked fur matted against his skin, and his mouth hung open, his fangs bared.

He certainly should have been a frightening sight, but he wasn't scary at all. He was majestic and beautiful, even in this mangled, beastly state. Because I could see past it all. I could see who he really was, and I had never wanted to be near anything so much in my life.

I knelt down slowly, savoring the closeness. After today, I would never have this again. I lied on the ground, face-to-face with Abram. His eyes were closed, but I reached out, stroking his cheek. Sparks lit up my hand every time I touched him, and now was no different.

The tears scraped down my face like needles dragging against skin, leaving my cheeks raw and sore. But I settled my breaths. If these were to be the last moments I would ever spend with Abram, I would not to cry through them.

"This isn't over, Supplicant."

Satina was behind me, standing over me and robbing me of this, too. Intruding on these last moments, stealing my chance to say goodbye. In her hand, she held the display sword I'd threatened her with earlier.

"Leave me alone," I muttered, defeated.

"And if I did, what good would it do? Fate has plans for you yet, plans that will take you to places near and far." She inspected the not-so-sharp blade of the sword and frowned. "You have not yet seen what you need to see, not yet done what you need to do, and not yet loved in the way that will save us all."

"Just shut up!" I screamed. I'd had quite enough of this. "Shut up and go away!"

"Why do you think Abram did this, Supplicant? Why would Abram go through this nightmare? Why would he give up so much for this crusade, for you? Answer that, and I'll leave you...if you still wish me to."

"I don't know," I answered, still sobbing painfully. I put my head on Abram's chest, resting against his soft fur.

Satina stabbed the sword into the ground and rested her hand on it. "Yes, you *do* know."

"I don't!"

Her hand gripped the sword handle, and her gaze cut into me like a razor. "Answer my question, and I'll leave."

"I thought—I thought he loved me," I said, squeezing my eyes shut. Maybe that would make her go away, or maybe she just wanted to rub salt in the wound. None of it changed how *I* felt about *him.* "But I was wrong."

"And yet, here you are, still alive. Because he knew there was more ahead for you. If you loved him, should you not honor his sacrifice?"

I stared up at her defiantly. "Why should I?" I asked. "Why are you letting him die? Why can't you just bring him back?" I sat up now, wild with need. "Use my blood or something. Satina, you can't let him die. You can't. You could help him, I know you can."

"Oh, child," she said with a sigh and a slight frown. "You still don't get it. Today is nothing"—she waved her free hand dismissively—"compared to the many trials you will face yet. You need this moment in your life to prepare you. There are worse days ahead than this one. Great lovers and more painful heartaches. Believe me."

She didn't know shit. I glared at her. "Nothing could be worse than this. Now do something," I growled through my teeth. "Save him!"

Satina pulled the sword from the ground and dragged it behind her as she practically floated over to me. Setting the display arsenal on the ground beside Abram, she crouched at my side and placed her hand on my arm. I would have expected my skin to crawl at her touch, but the action seemed surprisingly...gentle. Caring, even.

"He's not gone, Charisse," she said, her voice soft.

"You're gonna save him?" My voice was barely above a whisper, too afraid to convey hope.

"I don't have to," she said, smiling. "You already have."

"What do you—"

She swiped her fingers under my eyes, smoothing away my tears. When she lifted her hand, her fingertips were red. My tears must have been streaming through the cuts on my face from when we broke through the glass back at The Castle.

Looking down, I saw a pool of my blood, of my *magical* blood, soaking up into Abram's skin. It glowed with the same golden signature it had the first time he touched it.

Oh.

Realization shot through me like a current of electricity. My tears had carried blood from the wounds on my face to Abram's beastly body. Could it really have...healed him? Of course I never would have thought of that...this whole having magic blood was new to me, and I still didn't know all that I was capable of. But was I capable of saving him? Even without the ability to perform magic myself?

My gaze trailed up to his face, and just as I looked at him, I felt it.

I felt him *breathe*.

My heart sped in my chest, and a rush came through my lungs. I stood stock-still, frozen, holding my breath, waiting for another, hoping it wasn't imagined, praying it wasn't an illusion.

"Is he... Is he..." I was afraid to finish the question.

"Yes, Supplicant. He's alive."

"My God," I whispered, my tears turning from ones of anguish to joy. "He's alive!"

"Barely," Satina said. "But, if he is left to heal and recuperate, he'll rejoin us soon enough."

"Well, then," said another voice in the distance.

My head snapped up. *Dalton.*

He moved toward me, already changing into a monster himself, one dead set on tearing me from limb to limb. "Looks like I'm going to have to put a stop to that."

CHAPTER 32

The sight of Dalton standing there, half beast and half something much worse, sent spikes of panic coursing through my veins.

Abram was still out. He wasn't dead, which was a step above his condition a few moments ago, but he also wasn't in anything close to fighting shape. My body tensed as I mentally recounted the last confrontation I had with Dalton. That hadn't gone so well for me. In fact, I still bore several injuries from that attack, although, if I knew how my blood worked, that could be what saved my big beautiful ass. Unfortunately, I *didn't* know that. Not even a little.

Dalton's gaze violated every inch of me. It seemed impossible now that I had ever thought of him as desirable, as anything other than some horrific monster. It was all over him, in the wicked crook of his lips, in the sly way with which he slinked closer.

And then something unexpected settled over me.

Guilt.

He hadn't always been this thing. Dalton was once the boy I grew up with. He was Lulu's brother, who chased us around ponds, holding up frogs like they were knives, the boy who hid behind trees and assaulted us with snowballs every winter. He was just a boy, just a person. And now, in part because of the sickness that threatened to destroy him, he was something else.

But that was no excuse. I'd lived alongside my mother in that world for years, and no one else with his diagnosis had attempted the things he was attempting.

"I won't let you hurt him," I murmured, my hands pressed against Abram's barely living body.

"Is that a joke, Char?" Dalton grinned. "Because we both know there's nothing you can do to stop me, and lover boy over there doesn't look like he's in the mood to rescue you this time."

"I can take care of myself," I said through gritted teeth, echoing the conversation I had with him my first day back in New Haven.

"You keep saying that." He shook his head, pacing toward me slowly, as though he had all the time in the world. His hands were claws, stretched out and ready to tear me apart.

My hands balled into fists against Abram's chest. I would have liked to say there was some marked improvement, but his breaths were just as shallow and infrequent as ever. No, if we were going to survive this, it would be on me to make it happen.

"You're gonna wish you never came back here," I said, my voice surprisingly strong and steady.

"You gonna strike a pose at me, Runway Girl?"

I stood—angry, scared, and totally devastated. This would likely be my last stand. Before the sun came up, I would probably watch the last bit of life drain from the man I loved and then feel the last bit of blood drain from me.

Meanwhile, Dalton would no longer have to worry about mounting hospital bills. I could almost envy him that.

Still, if I was going to die, I would go down kicking. I owed Abram that. I owed my mother that. I owed *myself* that.

I spied Satina from the corner of my eye, which sparked an idea. I didn't know how to use my magic...but *she* did.

"You're gonna be really sorry," I repeated, this time with renewed vigor. Sticking my still bloody hand out for her to feast upon, I motioned to Satina. "Let's finish this."

"I'm afraid not, Supplicant," she said, and she might as well have added, 'I hope you're wearing clean underwear, because the cops are gonna see them as they're scooping you up.'

My entire body jerked toward her. "Excuse me?"

"This battle doesn't belong to me. It never has. The end must be the end, no matter how difficult it is." She leveled her gaze at me. "The object of pain is not to avoid it, but to outlast it."

"How very Dr. Phil of you," I muttered, feeling my pulse speed up to about ten times its normal rate as Dalton neared us.

"You can't trust a Conduit, Char." He chuckled loudly. "Figured your boyfriend would have warned you about that." His eyes flickered to Abram's unconscious body. "You know, the first time I caught his stench on you, it took me a while to deal with it. I really thought we had something special, me and you." He made a fake pout with his lips. "Turns out I was wrong. Oh well, just makes the prospect of tearing his throat out that much more satisfying."

"I won't let you touch him," I said, my voice nearly a growl.

"If you really want to save him, then step away from him," Dalton said sternly. "After all, you're the prize, baby doll. You're what the whole spectacle has been about. I'm sure you love that, vain as you are."

"And if I do step away?" I asked, a tremble in my voice. "If I went to you willingly, you would really let him go unharmed?"

"Come to me and let me lap up that precious blood of yours, and I give you my word as a gentlemen and a scholar that I won't touch a hair on his big bad head." He winked at me. "He'll have a good life, Char. Who knows, maybe he'll find some new precious little flower to desecrate."

"*Take the sword.*" Satina's voice went directly into my head, bypassing my (and presumably Dalton's) ears. Her command only made my anger burn hotter in my chest. Lord knew she wouldn't be any help—she'd told me as much herself. But I'd saved Abram without her, hadn't I? If I could trust Dalton about anything, it was that I couldn't trust Satina.

"It's fake," I answered, eyeing where she had placed the sword by Abram's side earlier. Did she really think I would fall for that? For all I knew, she was on Dalton's side.

"Take the sword," she repeated.

"I'm not an idiot," I choked out. "It's plaster and wood."

Dalton's determined gaze turned curious. Skeptical. Maybe even a little worried. "What the hell are you talking about?"

Satina's gaze burned into me. "*Touch* the sword, you stupid girl!"

"Oh, the hell with this," Dalton said, shaking his head like a bull. "Offer's off the table. I'm gonna kill him, Char. I'm gonna rip apart everything you love and bury it in places man will never touch again. But I like you, and I'll kill you first so you don't have to watch. You're welcome."

And with that, he sprung toward me in the air.

"The sword!" Satina's voice boomed through my cranium now. "Touch the sword!"

Seeing as I didn't have any better ideas, I reached for it, grabbing the hilt where Satina had tossed it minutes before. My hand, still coated in the blood from my own wounds, tingled as it touched the wood.

I lifted it off the ground and turned just in time to catch a glimpse of Dalton in full beast form, his mouth all fangs and anger, his eyes twisted and hungry. If there was any humanity left in the man, it wasn't there to be seen now.

Shooting up a quick prayer, I closed my eyes and swung the sword, hoping the plaster would at least be hard enough to disorient him. The other, more likely, possibility was that the plaster would shatter against his hulking body. And then I would die.

But there was no plaster. Instead, the sword whistled through the air, making a squishy *thwick* sound as it made contact with Dalton. He let out a yelp.

I opened my eyes to find Dalton on the ground, reared back and holding his gut. The sword in my hand shone brightly with blood and glinted strangely in the moonlight.

It wasn't plaster anymore. Thank the good Lord above, it

wasn't plaster anymore! I couldn't stop myself from beaming, even in my current predicament, as the revelation sent a surge of giddy adrenaline through me, replacing the sense of impending doom that had shackled me in fear just moments before.

My touch, my blood-soaked palm, had changed the fabric of reality. What was once plaster was now steel. What was once harmless and decorative was now deadly.

But that didn't make sense. My blood could be used for magic, yes, but not by me.

"You bitch!" Dalton growled through pained and twisted fangs.

I stood my ground, hovering close over Abram. "I know I said I could take care of myself," I rambled off quickly to Satina. "But I've never used a sword."

"You're destined for more than just taking care of just yourself, Supplicant. Don't be so self-limiting." She began to shimmer with light.

Dalton was starting to get up now, though, and Satina's riddles were of no help once he did.

"Okay, but what do I do *now?*"

"Outlast it," she whispered through the wind, and then she vanished into nothing.

Dalton stood upright now. No sooner did I register him than he came toward me. His claws struck at my side and knocked the wind out of me. I stumbled backward, but kept two hands on the sword's hilt. Swinging blindly, I came up with nothing but air.

His swing at me was much luckier.

He ripped into my forearm, spraying blood all over his claws and the ground. His affected appendage began to glow with golden ribbons.

"That's the stuff," he said breathlessly. "Now give Papa some more."

Pain shot up my arm, and a throbbing sensation threatened to rob me of my weapon, but I had to fight. This was my one chance. This was my *last* chance.

"I'll give you something," I said, arcing the sword at him again. Missing again.

But the sword felt less foreign in my hands now, as if it was speaking to me, telling me where to point it. Maybe the magic in my blood had something to do with it or maybe I was just a fast learner. Either way, I was open to any advantage I could get.

"Don't make this hard on yourself, Char," he said, circling me like predator. "I can make it quick. Drawing things out will only make it worse for you."

"You're just scared I can still kick your ass," I said, jabbing the blade forward. It nicked his side, but he spun too quickly for the blow to do any real damage. "You always were a sore loser."

"Don't be an idiot," he said, almost foaming at the mouth. "You don't have a chance here, and even if you did, you couldn't kill anybody. It's not who you are."

"You have no idea who I am," I cut out, narrowing my gaze at him.

I swung again. He grabbed the blade with his bare hand, and I yanked it hard, freeing it from him and slicing his palm on the way out. He yelped again and pulled back.

I may not have actually killed anyone before, but after this, after everything that had happened, I couldn't say what sort of person I was anymore.

"Fine," he said. "Have it your way."

He jumped again, and this time his feet came at me. He kicked me hard in the shoulders, knocking me backward. I tripped over Abram and tumbled to the ground. My head hit hard against a rock protruding from the lawn, and my vision dimmed. Then, I was being lifted upward.

Dalton's claws dug into my back as he raised me over his head. I clutched the sword's hilt tighter and made another swipe at him, but the angle made my attempt futile. Instead of doing any damage, it flailed back and forth ridiculously.

"I tried to warn you, Char. Really, I did." He threw me, and as I passed through the air, I saw everything: Dalton standing there wickedly, Abram lying on the ground beside him, the full moon hanging in the sky and marking some horrible countdown to Abram's curse.

And then there was the tree.

I slammed hard into its trunk. Something in my chest cracked as I slid to the ground. I tried to calm myself, to breathe, to ignore the pain. But it was no use. The entire world was spinning. Pain flashed through me, intense and damaging. I had been hurt. Badly. And it wasn't over yet. I could see my own blood covering me, yet doing nothing to heal my own wounds. I still had no idea how any of this worked. All I knew was that if I lost this fight, Abram and I were both dead. And who knew how many more would follow us.

Through bleary eyes, I watched Dalton come toward me. I grappled for the sword, but it was nowhere to be found. It must have dropped it at some point between Dalton's arms and sliding to the ground.

I tried moving, but a stabbing pain ran up my chest. Yep, I had definitely broken a rib or two, just like that time I fell off the top of the monkey bars in first grade.

"I really wanted to do this the easy way, Char," he said, lumbering over me. "But you just wouldn't let me, would you? Everything with you has to be a challenge. Always been that way. You know, not everyone wants a girl who plays hard to get." His sharp teeth shone in the moonlight. His claws twitched by his sides, as though itching to rip into me. "I was gonna make it quick for you," he said, licking his lips, "but at this point, I'm about ready to hurt you, and I'm not going to feel bad about it."

I searched his beastly body for a weak spot. Certainly there had to be something to exploit. Certainly there was an area that I could attack that, even in his current condition, might still be vulnerable.

I grinned a little as the answer came to me.

"Funny," I muttered. "I was just about to tell you the same thing."

And then I kicked him right between the legs.

Pain threatened to rip me right in half, but I still didn't hurt half as much as Dalton did. The big lug keeled over, affording me just enough room to snake past him.

I stumbled away, holding my injured midsection. He would be back on his feet momentarily. These beasts never stayed hurt for long. I thought about running, but Abram was here. I needed to keep him safe. Love me or not, he would've done the same for me. And that was what mattered.

Through my pain-filled gaze, I caught sight of the sword. It hurt like hell as I bent over to scoop it up, but something about its weight in my hands felt right.

An almost howl was the only warning I got before Dalton collided with me. He knocked me to the ground mere inches from Abram and flipped me over. The sword flew from my hands again, landing too far out of reach.

He sat on my chest, all his bravado gone.

"I'm gonna make you wish you were never born, you fat bitch," he snarled.

Thrusting his arm forward, he dug into my chest. Blood splattered everywhere as I felt an intense rush of heat and pain. Suddenly, my broken ribs didn't seem so bad.

He dug again and again. The pain intensified and morphed into a strong and primal sickness. Bile rose in my throat, and my body began to wretch.

"This is where you die," he kept repeating. "This is where you die."

My blood was all over him now, and he shimmered gold in its presence. I turned my head, half to check the distance to the sword and half so that I wouldn't have to actually watch Dalton murder me.

I stretched my hand out, but the damn thing was too far. It wouldn't have mattered anyway. I was too weak, and this hurt too much. My vision blurred, the world paled.

Satina's words rang through my head again.

Outlast it.

But that was ridiculous. Dalton ran a claw deep into me now. I could literally feel his fingers inside of me, claiming my blood as his own. There was no way I could do this. Let him take the blood. Let him take it all. Nothing was worth this pain.

But then I saw Abram lying there. He was still alive, even if just barely. If he made it through this, he would make the next century unlivable for himself, thinking about all the ways he had failed.

No. I would live for him. *He* was worth it.

And with that realization, the pain sort of went away.

It seemed I had outlasted it.

I stretched my arm as far as it would go, threatening to pull it out of its socket, but pain or no pain, the sword was still just out of reach. My fingernail grasped helplessly at the dirt, trying to pull myself just a little closer. Dalton's weight on me made that nearly impossible, but I couldn't die. I just couldn't.

I mustered up all the will I could for another pull, and now the sword was just a fingertip away. I didn't stop until my fingers grazed the hilt, until I could pluck the sword closer.

Dalton didn't seem to notice. Instead, he kept drilling into me, covering himself in my blood.

"This is where you die," he said again. "This is where you die."

My fingers wrapped around the hilt. "Funny," I said, gathering up the last bit of strength I had, maybe the last bit of strength I might ever have. "I...was...about to—to tell you...the same thing."

And I throttled the sword straight at him.

It flew true, slicing its way through the air and hitting Dalton right in the neck. He didn't have time to yelp this time. He didn't react at all. His eyes went wide and then they lost their light. His body fell limp and lifeless against me, and I pushed it off. All but his head.

I had already taken that clean off.

CHAPTER 33

The minutes stretched as I struggled to catch my breath. Killing Dalton... I squeezed my eyes shut. God, I had killed somebody. It was the hardest thing I had ever had to do. Pushing him off me was only slightly easier.

He was heavy and slick with blood. Bile rose in my stomach, not only because I was touching a still-warm corpse, but because of who the corpse used to be. This was Lulu's brother. Lord, Lulu was going to be heartbroken. And how was I going to explain this? How would I explain any of it?

His headless body thudded onto the ground next to me, and I rolled as far away from it as I could. The night air mingled with my bangs as I settled close to Abram. I felt his breath, steadier now. That was a good thing—perhaps the *only* good thing—to happen this entire damn night.

Heaviness drifted over me as I lay there. The weight of all that had happened, of all I had done, of everything all of us had been through, was too much. And it was begging me to sleep.

I fought the urge as long as I could. I needed to be here when Abram woke, to make sure he was okay, and to explain everything he had missed. But it was no use. My body was too exhausted. And before long, my eyes refused to cooperate.

I woke in familiar arms. My entire body ached, my mouth was dry, and my head spun. But as my eyes opened, heavy and nearly unwilling, the sight they took in made it all worth it.

Abram sat over me, cradling me in his arms. He was a man again, bare-chested and sweating. But he wasn't hurt. And he sure as hell wasn't dead.

"You're not..." I muttered. My voice was cracked, low, and weak.

"Not on your life." He smiled at me. It was beautiful. *He* was beautiful.

"And I'm not—"

"You can thank Satina for that one," he said. "She came back. Healed you. Woke me up."

I bit my tongue to stop myself from saying something that might sound ungrateful. Sure, she'd healed my wounds, but she could have prevented them in the first place. I guess that was just who Satina was, though. She wouldn't do more to help anyone than abslutely necessary. Maybe she enjoyed seeing me suffer, even if she didn't want me to die. At least I was here now, still breathing.

Abram's dark eyes gleamed in the quickly brightening sky. He was everything I had ever wanted. Even if he could never match the way I felt for him, it was okay. I didn't care, so long as he was alive.

He had given me this gift. He had shown me that love, real live honest-to-God love, existed. It was pure and beautiful. It would change you in the most unexpected and glorious ways. And it hurt. It hurt in ways you never knew were possible and in volumes you hoped would never stop.

He had shown me love, even if he could never return it. And right now, in the glow of the early morning, that was enough.

"Don't try to talk," he said over me. "You saved my life, you know."

"Now we're even," I answered, against his protests.

Bracing myself on his shoulder, I pulled myself up. The entire world was shaky, and I was somehow even less stable than that.

He took hold of my hand in his. "Do you need water?"

"No. Just you. I just need to sit here with you for a minute." The tears that welled up behind my eyes surprised me. "I thought you were dead."

"I was..." He shook his head. "Or at least, that's what she told me while she was healing you. Apparently you brought me back from even death, which I would venture to say makes us not so even after all."

"I'm sure you'll find some way to make it up to me."

"I can think of more than a few alternatives," he said with a grin, that smoldering look in his eyes making my knees go even weaker than they already were...but this time, for a completely different reason.

Just like that, the dread and worry that had laid so heavily on my shoulders melted away. Against all odds, we had won. There were no more best friends' little brothers hoping to bleed me dry. It was just Abram, me, and eternity.

And a third beast we still hadn't found...

"What about the other beast?" I asked warily. "I spilled a lot of blood..."

"You spilled enough blood for Satina's spell to block that beast for a month," Abram said with a low chuckle. "But I'll get him...or if that fails, I'll just toss you a sword next time he's around."

His simplicity in that moment solidified everything I felt about him. "I love you," I whispered, letting him fold me into his embrace. "You don't have to say it back," I said against his chest. "I know it's too soon for you. Just know that it's true. Just know that I feel it."

He tensed up and, when my mind slowed down enough to register the quickly greying sky, I remembered why.

"The curse," I whispered. "It's permanent now."

"Not yet." He caressed his hand down my back. "When the sun comes up."

I held him a little tighter. "There has to be something we can do," I said, dreading my sentiment wasn't true. "We've come this far."

"We have," he said, his hand tracing small circles at the bottom of my back. "Don't worry about the curse. It doesn't matter. This is who I am now. I've made peace with that."

I tilted my head against his shoulder and listened to the beating of his heart. It was so strong now, so alive.

"Don't you miss it?" I asked. "Being human?"

"I try not to," he said, but his voice was quiet and strained. "But there are...things that I would love to experience again."

"Like what?" I asked, lifting my head and meeting his gaze.

"Dreams," he said ruefully. "I can't—my kind doesn't dream." His eyes glazed over. "And that would be all right if not for my sister." He bit his lip. "She died when I was twelve. Paintings were expensive then, and my family didn't have any money. But I dreamt of her almost every night. It kept her face fresh in my mind." He pulled my body back against his again, maybe so I wouldn't see the pain etched into his expression. "I'm not sure I even remember what she looks like now."

I kissed his chest and twirled my fingers through his. "I'm so sorry."

"Don't be," said a voice from the other side of the room. "He does it to himself."

Satina.

She stood just a few feet away, although, floating might have been a better word for it. Every inch of her skin shone with light, and despite her few acts of kindness, I still found it odd that she wasn't cloaked in shadows instead.

"Satina, don't," Abram growled.

"What is she talking about?" I asked, unease creating a pit in my stomach.

"Nothing," Abram said. "Just ignore—"

"The curse is his to break, Supplicant. All the pieces are in play."

"What does that... *Oh*."

But before I could even finish my sentence, it all fell into place. Like a runway show, the idea coming to life as finally the make-up is applied, the hair styled, the wardrobe divvied up. Where I could not see the designer's vision before, it was all very clear to me now.

"Oh, God," I murmured, my gaze rolling back to Abram. "You *do* love me."

His eyes went wide, but the rest of his face steeled over. Still, I knew the truth. I had wormed my way into his heart, and he wouldn't admit it.

"He has to say it, doesn't he?" I asked, turning to Satina.

"Before the sun comes up," she answered, looking at the almost bright sky. "He has two minutes."

"Abram!" I said, spinning around to him.

He shook his head, tears gleaming in his eyes.

"I should have known," I said. "I knew you couldn't have kissed me like that, couldn't have touched me like that, if you didn't love me. I knew it was true."

He cupped my face in his hands. "Charisse," he said, his voice firm, "you need to let this go."

"No way!" I pushed his hands away from my face. "You have a chance to be human. We have a shot at a real life. We can have a future. Abram, I know you feel it, all you have to do is say it."

"Absolutely not," he muttered.

"Don't be so hard headed! What is your issue? You waited over a century for this. Please, I'm begging you. Just—"

"What is it you think would happen if I said it, Charisse? That we would go skipping off into the sunset?" He waved his hand. "Dalton wasn't the only one after you, remember? You're a commodity. There's always going to be someone out to steal what makes you special. Satina told me about the future. Your trials aren't over, and that means neither are mine. You are always going to be in danger, Charisse. And I'm sure as hell going to make certain I'm able to save you."

"*I* just saved *you*," I shot back, incredulous. Ugh. I didn't have time to deal with his sexist views right now, and I was kicking myself for not making more of an effort to get him over them sooner. "I can take care of myself. Surely you have noticed this by now!"

He scowled. "And if you do, then what good am I?"

"I love you, you moron. That's what good you are. Now for the love of God, you're running out of time! Stop being so goddamn self-sacrificing."

His eyes narrowed. "I'm not a martyr, Charisse. If I'm human, if I can't save you, then you're gone. And what am I supposed to do then? Would you just expect me to go on without you? Because I have lived over a hundred years, and I have made it through things that would tear mortal men apart, but I can tell you without a shadow of a doubt, I would never make it through that. Not for a day. So no. I'm not doing this for you. I'm doing this for me. For me and for us."

He leaned in and pressed his lips square against mine, and something in me shifted as we kissed. Gold light shimmered across him. The sun was up, the moon on the window was full. The curse was permanent.

He pulled away and took one of my hands gently in his own.

"I do love you," he said, and with his free hand, he swiped a tear off my cheek with his thumb. "And I always will. Now and forever."

EPILOGUE

Two weeks later, they laid Dalton to rest. It took all I could do to sit there without squirming out of my own skin. He was a monster. He wanted me dead. If he'd had his way, I would be the one they were lowering into the ground right now, nothing more than a bloodless husk.

But the townsfolk didn't know that. To them, sitting all teary eyed and justified, he had been a victim of Abram's. Even if they still couldn't quite put into words what Abram had turned into (and, as a result, were beginning to make stupid and mundane excuses about it), the narrative still stated the obvious. Abram was a murderer, a villain they needed to bring to justice.

Even if he hadn't been seen by anyone in town since that night.

Anyone but me, anyway.

Some believed he died and that wild animals had dragged off his carcass, but others thought he was still alive, out there, on the prowl, ready to strike again at any moment.

Because everyone knew about his place in the woods, Abram had been forced to hide out in an abandoned farmhouse in the next town over. It wasn't much, but it was off the beaten path, close enough for me to stop by every day, and there was a basement with enough space for him to stay when the sun went down.

People were still after him, and they were looking for both a man and a monster. We couldn't be too careful. Still, it was only a temporary solution.

Things at home didn't get any better, either. Lulu was despondent after the death of her brother. And though she didn't come out and say it, I could tell she blamed me at least in part for what happened. She knew I had sided with Abram, and since the town never was able to confirm whether Dalton had died before or after they had supposedly killed Abram, for all she knew, Abram was responsible for her brother's death.

Dalton was a hero not only to her, but to the entire town. And though I was a victim in their eyes as well, I was also a facilitator. And they weren't going to let me forget it.

Doors got closed in my face. Children sneered at me. It was like the entire place was filled with Esters. New Haven had finally realized how much I didn't belong here, and I absolutely agreed.

A week after Dalton's funeral, I left town. Lulu was still talking to me. God bless her, she was trying to move past things. But I could hardly look at her. It was me who had snuffed the life from her brother's eyes. And whether he deserved it or not, that fact weighed on me heavily.

"You're like my sister, you know?" she'd said before the taxi pulled up to get me. "Nothing's ever going to change that."

There were tears in her eyes when she hugged me goodbye. And there were tears in mine when the cab pulled away.

I met Abram two days later on the island of Grimold. It was a tiny dot of a place in the Mediterranean that I had never heard of, but the instant I stepped off the plane, I knew I had made a good choice.

When Abram had first told me we were leaving, I hadn't wanted to go. Not with a third beast still roaming New Haven. But

Abram promised me he would hunt that one down before meeting me in Grimold, and he'd held true to his promise. In a way, it wasn't someone I knew being a beast that really scared me, though. It was that there were so many who were complete strangers, insignificant in the scheme of themes yet ingrained in my life in the worst possible way.

But now was not the time to linger on those thoughts. Abram was finally here with me. New Haven was safe from the beasts and Abram was safe from New Haven. He stood on the tarmac, dressed in white, all tanned and rested, his hands hanging freely at his sides. Seeing him was like coming home, and his easy smile made me feel as though everything would be okay.

"What do we do first?" I asked after he gave me the sweetest, longest kiss of my entire life.

"Whatever you want." He ran his hands down my back and resting them near my big beautiful butt. "We've got the rest of our lives. All we have to do is live it."

* * *

On our third day in Grimold, Abram took me for a walk along the ocean. The mist of all that had happened dissipated there. Our dark past was no match for the sun, sand, and sea. No match for the man standing next to me or for the way I felt about him.

"Tell me again," I demanded, smiling and leaning into him.

"Again?" he asked with a secretive smile.

I kissed his bare arm. "You owe me."

"I love you," he said, and he dropped a kiss on my hairline. "I love you," he repeated, kissing me again. "I love you. I love you. I love you. A thousand times over, Charisse, I love you, and I always will."

Satisfied by his proclamation, I let my cheek rest against his shoulder, my fingers entwined with his, breathing in the smell of salt and sun on his warm skin.

This was my life now. Unending happiness.

Until I heard *her*.

"This sounds familiar."

Satina's voice was about as welcome as a hangnail. I spun around to find her standing along the shore in a fringe bikini. The crystal clear waves lapped at her feet, and she had one of those ridiculous drinks with the little umbrellas.

Abram's body tensed against mine. "What the hell are you doing here?" he asked, his voice dropping to a protective growl. "How did you find us?"

"Two questions with but one answer," she said, her voice lilting. "I told you fate wasn't done with your little Supplicant here. There's more to your story."

"No," Abram said flatly. "We are done with this, Satina. Leave now."

"I could," she said. "And I will. But that won't change anything. These things will happen whether I'm here or not. So I suggest you hear me out and prepare while you still have time."

I stepped forward, half terrified and half resolved to hear what she had to say.

"What?" I asked, crossing my arms in a poor attempt to stop my hands from trembling. "Skip the riddles and cut to the chase."

"I have the answer to the question you never asked," she said, tilting her head. "You know—how you used magic. Supplicants can't use magic, Charisse. They can only facilitate it. And yet your blood performed magic without a Conduit to conduct a spell. Don't you find that strange?"

"Well, I guess you were just wrong then," I said, rolling my eyes.

She pressed her lips together and shook her head. "Yes and no. I was wrong about *you*, but now I know why. You aren't just a Supplicant, Charisse. You're the bridge. You're the fuel *and* the fire."

"What the hell does that mean?"

"You're not just a Supplicant. You're a Conduit, too."

I stepped back. "No, I'm not."

"You are," she insisted. "And you'll either be the key to fixing this mess or the key to destroying our world, so I suggest you take what I have to say seriously. The hunt for you will not end here. Mystics all over the world have been prophesying about you, and it won't be long before every Conduit on this planet knows who you are and what you are. And they will come for you."

I shook my head, trying to will away everything she had said, but there was no unhearing her words. "But Conduits turn into beasts," I said, finding satisfaction in unearthing the flaw to her logic.

"Abram is a beast, but not a Conduit," she said, matter of fact. "And you a Conduit, but not a beast. Perhaps you can thank your Supplicant nature for that, but I promise you, it's not less true."

"Fine. Let's say you're right," I said. "What happens now?"

"What always happens, Charisse. The next."

"Enough," Abram barked. "You promised me you would give us—"

"I already gave you time!" she shouted, a storm taking over her features. "I gave you as long as I could. There is no more time, Abram."

Abram clenched his jaw, and he stepped past me, right up to Satina. His body was hulking compared to the body she had borrowed. "I said we're done, Satina."

"Uh-uh." She didn't even flinch. "Sorry, lover boy, but your romance will have to wait. *What is* will turn into *what needs to be.*"

"Great, more riddles," I mumbled.

Just then, a mass fell to the shore, landing with a thud and bursting in warm red ribbons.

No. Not ribbons. *Blood.*

It splattered against my legs and the skirt of my sun dress. And that mass...it was a man. A very dead man, with two simple words carved into his forehead.

She sleeps.

I covered my mouth, holding back a horrified gasp, and lifted my gaze to Satina. "What does it mean?"

"It means," Satina said, waving her drink to the side, "that you two have your work cut out for you."

The End

Continue reading the Conduit Series with Book 2, Sleeping with the Beast.

ABOUT THE AUTHORS

Conner Kressley is a USA TODAY Bestselling Author represented by Rossano Trentin of TZLA. He is an avid reader and all around lover of storytelling. His book "The Breaker's Code" is the first in the epic "Fixed Points" series that pits free will against fate and true love against good intentions and bad situations. You can learn more about Conner and his books below.

Visit His Website: http://connerkressleybooks.weebly.com/

NEW YORK TIMES, USA TODAY, AND WALL STREET JOURNAL bestselling author Rebecca Hamilton writes urban fantasy and paranormal romance for Harlequin, Baste Lübbe, and Evershade. A book addict, registered bone marrow donor, and indian food enthusiast, she often takes to fictional worlds to see what perilous situations her characters will find themselves in next.

Visit Her Website: http://www.rebeccahamilton.com/